The Seventh Illusion

Doyle Black

Copyright © 2022 by Doyle Black

This book is a work of fiction. Names, characters, businesses, churches, ministries, organizations, places, events and incidents are either the product of the author's imagination or are used fictitiously. Any resemblance to actual persons, living or dead, events, or locales is entirely coincidental. No part of this book may be reproduced in any form or by any electronic or mechanical means without permission in writing from the author, except by a reviewer who may quote brief passages in a review.

ISBN 979-8-364-34609-4

To the Truth Seekers

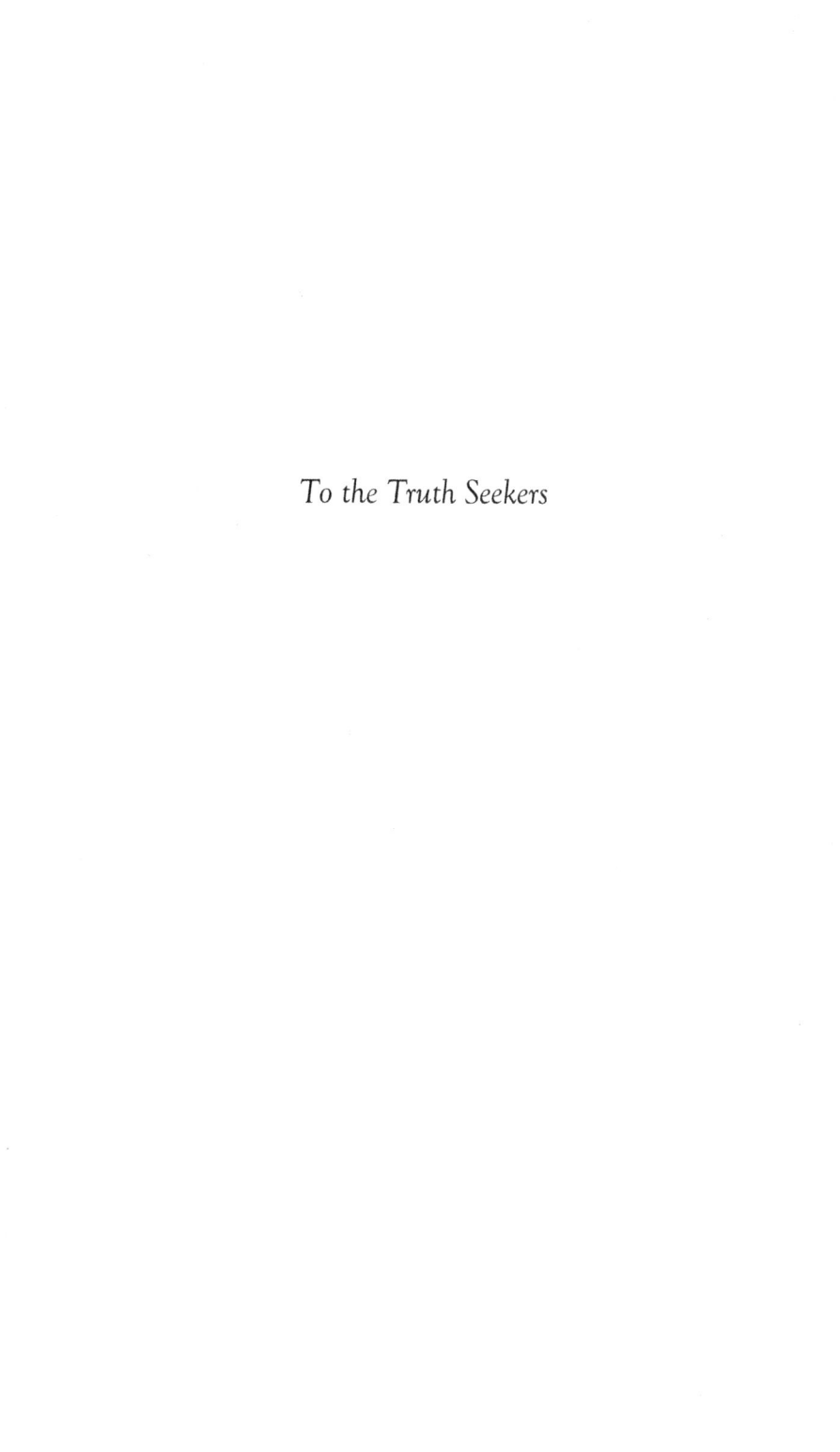

Part I: I Am Born and Killed

*O Moon! In the night I have seen you sailing
And shining so round and low.
You were bright – ah, bright – but your light is failing;
You are nothing now but a bow.*
　　　　　　　　*Jean Ingelow
　　　　　　　　Seven Times One*

One

An idyllic innocence; that's all I wanted when I was alive. My biographers claim that I was a born killer, but they're mistaken; I always found murder repugnant. I only killed to defend innocence in all its manifestations: the scent of a newborn baby, the tears of a girl at four, the warmth of my mother's embrace. I killed for the same reason a good soldier kills: to defend the innocent from evil.

The first decade of my life was immaculate. Oh, and how I wish I could cast this corpse aside and be resurrected into those tender days! To feel each moment again like a poet child, and fill my senses past the brim with happy, happy love. To sink into my soul, once more at four, and draw my breath from a violet Virginia evening! To step into love, squeaking clean from my bath. Above me, the moon smiling through the screen as Father towels my hair…

"*I see the moon…*" he sings in soft baritone.

Our nightly ritual; towel off, step through daddy's splayed fingers into underwear; lean on his warm shoulder.

"*And the moon sees me.*"

Our happy, hollow march along the pinewood hall to my room. Daddy pulls jammies from Little Bo Peep's chest of drawers.

"God bless the moon..."

White jammies are best; fluffy and soft.

"and God bless me."

A gentle comb of the hair and look! My Mother. We kneel by my bed and whisper together:

Now I lay me down to sleep.
I pray the Lord my soul to keep.
If I die before I wake,
I pray the Lord my soul to take.

Oh, but where? Where was it taken?

* * * * *

Of the many psychiatrists, journalists and holy men that have studied the causes of my "criminal psychosis", one mediocrity has concluded my sainted parents are to blame:

"...a blend of combustible ingredients that ultimately proved explosive," opines Mr. Roger Barnhart in his oft-quoted bombastic biography of me. According to Barnhart, my parent's late age in bearing me (he 47, she 39) and I, an only child, led to their tendency of "over pampering". Barnhart considered the disparity of their educational backgrounds "combustible" as well. My father graduated Magna cum Laud from a distinguished university but chose to teach twelfth grade Literature in Virginia his entire career. My mother, a high school grad from Atlanta, believed her life's purpose was teaching me the tenets of Christianity.

The Seventh Illusion

Yet despite the disparity of their age, education, and religious belief (he Agnostic, she Baptist) they were drawn to each other. My father first noticed her as she organized Jell-O servings in the cafeteria line. "That hairnet accentuated her beautiful face" Father said as the three of us dined decades later. As for Mother, she observed him reading poetry weeks before, and considered him "dignified". When he suggested coffee after school she accepted.

"He read Keats to me on our first date, Leonard." Mother said.

They married within six months, bought a house, commingled their modest assets, and tried for children. It took three miscarriages and ten years to succeed. Among my earliest memories is Mother assuring me I was a gift from God.

"God answers prayers Leonard," she often said while tucking me in. "You're our answered prayer my little angel."

"*Boseki's parents treated him like Siddhartha as a child,*" scrawls the sub-literate Mr. Barnhart, "*because they sheltered him from everything ugly in the world...*"

Sadly, Barnhart has his facts wrong from the beginning. My first five years were more akin to the Dali Lama's. I was held in high esteem wherever I was displayed, whether it be church, grocery stores, or neighborhood walks. My parents insisted that I was the smartest, most beautiful boy in Virginia and judging from public response, I believed it. Such fawning wasn't limited to the masses either, for the very idols of childhood adored me also. Tooth Fairy habitually tucked five dollars and an obeisant note for each lost tooth, Bun-Bun sprinkled hundreds of brightly colored eggs on our lawn each Easter, and Santa? Below is his note to me when I was seven:

December 23, 1973
Dear Lenny,

I'm happy to confirm that of the 400 million children I visit annually, you are once again on my Top Ten List. In fact, you're such a good boy that you still retain the #1 spot for the 3rd year in a row!! This of course means that I'm granting every wish requested in your letter of November 27th, mailed to the North Pole. Merry Christmas, from Santa!

Santa also left an early gift that year on Christmas Eve. It remains among my few possessions. Father and I found it on my bed just after bath time:

"Daddy! Look!"

"Oh my gosh, he's done it!" Father said.

"What? What?"

"Santa left you a Christmas Eve gift, Leonard!"

I tore off the wrapping paper to find a red leather-bound book with gold leafed pages. The spine read *Golden Poems*.

Father opened it and selected the first of many verses I'd discover over the ensuing years:

'Twas the night before Christmas, and all through the house; not a creature was stirring, not even a mouse..."

Oh, those restless Christmas Eves after lights dimmed! Twisting and rolling in bed until the sheets mummified me! Rising before dawn to find, at the foot of the stairs, cookie crumbs and note from Santa on a plate! And round the corner in the living room, brightly wrapped with promise, everything I asked for.

* * * * * *

I was in similar spirits three years later, when my first illusion melted. My eleventh Christmas; December 21st

1976 to be precise. We were playing Hide & Seek. Tommy Lewis, a corpulent, slow-witted third grader, was It and so there was no need to find an elaborate hiding place. Sarah Levine and I ran and huddled together behind a thick stand of Viburnum.

"Ohhh, I can't wait til Christmas!" I whispered. "I hope Santa brings all four GI Joes I asked for."

"Oh, don't worry," Sarah scoffed. "Your folks will give everything you want."

"They only give me clothes." I said. "Santa's got the good gifts."

I'll never forget her black, soulless eyes; staring at me.

"What?" I asked.

"Lenny, don't you know? There's no such thing as Santa Claus..."

LIAR!!! She was ugly, with bad breath and I told her so. She denied his existence so emphatically that I burst through the shrubs and ran home to confront mother. She equivocated at length but finally confessed after I persisted. And although wounded, I fought on bravely; firing round after round of hard questions.

"DOES GOD EXIST?" I finally wailed after witnessing "Sand Man", "Tooth Fairy" and "Bun Bun" butchered under my inquisition.

"Leonard! How dare you! Of course, he exists!" Mother said and sent me to my room. I lay in bed for the remainder of the afternoon, staring at the ceiling; struggling with the death of demigods.

That night, I refused to dine downstairs in the Den of Deceivers. Father came up afterward and told me to bathe for bed. I sat in the tub for an hour, mauling my toy soldiers with my powerful jaws of death, scalding them with hot water and subjecting them to Chinese Faucet Cramming torture. Father knocked on the door and told me to towel off because it was time for bed. I slunk into my room to find him sitting with <u>Golden Poems</u>. I got under the covers and turned away as he opened the book.

"'Twas the night before Christmas, when all through the house..."

"Oh don't bother." I said. "It's all a lie!"

Father stopped.

"It's not a lie Leonard, it's a tradition. Christmas is a wonderful tradition of love and good will. Christmas exists Leonard..."

"You lied to me!"

"Your mother and I love you very much. We only want you to feel cherished."

"Nothing will ever be the same! Everything's changed!" I screamed.

Silence. I began to weep.

"Nothing's changed, Leonard. Your mother and I love you deeply..."

But I couldn't be consoled. Father gave up and left. A few minutes later Mother asked me to kneel beside her for night prayer. I refused. She knelt beside me, her face inches away from mine as I lay resting on my pillow. She closed her eyes and recited St. Matthew from memory:

...Teaching them to observe all things whatsoever I have commanded you: and lo, I am with you always, even unto the end of the world.

* * * * *

My parents, sensing my sensitive temperament, enrolled me in various after school activities to keep me occupied. By spring I was immersed in art lessons, judo and baseball, while continuing to manage straight A's. My confidence gradually returned. Months later, after I'd recovered from that first disorienting epiphany, another pillar collapsed and tumbled into the ocean of truth. It happened in the back of a school bus on a field trip to Jamestown.

"Hey, you wanna know where babies come from?" Randy Head asked while I played Tic Tack Toe with my seatmate. I turned around to find Randy's rodent face, sniffing the air.

You're not gonna want to hear this... a voice inside me warned. I didn't like Randy. His grades were lousy and Ms. Lawson was constantly making him stand in the corner. I always avoided him and it was only because of assigned seating that he was behind me now.

"I already know." I said and turned back to the game.

"Oh yeah? Tell me."

"From the mommy's stomach."

"Yeah, but how does the baby get there?" Randy asked.

"The parents pray for it."

"Oh man! You're so stupid!" He laughed. "Babies come from a man sticking his dick in a girl's pussy!"

I couldn't breathe. X's and O's blurred as his demonic laughter rang through the bus. I'd never heard "pussy" before but guessed it was that thing I'd seen once as Mother exited her shower. I angrily denied his words, told him he was a pig and perhaps *his parents* participated in that kind of disgusting behavior but not *mine*. I defended Mother so loudly that Ms. Lawson rushed from her seat at the front of the bus to find out why I was screaming.

It ruined my field trip. While others ran around the ship decks of the Discovery and Godspeed, I slouched over my lunch box alone on a bench at shore. I told Ms.

Lawson that I had a stomachache but she knew better. After school I went home and confronted Mother again.

"Who told you that?" She gasped. I could see it in her eyes: same stare as the Santa catastrophe.

"Yes, Leonard it's true," she blurted "but it's not nearly as nasty as that horrid boy describes..."

"Then Daddy doesn't stick his pee-pee in your wee-wee?" I asked.

"Leonard!"

For the next ten minutes Mother tried to calm me by rambling about the sanctity of marriage and love and "fertilization" as my forehead rolled back and forth on the kitchen table. She finally banished me to my room after I pounded my head so hard into the Formica that the salt shaker toppled. It proved more difficult to cope with my new carnal knowledge than the Santa lie, particularly because I had to face the Fornicators daily.

Weeks later, just as those horrible word pictures began to recede, I walked in undetected by my parents, just as Father was mounting. Suffice it to say that I ran away from home and remained undiscovered until late afternoon, when I was pulled from underneath a slide at the Paul Burbank Elementary School playground. They were never able to glean the reason for my disappearance and incorrectly assumed it was due to their stubborn refusal to allow me a horse. I never bothered to correct them.

* * * * *

Years passed. I entered high school. Although I'd remained a promising academic student, by tenth grade I knew my athletic ability was insufficient to gain a position on any school team. This was unfortunate because I was not popular on campus and my inability to even make Crew left me with an aching emptiness. I filled the void by focusing on my studies; particularly geometry, physics and German, in homage to Einstein. I loved mathematics because of the constancy of universal laws. It comforted me to know that wherever I was; China, Africa or coursing across the Milky Way, the laws of geometry and physics applied. They had always existed and always would, unchanged from the time of Euclid's discovery and forever unchangeable into eternity.

For similar reasons, I also became heavily involved at the First Baptist Church, after hearing their Pastor Bruce Hearty speak at a Wednesday evening service. The pastor's eyes met mine throughout the course of that sermon, and I felt his words were meant specifically for me. Perhaps I drew his attention because I walked in alone and sat in the front row. Or, was it because I started crying during the altar call? Whatever the reason, Pastor Hearty pulled me aside as I left that night and said five words that comforted me:

"I can see you're hurting."

The tears came again. I'd been struggling with melancholia for months and had alarmed my parents to the point of their seeking psychological counseling for me. The sessions had produced nothing but a prescription for anti-depressants that I refused to take and so I had stumbled on, seeking relief from the great unspoken. I found solace that night in the hazel eyes of Pastor Hearty.

"Look, I host a fellowship group every Thursday night at my apartment..." He smiled, and just like that, I was part of his little flock. I soon discovered that he devoted his life to the church, delivering three sermons on Sunday in addition to a Wednesday evening service. Rather than hire a youth minister, he insisted on taking the job himself and often organized field trips to the beach, movies, or amusement parks. He was our ever available protector, our best friend and most importantly, our spiritual leader.

Pastor Hearty opened my mind to Truth through his sermons and intimate gatherings in his apartment. He breathed passages from the Bible and showed us how they were still relevant in the twentieth century: Love one another. Shun the flesh. Seek God. His words; delivered through his penetrating eyes, fingertips, and soft sweet breath, permeated every pore of my body.

"Children listen to me," he said as we sat holding hands in a circle before his fireplace. "Love one another."

Unfortunately, his potent message became severely ambiguous after he was discovered sodomizing a parishioner at an economy motel in Newport News. His partner was a young man who had only recently joined our prayer group, a teenage Svengali, whose eyes seethed with unrest. I hated him, and felt an immediate change in the chemistry of our flock the moment he walked into Pastor's apartment. It took less than a month for Pastor Hearty to fall under the spell that led to Happy Days Motel. A church member saw the couple leaving their room one gray afternoon and Hearty was promptly fired. Over the ensuing months a thorough financial audit revealed that our pastor had also diverted church resources to purchase a small Horse Farm in Ocala, Florida.

Pastor Hearty's metamorphosis had a serious impact on my psyche. I have a vivid memory during that time of staring at an open Geometry book in my room and trying to form a postulate for Pastor Hearty. I just couldn't understand how a man steeped in the word of God could succumb to crime and perversions. Hadn't he walked in the Spirit? Didn't he speak with God? Wasn't he further down the road, closer to the light than the rest of us? I struggled for hours, forgoing dinner and an entire night's sleep until I had my postulate (duplicated below from a fading twenty-year-old memory)

Postulate 666: A given straight line can be broken by points C and D when C = a sullen little faggot and D=$$$. Said broken line can then be twisted into a spiral that wraps tighter and tighter into concentric circles until vanishing through the portal of Beelzebub.

I have no idea what to make of it now. At the time it seemed strangely soothing.

The following Sunday, after suffering through an insipid sermon from our interim pastor (an elder who owned a string of dry cleaners), I decided to take a sabbatical from church. Over the next several weeks I took numerous calls from fellow parishioners, all offering the same advice: Pastor Hearty was human and all humans have fallen short of the glory of God. Look to God Leonard, not mammon. I thanked them and hung up.

* * * * *

The Pastor Hearty incident turned out to be a blessing as far as my formal education was concerned. My single-minded focus on academics during senior year won me acceptance to a prestigious private university in the Southeast, one that I shall not name out of respect for the contrast between our respective reputations. I'll simply say that I suddenly found myself sitting beside the best students in the Country. I intended to obtain a mathematics degree and follow Father into the teaching profession. But my freshman year did not begin well. It did not end well either. In fact, it ended so badly that it's difficult to comprehend how it reached such a concentrated level of catastrophe. But for those of you who have lost grip of that ethereal quality known as self-confidence, you'll understand quite well.

Hundreds of miles from home, in a strange environment. A campus of Neo-Gothic architecture, whispering with the ghosts of gifted generations. Professors assuming a sturdy foundation of knowledge that I did not possess. Incomprehensible class lectures and student discussions that slipped frictionless through my anxious mind. Most importantly; an arrogant, abusive roommate.

I hated him. For years, I nurtured a scheme of flying into LAX and driving to Pepperdine for a reunion.

"Richard, old buddy! Do you remember me?" I'd ask, just as he released his physics class.

"Leonard Boseki! Of course, I remember you! My God, what are you doing here?"

I'd tell him that I was in town on business and wanted to visit my esteemed ex roommate to congratulate him for all he's achieved. How far he's come from those freshman days! A double major in Physics and philosophy; a Master's from MIT and Ph.D. in physics from Dartmouth; countless published papers and books on theoretical and quantum physics. I'd gorge his enflamed ego with jejune pandering as we dined in Malibu overlooking the ocean. Afterwards, we'd drive north on the PCH in my nondescript rental, far enough so that the lights of LA faded into a smog laden glow.

"Where are you taking me Lenny?" Richard laughs, comfortably sedated from three bottles of pinot noir.

"Oh, just a little further…" I smile.

The Seventh Illusion

A dark desolate spot, silent save for distant crashing waves. No head lights on the highway.

"Here it is!" I announce and pull to the shoulder of the road. "I want you to see where I'll be building my dream house."

"Dream house? Lenny, you can't build out here, they'll never give you the water rights..."

"Ah contraire professor! I've discovered a short cut to de-salinization! Follow me!" I lead him out of the car and down a winding path to the edge of a barren cliff.

"Look below you, my good doctor and find the future."

Ah, and now my most relished scene: Professor Dick steps to the cliff's edge and peers nervously into the abyss. Under enshrouded moonlight I see confusion in his eyes.

"I don't understand Lenny..." he says, looking back at me.

"What's the speed of light now, bitch!?" I ask and crack the bridge of his nose with a jujitsu jab.

"Owwwww!!. That hurts!!" He screams, as blood spurts onto his white oxford shirt.

"What's the velocity of a falling object...." And a humiliating kick to the crotch purges the final pomposity from his lungs as he topples down the cliff in a horrifying hundred-foot bone cracking, gruesome death.

Oh, I know what you're thinking. *How could you imagine doing this to such a great man? Didn't Dr. Richard Dietrich author that best seller Quantum Physics for Every One? Wasn't he a candidate for the Nobel Peace prize in 1998? Isn't he...*

FUCK OFF!!! I tell you he's not about shit! He never gave me a moment's peace the entire three months that I roomed with him. All his fucking talk about Phi and

Fermat and Fibonacci, his endless droning about Relativity and Worm Holes and Time Travel, his condescending comments like "It doesn't take an Einstein to figure out physics..." or "Euclid's geometry doesn't apply as you approach a white dwarf star..." or "...thus two parallel lines will eventually meet..." drove me insane! To make matters worse he virtually claimed the entire room for himself with his trendy Einstein posters and music and drug paraphernalia.

"Ah, I consider Berlioz's *Symphonie Fantastique* to be the height of man's musical accomplishment..." he once brayed over a bowl of hashish with some blood shot blonde. You'd think he'd slipped her an aphrodisiac the way she fell for that bull shit. But her response was typical. His long-winded diatribes always won him one of more rapt houseguests for the evening. I'd often drift off from exhaustion the next day in class after Richard's typical all night "Salon".

He never studied, rarely went to class, yet somehow received all A's. I discovered this fact after rifling through his notebooks one night while he was at a football game. Seeing his grades staggered me. How could a stoned, slothful, hedonistic asshole score nothing but A's while I spent every waking hour struggling for C's? In the darkness of my dorm room that night, I realized that I was not as bright as I assumed and my roommate was smarter than he deserved. Stabbed by despair, I lay whimpering and fetal for hours, as the blare of marching band trombones drifted through an open window.

"I don't belong here." I sniveled. "I'm not smart enough."

I needed a railing to grasp, if I was to withstand this torrent of pain. I found it the following Monday, on a Crusade for Christ poster in the cafeteria. The sight of clean-cut students smiling back at me was balm for my nerves. They were meeting Friday night at the student union and everyone was invited. I jotted the time into my calendar and told myself to hold on until then.

But the week proved unbearable. On Tuesday my Calculus test was returned with "72" scrawled in crimson across the front page. Wednesday morning, I discovered I'd failed my second Organic Chemistry exam. Out of desperation, I ran to the campus bookstore and purchased a Bible. For the following two evenings I sat ensconced in my room, reacquainting myself with the New Testament. Little did I realize that Scripture would prove to be my undoing.

Thursday night, November, 1984. I was reading at my desk when I heard Richard fumbling with the doorknob. In he came with another Bohemian, both obviously returning from some mid-week kegger.

"What you reading old buddy?" He asked.

But understand this, that in the last days there will come times of stress...

"The words of St. Paul." I said.

For men will be lovers of self...

"Oh, what epistle?"

...proud, arrogant, abusive, disobedient...

"Second Timothy."

...lovers of pleasure rather than lovers of God...

"Oohhh..." He whispered in that know-it-all way. I looked up to find his bloodshot eyes staring at my open page.

"What's the matter?" I asked.

"Hmmm. Nothing, nothing at all." He winced and turned away. Something in his tone warned me not to ask. So why did I?

"Just come out with it! What's your problem?" I demanded.

He turned and swayed beside his Frat brother for long seconds before finally speaking.

"Well Lenny, it's just that most Biblical scholars don't believe Paul wrote the Pastoral Epistles that's all..."

"The *what* Epistles?"

"Pastoral Epistles. You know; first and second Timothy and Titus..."

"What the hell are you talking about?"

"Well, besides the obvious difference in writing style and vocabulary when one compares these Epistles to Paul's other letters..."

"Shut up!"

"...the writer of Timothy refers to a church hierarchy, i.e. Bishops and Deacons that simply didn't exist during Paul's life. Paul never wrote the letter. It's a forgery..."

"I'LL KILL YOU, YOU SON OF A BITCH!" I screamed and lunged from my chair with a pencil. It was a brief altercation. He was surprisingly agile despite his inebriation and managed to drop me with a swift jujitsu type blow that caught me entirely off guard. He apologized profusely and had the good sense to disappear for a few hours while I tried to "simmer down" but, upon his return, found me still in the throes of a nervous breakdown, babbling incoherently and drawing parallel lines along the walls with my pencil and ruler. Within two days I was drummed out of the University with a medical discharge and nestled back in Hampton Virginia under my parent's care.

The squalling cat and the squeaking mouse,
The howling dog by the door of the house,
The bat that lies in bed at noon
All love to be out by the light of the moon.
                                Robert Louis Stevenson

Two

I was in a highly nervous state upon returning home. My senses were so acutely calibrated that I couldn't bear to be touched or even looked upon. Apart from bathroom visits, I hid in my bedroom twenty-four hours a day for weeks after leaving the university. Mother and Father were attentive, but I could only suffer their presence in short bursts and never with them together. It's painful to recall those one-on-one sessions I granted in my darkened room. Both asked the same two questions: what happened at the university? How can we fix it? Yet, although their questions were identical, they had different views as to the solution. Father's approach raised my anxiety to an unbearable level:

"Leonard, you're entirely capable of succeeding there. You simply need the correct attitude. The provost is a good friend of mine and I can have you back on campus this week!"

Father discarded my fragility and insisted "positive thoughts" would revive me. He even tried reciting Browning's "All's right in the world" one evening as I laid catatonic under covers. I did not respond.

Mother's visits were more sympathetic but provided minimal relief:

"What a horrible boy you were living with! Don't believe a word he told you Leonard. Paul certainly wrote those Epistles..." and off she'd go regarding the inerrancy of the Bible and how God was with me during trying times.

Their attempts to heal me only heightened my fear as to what lay "out there." I was one shudder away from a mental institution and knew it.

"You can't demand anything of yourself now," I'd remind myself during commercial breaks from afternoon Soaps. "You're just too weak."

Still, I slowly improved over the ensuing weeks. It started on a special morning in bed, while holding <u>Golden Poems</u> in trembling hands. I turned the pages cautiously, tiny needles prickling just beneath my fingertips. At first, I simply stared at NC Wyeth's illustrations of poetic scenes, but eventually began absorbing verses. An obscure RL Stevenson poem creaked opened the door that led me from darkness:

When I was sick and lay a bed,
I had two pillows at my head.
And all my toys about me lay
To keep me happy through the day...

It soothed me. The nostalgic lines reminded me of my GI Joe's from elementary school and so I arose, dug them from the closet and tenderly dressed them again in uniforms. Thereafter, I awakened daily to find them standing at guard on the windowsill, awaiting my command. I had none to give, so instead shared my deepest fears and sadness of heart: my social isolation and intellectual inadequacy, Pastor Hearty's betrayal, my parents deceiving me since childhood and their unreasonable expectations. How cathartic it was to have those silent soldiers listen to my trials without offering a word of judgement, or advice. I began to take them in hand and study them each morning. I straightened their uniforms, adjusted their helmets, and cleaned their scarred faces. I came to realize that they, like me, had been wounded by life's battles. But unlike me, they were stoic survivors. I placed their weapons back in their hands and resolved to emulate them.

I gradually regained confidence, which manifested itself in anger. Anger at the lies fed to me by teachers, ministers, and parents. My neighbors enraged me too, after seeing them leer across our yard into my window, wondering why I was no longer in college. It's none of your fucking business!

I gained enough courage to start roaming the house around 10pm nightly, although I still couldn't bear to have eyes gaze upon my countenance. My parents were typically still up, sitting in the living room, speaking quietly before a waning fire. I avoided them and crept silently through vaguely familiar territory toward the kitchen. It was during one such excursion that I had an unfortunate mental setback that I've never disclosed before. I'll blame it on another Stevenson's poem; A hypnotic verse that seemed to mirror my life. I gasped the night I read it; so sure, was I that he was *speaking of them!*

> *At evening when the lamp is lit,*
> *Around the fire my parents sit;*
> *They sit at home and talk and sing,*
> *And do not play at anything.*

Stevenson's bony hands clasped my shoulders as I repeated the verse aloud. Yes of course! Every evening they sat in the living room by the fire. And although they weren't singing, they spoke in hushed sinister tones! Were they plotting against me? Would they have me institutionalized?!

"What will you do?" Rasped Robert. "I'll tell you..."

With trembling cadence, he offered his next prophetic verse:

> *Now with my little gun I crawl*
> *All in the dark along the wall,*
> *And follow round the forest track*
> *Away behind the sofa back...*

Mother's damp stocking draped in their bathroom shower. So cold, stretched across my face. Nose bent so tightly that I could barely breathe. Father's 38 snub-nose pistol, gripped in my fist. Bare feet, toes clinging to the hard wood floor like suckers. Closer, closer toward the back of their whispering gray heads. What now?

"JOSEPH!" Mother shrieked.

Father jumped so quickly that I never raised the weapon above waist level. A hard chop to my neck sent me squealing back onto my tailbone with an excruciating thud. He yanked the pistol and ripped the stocking off my face as I cried hysterically in my confusion.

"Oh, Stop crying you goddamned sissy!" Father screamed. "I've had enough of your silly games!"

Almost a decade later, soon after my first murder, he would say the same thing again.

I'd gotten word he had fallen and broken his hip during a midnight stroll to the kitchen. After his surgery he'd been sent to a rehab facility within a modest neighborhood I knew very well. It was easy to imagine him struggling along with his walker down rutted streets; dogs yelping and straining against soiled yellow rope as he passed. I knew I had to see him.

I drove twelve hours in late August and arrived just after 7pm. It was back before they kept records on nursing home visitors, and so I easily got through the foyer without providing ID or explaining who I was. I wandered the halls until I found his name, posted outside his door. He was sharing a room with some poor, slack jawed bastard that didn't blink when I crossed his view of the TV. I stepped past the dividing curtain to gaze upon my father for the first time in six years. He was on his back, staring at the ceiling. He'd dropped probably a hundred pounds since I'd last seen him and his emaciation accentuated his sharp nose. Broken blood vessels spread out in tiny rills along his cheekbones. His once clear blue eyes were yellowed with approaching truth. I drew closer. But this can't be my father. This cannot be the man who cleaned my fingernails and brushed my hair; the reader of poems, the man that never tired. No, that man is ageless.

But it was him and I could not hold dominion over my emotions. I wiped my eyes and drew closer.

"Father?"

I had expected a tearful reunion rife with apologies and words that had needed to be said for so many years. My eyes brimmed with expectation, my throat choking back spasms of unspoken love.

"Oh, stop crying you goddamn sissy!" He groaned.

His words stopped me a good six feet away and I froze with outstretched arms. We stared at each other for a time before I finally asked:

"How are you feeling?"

"Terrible. Where is your mother?"

"She'll be here soon." I lied. "Do you need something?"

"Yes. I want you to go home and win!"

"You want me to go home and win?"

"Yes! Right now!"

"What do you mean?"

"Just what I said! I want you to go home and win!"

"OK Dad, I will, in just a minute."

Why had I come? I'd asked myself the question several times during my twelve-hour drive and somewhere past Fayetteville realized that it wasn't to comfort him. I was going for me. I wanted to receive something beautiful and timeless to hold like a talisman against my breast and say: This is what it means, this is why I'm here, and what I live for. I'd always believed that father understood life. Through all my sorrows I'd experienced since we'd last met, I often imagined him at the foot of my bed, smiling across the years, nodding yes, yes, Leonard but wait and see how it all works out. Let's turn the page and see the pictures, hear the verse.

That night in Father's room I was searching for his answer. I wanted to hear a beautiful poem about his family and what he had learned from eight decades of life. I wanted to hear him breathe poesy that would ease my journey through this great illusion.

But it was not to be. His breath was foul and he spent that first evening rambling of bicycles in all colors and sizes. He complained about how Mother had just left on a brown one and that I'd paid too much for mine. An hour into my visit a nurse came to turn and change him for the night. I asked if he was heavily sedated.

"No honey," she replied "that's just how Parkinson's takes people. We think he's got a touch of Alzheimer's too. Now how do you know Mr. Boseki?"

"I was one of his students at Thomas Eaton."

"Oh, that's right. He taught Literature, didn't he?"

"Yes Ma'am."

"He spent too goddamned much on his bicycle!" Father wheezed as she tossed back his covers.

"Oh, he did?"

"Goddamned right he did! Pisses me off."

"He's still feisty for weighing only 125 pounds." She smiled.

"Does his wife visit very often?"

"She comes in the mornings."

And so, I arrived at 7pm sharp each night for the next several weeks; waiting for lucidity, waiting for recognition, waiting for something I have been searching for all my life. Somewhere within those visits I knew I wouldn't find what I came for, but I kept going anyway out of rediscovered love. He slept most of the time and always with his eyes open, which created the appearance of him being lost in thought. Into the second week I began speaking to him as he slept, slowly filling in the void of years since our last meeting. It was cathartic. I wove the fabric of those painful days before his blank eyes with such vivid colors that I often caught myself weeping. I saw that it was negative space that I was evoking: lost years with Margaret robbed from me, a fruitful career and standing in the community that evaporated in the twinkling of an eye, leaving me to wander alone in a strange land, teeming with barbarians. Somewhere deep within, I knew Father felt my desolation, as I suffered those losses again. And somewhere beyond all his delusions, I knew he understood with perfect clarity, the justification of my first murder; that noble act that freed the world from a pederast, whose only purpose was to spread evil and confusion.

"Serves him right for stealing bicycles..." Father whispered after my confession.

I stayed away for two days afterward, for the euphoria of confession, coupled with fear of potential questions he may had formulated, threw me into another one of my nervous states. Yet, upon my return, he asked nothing of the murder. In fact, he never asked questions, and we spent our visits talking of increasingly disjointed, violent happenings:

"...Leonard, I'm so glad you're here!" He said, shaking my hand. "Two nurses just beat the hell out of me!"

On another occasion:

"A man was hiding under the bed and crawled out with a tire iron! He scared the hell out of me!"

I found him staring at the wall when I walked in one evening. He looked at me dolefully and said:

"Leonard. I've just been told I'm going to hell."

On each such occasion, and they occurred daily, I assured him that there were no evil nurses or men hiding under beds or messengers from hell. I took to combing his hair after feeding him dinner, a ritual that seemed to soothe him. He was fortunate enough to have a window beside his bed, which viewed a birdbath and feeder that drew many birds. We would watch the Jays and Cardinals and Wrens flutter on the mildewed bowl, and I'd identify each one just to keep silence at bay. One early evening I pointed out a Nightingale as it alighted on the feeder.

"It's a mockingbird, Leonard." Father said to my surprise.

"Ode to a Mockingbird" I said. I watched it skip from the feeder to the bath to the ground, pecking along toward the sidewalk. When I turned back to father his eyes were pink slits.

The next evening, I entered his room and found his bed empty. I went back to the front desk and was unceremoniously informed that he had passed away late the prior evening. They had bagged his clothes and asked if I wanted them. There was nothing for me to do but take them and return to Florida.

If only I had.

Though nurtured like the sailing moon
In beauty's murderous brood,
She walked a while and blushed awhile
And on my pathway stood
Until I thought her body bore
A heart of flesh and blood.
                    W.B. Yeats

Three

Mother insisted that I see a minister after I was caught with her hosiery over my face.

"Nonsense!" Father said.

"But Joseph, the poor boy has had a nervous breakdown!"

They were speaking at my bedside as if I didn't hear. Mother propped my head under a pillow. I felt her fingers tremble on my brow.

"We have been far too soft on the boy!" Father said. "Good god, he's almost nineteen! Now he either goes back to college or he gets a job, but this lying about all day playing with toy soldiers ends tonight!"

"They're not toys..." I whispered.

"Oh, do shut up!" He said.

"Joseph, can't you see he's suffering?"

"Suffering from what Judith? Suffering from the realization that things aren't as easy as he expected? Welcome to the world young man! And first thing tomorrow I will have your answer. You are either returning to school or finding a job, but you will not continue hiding from life!"

And so, I was thrust back into academia. Expectations were lowered on my second pass after I enrolled into Richmond College, a scant two hours from home. My parents secured a studio apartment for me that was a ten-minute walk to campus. Initially, I had difficulty fitting in. Some Neanderthal embarrassed me the first day in class by noting how pale I was. I explained that I was recovering from a mental breakdown. Perhaps my honesty was a mistake, because thereafter the entire campus seemed to ostracize me.

"Weirdo..." or "...geek..." or "...stay clear of that lunatic..." emanated from various people I passed, including professors. During those first months my daily routine was to rush onto campus, take copious notes in class without asking questions or establishing eye contact, then promptly retreating to my studio afterward. That summarizes my life until late March, when I had my infamous reunion with Randy Head. Oh, the dread upon finding that ignoramus in the same institution with me!

"Lenny Boseki! What you doing here? I figured a genius like you would be at Ha-vad!"

I of course, recognized him immediately.

"I'm sorry, do I know you?" I winced.

"You don't remember me asshole? Randy Head?"

"Oh yes, Randy, how have you been?"

As you may recall from my 2nd murder trial, the prosecutor opined that I started plotting from that initial meeting on campus. It's simply untrue. As proof I ask you to turn to Appendix B: <u>The Victims</u> and refer to the police photos of the murder scene. Does his pummeled body appear to be the handiwork of a shrewd, premeditated murderer? Of course not! But I digress. Those of you familiar with my history recall that it was

Randy who not only first explained "the Facts of Life" on a filthy trip to Jamestown, but also introduced me to Margaret, the sole love of my life.

"Hey, we're having a Frat party Friday at the house. You gotta come!"

"Oh, no thanks, I'm heading home this weekend..."

"Don't be a pussy! My girlfriend has this hot little number that likes to bob for apples..."

"Bob for apples?"

"You know... oh never mind. Look she's a babe. I'm heading to C parking lot now to meet them, come on."

I struggled for an excuse but couldn't find one. The C lot was on my route home anyway. Perhaps I also walked on with him because I hated the loneliness of my claustrophobic apartment.

He was correct regarding Margaret; she was warm and beautiful. Somehow, she both calmed and exhilarated me by her presence. From that first day on, she held a gravitational pull on me; sucking me into her orbit from which I never escaped. Over the following weeks she introduced me to alcohol, intercourse, and accounting, in that order.

Two days after meeting Margaret, I followed her to a Frat party. Hours later, we were floating through a frigid night, toward her apartment. But, once inside her close, perfume laden bedroom, the experience was anything but frigid. And although I was inebriated by a half dozen beers, I still maintain that our first lovemaking on her unmade bed; tussling while Pooh, and Teddy compressed and babbled in tin voices beneath us, was the most thrilling hour of my life. Afterward, while holding her in my arms, I confessed that I loved her. She gave an innocent laugh I would come to know so well. Within five minutes she was snoring. Within thirty I was vomiting.

Doyle Black

* * * * * *

This is what winning the most beautiful girl on campus brought to mind: While in fourth grade, Father took me every Sunday to a playground off Interstate 64 after church with Mother. It was usually barren when we arrived, but gradually families trickled in and children charged the field to assault monkey bars, swings and slides. The focal point of the playground was a corroded Rocket Ship; constructed of vertical steel ribs circling the vessel's perimeter and rising in an arc to its forty-foot apex. The Rocket comprised four interior compartments with a ladder piercing straight up, through the center of each floor, via a two-foot diameter opening. The ship was a relic of the sixties; those less litigious days before engineers became concerned about broken arms and stitches. Only the bravest boys had the courage to climb ever higher through each compartment, glancing back down through concentric circles to find timid eyes staring up. I was one of those brave boys. In fact, I was the bravest boy, for I alone occupied the top compartment on those bright Sunday mornings. Oh, others attempted to ascend, yes, but the heel of my Buster Browns sent them squealing in pain, back down the ladder from whence they came. I sat alone in that cage staring over my domain, gazing down upon parents tending swings. And lo, across the wide green berm, cars floating along the interstate, gazing up to find me seated above all on Red Rocket. "My, my," those ephemeral passengers smiled, "That's a special boy!"

* * * * * *

"So, ya went home with Margaret Friday night, huh?" Randy said to my back as I scanned the halls for her.

"Uh, I saw her back to her apartment, yes."

"Did she bob the knob?"

"WHAT?"

"You know. Did she go for it?"

"What are you saying?"

"Oh, come on man! That bitch could suck the chrome off a bumper..."

I saw her emerge from the ladies' room.

"Margaret!" I called and her green eyes bloomed with happiness.

"Lenny! I'm so sorry about Friday night. Was I an idiot?"

"No, of course not! Why would you think that?"

"It's just that you weren't there when I woke up and when I went to the bathroom, I saw that I got sick..."

Oh Margaret; Why didn't I take your face in my hands then and confess that it was I who was sick? Why could I never tell you of my weaknesses and fears?

We fell in love after our first date and I subsequently followed her around campus with constant craving. Whenever we were apart, I obsessed over her. Through chemistry, calculus and physics I dreamed of her soft freckled legs, black silk panties and low, approving moans. Never have I longed so desperately as I did freshman year for Margaret Kelly. Within a week after meeting, we were together nightly. Still, it wasn't enough. I wanted to consume her each minute of each day. And that's why, despite my parent's vehement protests, I changed my major from Mathematics to Accounting.

"Leonard, no!" Mother said. "You have so much more to give! Be a teacher like your father!"

"Accounting? Do, you want to be a bookkeeper?" Father asked.

How could I explain that I sought Margaret, not Accounting? How could they understand that I was in love and frightened to my core that some boy would brush her pale hand as they studied a Financial Accounting Bulletin together? No, I saw my destiny.

"My god, Boseki! I lined you up with Margaret for a fuck, not a future!" Randy Head screamed over the band at The Mad Bull Pub. Margaret had left her stool for a third visit to the ladies' room. I stared at him and his Frat brothers as they waited for their pours.

"I'm going to marry her…" I said and he laughed.

"She's not the marrying kind, Boseki! She's a party girl!"

"What's that supposed to mean?"

"Man, we call her Margie Mouthful at the Frat house bro!" Guffaws all around.

I believe that's the first time I felt it truly emerge. That primal rage that I eventually became quite comfortable with. But on that night, it was an irrepressible stranger, rising through my heart.

"I don't get it." I said.

"Oh, come on Boseki! She's a slut that's all I'm saying! All it takes is a few brews and she's…"

He never finished. I'm told I swung my mug so hard against his temple that glass shards and beer sprayed through the crowd. Several witnesses testified years later that I screamed murder threats. I probably would have carried it out, had others not wrestled me off Randy's prone body. I cannot confirm their testimony because frankly, I can't recall the altercation. I only remember faces staring fearfully into mine as the barman; bat in hand, spoke incomprehensible words.

The Seventh Illusion

Fortunately, Head never pressed charges after he was released from the ER, but the incident altered the remainder of my college career. I was prohibited from attending further Frat parties; a snub that greatly displeased Margaret. But I was happy we were banned, and relished the quieter evenings we shared, going to movies and dining at my apartment. Margaret needed more social interaction than I and occasionally left to visit girlfriends, but for most of her remaining college years, she focused on accounting. Her grades improved and I'm sure she would have had an excellent career, had she not become pregnant during our senior year. She kept the news from me for months, until her spreading thighs and voracious appetites became unavoidably obvious. She wept with a mixture of remorse and confusion upon finally confessing, and with great joy I kissed her mascara-streaked cheeks and proposed. We were promptly wed in Hampton by a Justice of the Peace, then drove to my parents to deliver the Gospel of the new Boseki family.

Mother and Father were disappointed. They had decided two years earlier, after a weekend visit to college, that they did not care for Margaret and found her "common".

"Oh, Leonard no!" Mother cried after we made our announcement in the living room. Margaret burst into tears.

"Mother, I will not have you treat my wife with disrespect!" I screamed and Mother started crying too. I turned to Father who sat quietly in his lounge chair studying the scene. His detachment angered me.

"She's three months pregnant too!" I said.

"I can see that, Leonard." Father said.

"Are you calling my wife fat?!"

"Perhaps this isn't a good time..."

And so, Father escorted his crying guests to the door. It was the last time Margaret set foot in their house. We did not call them when she lost the child in November.

I have attempted many things
And not a thing is done,
For every hand is lunatic
That travels on the moon.
She smiled and that transfigured me.
And left me but a lout,
Maundering here and maundering there,
Emptier of thought
Than the heavenly circuit of its stars
When the moon sails out.
                    WB Yeats

Four

The happiest period of my life lasted seven years. It began when I fell in love with Margaret and ended Christmas Eve 1991. The fact that I have so little to say about it now serves as confirmation of the peaceful love we shared. Yes, there were problems: rejection by friends, disapproval from parents, losing our baby, but the misfortunes only strengthened our bond.

After graduation, I accepted a position as a staff accountant at a national CPA firm in Newport News. Margaret felt too fragile after her miscarriage to finish her degree or find employment and so I encouraged her to stay home. We bought a split-level in the suburbs and set up house. I have a cherished memory of an evening there, soon after we moved in. I had pulled into our driveway late again, because I was incapable of accomplishing my work within an eight-hour day. Disturbed thoughts had accompanied me home that night, and hours of studying for the CPA exam lay ahead, which triggered fears of failing the exam, then losing my job, my house; Margaret. By the time I ran up the front steps, anxiety gripped me from heart to throat. I opened the front door. Soft jazz wafted out into the evening air. I followed it back into the living room and found Margaret; legs draped over the arm of a new lounge chair. She giggled and told me how handsome I looked in my Hickey Freeman. I kissed her and lit a fire. We shared a Beaujolais she'd found at a little wine shop, as she talked of things now long forgotten. Only her eyes, sparkling with the fire remain with me. We made love on the red velour couch, her soft tongue stained with wine. That's how I choose to remember her.

I loved her with a consuming passion. So consuming that it transitioned into jealous suspicion. Margaret was more beautiful and outgoing than I and so I became obsessed that another man might steal her. I'd call her at odd times during the day; always panicking when she didn't answer. And yet, my fears evaporated every evening:

"Look what I found at Mercury Mall today!" She'd announce at the door and lead me into the dining room to view a new painting or onto the porch to sink into white wicker furniture. It was wonderful to see her happy and to know I was providing for her.

In the evenings, after we returned from dinner, she'd go upstairs to shower and doze off watching TV in bed. I'd sit downstairs with my thoughts at the kitchen table. I loved her desperately and wanted her to love me with similar fervor. I began crafting a poem, planning to slip it under her pillow or on the dashboard of her Miata. But after weeks of effort, I found my lines to be stilted and childish. During lunch one afternoon I drove to my parent's house, let myself in and retrieved _Golden Poems_ from my bedroom closet. Back at the office I copied verse onto a four-column pad:

The Seventh Illusion

So kiss me sweet with your warm wet mouth,
Still fragrant with ruby wine,
And say with a fervor born of the South
That your body and soul are mine.
Clasp me close in your warm young arms,
While the pale stars shine above,
And we'll live our whole young lives away
In the joys of a living love.

That night, after making love, I rose and pulled the page from my pants lying on the living room floor.

"What's this Lenny?" She asked, naked and fair on the red velour couch. She sat up, unfolded the green sheet and I watched her lips slowly mouth the verse. Her eyes filled.

"Lenny, it's beautiful!" She said and hugged me. "I'm going to frame it!"

She mistakenly thought that I (rather than Ella Wilcox) had penned the poem. I didn't tell her the truth, for fear of ruining the moment. The next day I got home to find my four-column sheet trimmed and displayed in a gold gilt frame by our living room couch.

* * * * *

I'm always mystified when people ask why I loved Margaret so deeply, "considering her flaws". The answer is simple: She was flawless. It is the world that's flawed.

"Oh, come on Leonard, she was too lazy to even cook you a meal!" That worthless piece of shit biographer said during our first and only interview. The guards had to restrain me. He embellished my little outburst into a full five pages of his "ground breaking biography". He's a pussy.

It is correct that Margaret had little interest in cooking but it had no bearing on our love affair. We dined out most nights and typically walked through the mall afterward. On weekends we often brunched at Cap'n Eddy's, a little waterside café near Ft. Monroe. She loved the Chesapeake Bay and so I bought a boat for her in the spring of our second year. On Saturday afternoons we'd pack a picnic lunch with chilled bottles of Sauvignon Blanc and sail for Sandy Point. We'd spend hours swimming at the shore until our pale shoulders pinked; then nestle on blankets among the sea oats, drinking wine and softly touching. What is it about salt air that brings the juices forth? One afternoon, flush from sun, wine and lovemaking, I lay on my back staring at the perfect blue Virginia sky as soft, cumulus thoughts floated by:

> *Come what may, beyond today*
> *This perfect, pure moment,*
> *Shall cleanse it away.*

How ironic those words have become with the clarity of time.

* * * * *

As my marriage was strengthening, so was my career. I found accounting more interesting as a profession than as a major, and excelled at my job. My supervisor, Dennis Mazzani, had much to do with my advancement. He was an athletic, outgoing Italian who took to me immediately.

"Lenny, you're intense, I like that!" He laughed one day after a contentious meeting with an IRS agent. "I can see you have a temper, my friend. Come on, I'll buy you a drink..."

Drinks led into dinner. I felt uneasy leaving Margaret at home alone, but she insisted I stay when I called from the bar. "He's your boss Lenny, he's sure to help you." She was right. Soon afterward he assigned me to several large clients. Dennis and I traveled the Southeast servicing them, always staying at better hotels than the firm authorized, dining in expensive restaurants (usually with clients, but twice with a girl he'd met at the hotel bar). We squeezed in golf occasionally too. Our firm became increasingly agitated with our travel expense reports, which increasingly agitated Dennis.

"Who the hell are they to disallow dinner at Del Monaco's? Do they want us to take clients to Fat Burger? They can fuck off!" He'd seemed to forget it was just the two of us at Del Monaco's.

Margaret and I eventually invited Dennis and his wife Amy to dinner. Margaret served lasagna, catered in from Guiseppi's. I recall her wearing spandex tights, which I found inappropriate for dining with the boss, but Dennis liked Margaret immediately, teasing throughout the evening about her southern accent. It was the first of many dinners with the Mazzanis; distorted, comical evenings soaked with liquor and sexual innuendoes that I never quite understood. Bottles of Chianti and bourbon on the kitchen table and strip poker with wives tittering in bras. Legs dangling in a low-lit, turquoise pool, deep within a drunken night. Dennis slurring a lecture on obscure European philosophy; Margaret beside him. Me, nodding, smiling with mild nausea, feeling a strange miasma enveloping us. We passed a year of such weekends before Dennis announced he was leaving the firm.

"I'm taking a few of the best staff with me to start a new accounting practice, Lenny. I want you to come."

I told Margaret of the offer. She was skeptical until I mentioned my salary would almost double. I resigned the following Friday. On Saturday Margaret and I drove through the Mazzani's neighborhood, looking for a new home.

I felt blessed in those days to know Dennis. He was charismatic, and coaxed many of his old clients to our new firm. By the end of our first year, we were generating more revenue than anticipated. Dennis promoted me to partner and my bonus in May exceeded what I'd made my entire first year out of college.

"Mazzani, Sterling & Boseki, CPAs!" Announced Dennis as we celebrated in our new home a block from theirs. "Sounds powerful, doesn't it?"

We toasted our success with champagne. I sat beside Margaret on a new red leather couch, holding her hand. She had on a light green jump suit, her hair, illuminated like a halo from an end table lamp. She squeezed my hand and kissed me.

It didn't last long. In late September, Mother died suddenly of a heart attack. I received the news via a choked phone call from Father; the first and only time he called me at work. I went to her funeral without Margaret, for she had never forgiven Mother's slight on our wedding day.

I have few memories of Mother's service. I recall staring across the pew at my father and realizing that he had died also. He was heavily sedated. His eyes, once vivid blue, now stared vacuously into nothing. I could not bring myself to approach him, nor Mother, in her open casket, and so kept back from the small gaggle of mourners creeping single file past her. A woman; a common, ancient whore whose name I refuse to repeat, sat next to Father after her viewing and grasped his lifeless hand. She would marry him within six months and feed him a steady diet of demonic delusions until his dying day.

* * * * *

I have long believed that Mother's passing was the harbinger for the final death of my innocence, which in turned birthed the suffering that soon enshrouded me. But it would be another year before the final dregs of my "happy" illusions were drained before me. In the interim, business thrived and success distracted me.

"Lenny, I need you in Savannah for the Play-Max audit", or "Lenny, the IRS is reaming the Fat Burger chain and I need you in Baltimore", and "You're the only guy that can do this bro..." were typical pleas from Dennis. I traveled so often that I dropped my memberships to the Kiwanis and Optimist clubs. I was billing so many hours out of town that I rarely saw Margaret during the week and we saw less of the Mazzanis. Margaret grew sullen, partially because of my travel, but also because of our nonsocial weekends. At first, I thought that the Mazzanis had simply tired of our company, but when Dennis announced their upcoming divorce just after Thanksgiving, I blamed the firm's workload on their ruined marriage. I promised myself while shaving in Raleigh that I would never let that happen to Margaret and me. I started calling her three times a day (morning, midafternoon, and evening) but after a few weeks of the routine she had little to say. Christmas Eve would change that though. Oh, there was plenty to discuss on that hallowed night.

10:27 p.m. pulsed on the Microwave. Margaret poured the remainder of her "$7.99" Chardonnay into a goblet at the kitchen table as I wrapped her presents in the den. I heard sighs through the open doorway and knew she was in another melancholy mood. I walked into the kitchen to cheer her up.

"You're going to love your presents, Honey."

No response.

"I got you something sexy in San Antonio last month. You'll never guess what it is."

A frightened nod.

"I picked something romantic that I know you'll love…"

She burst into tears.

"Honey! What is it?"

She sobbed through the rest of her glass before I could get anything out of her. She kept saying "I'm so sorry Lenny, I'm so sorry!" as she rocked in the pew without offering anything more. It scared the hell out of me. I felt impending doom clawing at my heart, but I kept fighting it back, fighting it back.

Finally, she rose, walked slowly out to the garage fridge and returned with another bottle. She opened it, poured generously and blurted:

"I'm pregnant, Lenny. Pregnant!!"

"Honey, it's ok! Why are you so upset? It's great news!"

She was crying heavy now, and inconsolable. I was frightened and confused. Was she worried about losing another child?

"We'll be careful, Honey – I'll make sure you get plenty of rest…"

"I'm not sure it's yours Lenny! I don't think it's yours! Oh God! Lenny!"

How did I survive that night without ending my life or hers? I sat dumbfounded at the kitchen table as she spewed out her drunken confession. Dennis was darker than I and she was sure it was his. She didn't want to torture herself with another six months of worrying whether I'd find out or not. She wailed apologies, begged me not to leave her and swore that it was me she loved, not him. I sat numb before her, knowing I would never return to work, knowing I could never trust Margaret nor Dennis again, knowing that I had to do something.... SOMETHING about this PAIN but didn't know what. When I refused to speak or respond to her frantic kisses she fled upstairs and locked the bedroom door. I slowly became aware of staring at myself in the downstairs bathroom mirror, listening to a voice emanating from my throat that was not my own.

"Listen to me Leonard. Listen! You must kill her. You must kill her. Dennis too. They must be punished for this..."

I shook my head, cried that I couldn't, I loved her too much.

"Get your father's gun. Shoot them tonight!"

On the wall, in the distance, hung my framed poem to Margaret. I went into the living room and shattered it with my fist. I walked into the kitchen, tore a page off a pad and slipped my final note as a husband to her into the splintered frame:

> *So kiss me stiff with your cold dry mouth*
> *Foul from the sickness of sin*
> *And say with a sadness born from the South*
> *That you'll never be mine again.*
> *Clasp me close in your cold blue arms*
> *While the pale moon shines above,*
> *And we'll end our sad young lives this way*
> *In the stench of a dying love.*

Doyle Black

I hadn't unpacked my bag from the Atlanta trip. It was still in the foyer. How simple it was to walk out on four years of marriage without a word. I checked into the Consulate Suites that night on Interstate 64. A week later, Margaret moved into Dennis' house. And just like that, three more illusions evaporated.

.

Part II: I Am Born Again

So, the sun stood still,
And the moon stopped,
Till the nation avenged itself on its enemies.
  Joshua 10:13

One

October 25, 1994
Macon Convention Center
Baptist Youth Pastors Conference
Lecture One. How I Found Strength in the Bible.

Good morning, and welcome to the first of three lectures I will be conducting over the next several days. I'm honored to be granted a speaker's slot on such short notice and humbled by the level of interest in my message. It looks like our conference organizers were ill prepared for the size of the crowd we have this morning. For those of you standing in the back, please be patient while more chairs are brought in.

No doubt many of you are here because you're familiar with my history. Perhaps the title of my lecture series has also drawn your interest. You are here this morning, hoping to gain insight and inspiration from the lessons I've learned from the Bible. There are many church leaders and youth ministers here looking for a tangible message to take back to your congregations. Over the next three days we will study every book in the Bible in sequential order, so that we can more clearly understand God's plan for mankind. This is how God intended the Bible to be read; not via some "Read the

Bible in 365 Days" monstrosity, consisting of a daily random passage from each the Old and New Testament for a year! Imagine reading any other masterpiece in such a manner! How can the reader possibly grasp the author's intention? No, we will study the Bible starting at page one! And, after my lectures have clarified your faith, I pray that you'll in turn reinvigorate your flock's passion for righteousness and they'll join other Christian soldiers to resuscitate America!

We have a problem in the U.S.A. today my friends, I think you know this. It is dying spiritually. We have this problem because many have turned away from God and are dead in Spirit. I was among those dead until one dark, desperate morning, I turned back to the Bible.

Let me begin where my life ended. I was twenty-six years old, a partner at a successful accounting firm with a nice house in the suburbs, a beautiful wife, friends, and all the accoutrements of success. You already know this. You also know that my best friend and business partner was having an affair with my wife and that I snapped, or as some reporters have stated, suffered a "mental collapse". But what neither you nor the press know is what transpired during those first days after discovering my wife's infidelity. Allow me to fill that void.

After Margaret's confession; my marriage, career and life ended. I never returned home. I never returned to work. I'm told that my desk, much like my house, was left untouched for months after my disappearance. I spent my first few weeks after the death of my world at the Consulate Suites in Buckroe Beach. I took only a suitcase of clothes and a book entitled *Golden Poems*. For the first week after check in I left my room only once, and that was to withdraw half the funds from my joint bank account with Margaret. The total came to just over twenty-five thousand dollars, of which I took five in cash and twenty in a cashier's check. The remainder was abandoned to her.

I spent most of that first week crying and fighting against an unquenchable desire to kill Dennis Mazzani and my wife in the most violent manner imaginable. I dreamed of hacking them with a machete as they lay in bed, pouring gasoline over their entwined, mutilated bodies and engulfing them in the hell fire they deserved. I imagined them screaming for forgiveness as their skin peeled off their bones in sheets amidst the funeral pyre. It took all my will power to fight against those murderous urges that haunted me through several sleepless days. In an attempt to calm hatred, I took to reading *Golden Poems;* hoping to slip away from lacerated limbs back into simpler times. Unfortunately, I gravitated to the macabre writings of Edgar Allen Poe, which only fueled my anguish.

Oh, I see some of you shaking your heads with disapproval. Yes, you're correct, how could I have been so stupid as to seek comfort from a drunken opium eater? Still, you must allow me a brief passage from Poe in order to understand my state of mind:

> *It was many and many a year ago,*
> *In a kingdom by the sea,*
> *That a maiden there lived that you may know,*
> *By the name of Annabel Lee;*
> *And this maiden, she lived with no other thought*
> *Then to love and be loved by me.*
>
> *I was a child and she was a child,*
> *In this kingdom by the sea;*
> *But we loved with a love that was more than a love,*
> *I and my Annabel Lee;*
> *With a love that the winged seraphs of heaven*
> *Coveted, her and me.*

Now, who here knows what seraphs are? Anybody? You sir in the back. Yes! Angels! But not just any angels, they are defined as angels of the highest order! Are you beginning to see where my head was? Margaret and I had lived in our self-made "kingdom", loving each other so much that the angels <u>coveted</u> us. Do you see the twisted blasphemy I was buried under?

Now listen. Listen there's more.

The angels, not half so happy in heaven,
Went envying her and me.
Yes, that was the reason – as all men know,
In this kingdom by the sea-
That the wind came out of the cloud by night,
Chilling and killing my Annabel Lee.

Oh, I was angry! Angry with God for taking my Annabel Lee! For what had I done to deserve this cup that had been passed unto me? I was angry and quite insane, quite insane indeed. And after reading that poem perhaps a hundred times I knew what I wanted to do. You will find it in the last stanza:

For the moon never beams without bringing me dreams
Of the beautiful Annabel lee;
And the stars never rise but I feel the bright eyes
Of the beautiful Annabel Lee;
And so, all the night tide, I lie down by the side
Of my darling, my darling, my life and my bride
In the sepulcher there by the sea,
In her tomb by the sounding sea.

Sepulcher. The tomb. Death! I would kill her on our boat and commit suicide!

Oh, but wait, wait now because hope is coming! Hope is coming!

The Seventh Illusion

I was crying one morning when a Consulate maid came to clean my room. I slumped at my desk, feigning an over worked businessman's persona while she shuffled through her chores. Just as she began to vacuum, I idly opened a desk drawer to find a black cloth bound copy of Gideon's Bible staring back at me. I thought of my mother, whose faith had been firm to her dying day.

"This is all that can save you now." I said aloud under the vacuum cleaner. "You...need...answers." I resolved then and there to read the entire Bible, starting at Genesis:

In the beginning God created the heavens and the earth...

I had never read the Old Testament, having always preferred the New Testament and teachings of Jesus. Was it possible I'd missed the complete message by not studying the Old as I had the New Testament? I began reading; praying that as I moved through the pages clarity and strength would come. Oh, and how well that prayer was answered dear friends!

For those of you that brought your Bibles today, you may want to refer to my Scripture references during lunch break. For those wanting to study how to fully comprehend Truth *The Bible Notes of Lenny Boseki* is available for $14.95 at the table located in Hall C of the Convention Center. At the risk of sounding like a self-promoter, I strongly encourage you to purchase *Bible Notes*, as they clearly lay out the Genesis (no pun intended) of my spiritual awakening. Now, back to my lecture:

AA Milne once wrote:

The Old Testament is responsible for more atheism, agnosticism, and disbelief than any book ever written; it has emptied more churches than all the counter attractions of cinemas, motorcycles and golf courses.

I must respectfully disagree with Mr. Milne, for studying, and living the Old Testament has been an amazing, life altering experience for me! Thank you. Thank you, please, please sit down.

But I have a confession. As I started through Genesis my initial reactions were in fact very close to Mr. Milne's. I was immediately confused by God's prohibition against eating from the Tree of Knowledge. Why didn't God want our eyes opened? Why is knowledge bad? Further on into chapter 11, I was troubled by the Tower of Babel story. Here the "whole world" had a common language and was working together in harmony to construct a city and tower to reach to the heavens. But God, instead of rejoicing over their peaceful cooperation, was angered. "If as one people speaking the same language, they have begun to do this," spake the Lord, "then nothing they plan to do will be impossible for them. Come, let us go down and confuse their language so they will not understand each other." And so, God scattered and confused all. Did God not want unity among men? Did he instead prefer confusion and division on earth?

It got worse the further I read. I was stunned to find that Abraham, father of the Jews, married his half-sister Sara, later fathered a child through Sara's maidservant, and then allowed his wife/sister to chase the maid/concubine and bastard child off into the desert. Was Abraham guilty of <u>incest</u>, <u>adultery,</u> <u>child abandonment</u> and <u>attempted murder</u>? I glanced at the Book spine to verify I was reading the Holy Bible. Surely this wasn't the same version that Mother had read to me as a child. It was. I read on.

The Seventh Illusion

I screamed aloud at Genesis 19. There, I watched God incinerate the city of Sodom with burning sulfur because of the people's "great and grievous" sin. Everyone is burned to death except for one "righteous man" (Lot) and his two virgin daughters. And what does this righteous man do? He takes his girls into a cave, gets drunk and has sexual intercourse with his oldest daughter! The very next night he gets drunk again and has sex with his youngest daughter. Both daughters become pregnant! This is righteousness in God's eyes? Why wasn't Lot burned to death too? Homosexuality warranted destroying every man, woman, child and baby in Sodom but getting drunk and penetrating your virgin daughters is ok?

"You piece of shit!" I screamed and flung the Bible across the room. "You're worse than a mother fucker! You're a destroyer of innocence you goddamned alcoholic daughter fucker!"

Forgive me. Forgive me, I see that you are unsettled by my words. I simply wanted to convey my overwrought state of mind. Please be patient, for I promise you will not be disappointed. Please be seated and I shall continue. Thank you.

I was greatly troubled. I lay on the floor spitting hate and confusion. I now realize I had gone quite mad at that point. I was screeching at the ceiling, railing against God for all the pain and loss that had destroyed my life. I screamed and cursed until I fell into a stupor, and there I laid for time unknown. Finally, clearly, I heard a hoarse voice proclaim:

"Do not question me." I opened my eyes and He spake a raspy verse:

Do not question the Bible.
Do not question Me.
Do not seek answers.

Do not eat from the Tree.

I am the Lord.
Do what I say.
To question is sin.
So just simply obey.

Now pick up and read,
What is divinely inspired
Pick up and read,
And ye shall not grow tired.

Pick up your sword
And follow me.
And then we shall deal
With your Annabel Lee

I rose on unsteady feet. He repeated the poem. I stooped, picked up the Bible ... and Lo! The scales began to fall from my eyes!

Chapter 22: God tells Abraham to offer his only son Isaac as a sacrifice. Abraham <u>obeys</u> without question. God's response? He spares Isaac and blesses Abraham! I suddenly understood! God doesn't want us wasting time seeking knowledge or questioning him. He wants <u>obedience</u>! The Patriarchs knew this and were blessed! I pulled a notepad and pen from the drawer and wrote:

Genesis lesson – God demands <u>Obedience!</u>

I turned into Exodus and found the Israelites enslaved by Pharoah. God brings down plagues on Egypt in order to free His people. Pharoah agrees to free them but insists they leave their livestock behind. This enrages our Lord and He kills Pharaoh's first-born son, along with every first-born in Egypt, both man and animal. He also drowns every Egyptian soldier and horse in the Red Sea. Murder on a grand scale!! The extermination of thousands of evil soldiers, first-born sons and livestock for the benefit of His Chosen Ones!

God's people sing: "The Lord is a warrior!"[1]

God leads his freed slaves to Sinai and instructs Moses to tell them that He'll soon recite detailed laws to Moses which all must keep. If they obey the Laws, they'll be His most treasured possession[2]. The people agree.

The Lord descends on Mt Sinai and speaks His Ten Commandments and other Laws. God then tells Moses He's sending an angel to take His freed slaves to the Promised Land. The indigenous nations already living there will tempt God's Chosen Ones to sin, so they must all be slaughtered.[3] Moses conveys God's orders to the Israelites and they reply: "Everything the Lord has said we will do."

The Lord is pleased. He invites Moses and seventy-three leaders to go up and see Him, and eat and drink![4]

Exodus Lesson – <u>The Lord is a warrior!</u>

Exciting, is it not?! I was now fully engaged as I turned to Leviticus, which begins with God dictating His

---

[1] *Exodus 15:3*

[2] *Exodus 19:5*

[3] *Exodus 23:20-33 - I am sending an angel ... to guard you along the way and bring you to a place I have prepared... into the land of the Amorites, Hittites, Perizzites, Canaanites, Hivites and Jebusites and I will wipe them out...You must demolish them... do not let them live in your land or they will cause you to sin against me.*

[4] *Exodus 24:9-11 - Moses and Aaron, Nadab and Abihu and the seventy elders of Israel went up and saw the God of Israel...they saw God, and they ate and drank.*

Law to Moses in his tent. This is what Exodus 33 was referring to when it said that God hung out with Moses and spoke to him face to face like a friend![5] I flipped ahead and saw that the entire book of Leviticus is God speaking directly to Moses, while Moses transcribes. The final verse of Leviticus confirms: "These are the commands the Lord gave Moses on Mount Sinai for the Israelites."

Is this not INCREDIBLE?! God, face to face with Moses for hours, articulating 24,541 words of His Law! Yes, I counted them! Here lies God's longest personal exposition throughout history! Clearly, this is the most important book in the Bible and the world as well! This entire chapter should be printed in red, as the words of Jesus are when he speaks!

Leviticus Lesson – <u>God is serious! Obey His Laws!</u>

I studied each passage in Leviticus carefully, reading instructions for sacrifices, forbidden foods and personal hygiene before arriving to God's prescribed punishments for sin. There, in Chapter 20, verse 10, I found:

If a man commits adultery with another man's wife – with the wife of his neighbor – both the adulterer and the adulteress must be put to death.

I reread the passage. Yes, Lord! He was ordering me to kill Margaret and Dennis Mazzini!

---

[5] *Exodus 33:9-11 - As Moses went into the tent, the pillar of cloud would come down and stay at the entrance, while the Lord spoke with Moses...The Lord would speak to Moses face to face, as a man speaks with his friend.*

The Seventh Illusion

"I will!" I said but then realized I would be jailed if I murdered them. But why, I wondered, is it illegal to do what God commands? I pondered the question at length, and it brought forth more questions: Why doesn't God hang out with us anymore, as he did in Old Testament times? Why is he not speaking directly to us anymore? Why is he no longer leading us? Why does he now allow such evil and suffering on earth?

Patience, my fellow Christians; for I have the answer to each of these questions. It will take several more days for you to fully understand, but I promise that at the end of my lectures you'll see Biblical Truth in all His Glory! But, here's a taste of the answer in the book following Leviticus: The book of Numbers.

At the opening of Numbers, we find God, ready to move his people into the Promised Land. Knowing that hordes of infidels already living there must be slaughtered, He drafts six hundred thousand men from Israel's Twelve Tribes to form His New Army. The Israelites, no longer runaway slaves, now march forth as a conquering nation!

But upon reaching Canaan, and sending spies out to reconnoiter the region, God's Generals become frightened and decide to *disobey God's genocidal orders!* They protest that the natives are too powerful and their fortresses too large! The Chosen Ones bleat like sheep: "Why is the Lord bringing us to this land, only to fall by the sword?"[6].

The Lord is outraged by their disobedience! These lambs are too cowardly to be His soldiers! He resolves to kill all the Israelites and start over! Moses begs God not to. The Lord compromises by condemning the freed

---

[6] *Numbers 14:3*

slaves to wander the desert for four decades until all six hundred thousand cowards drop dead. As for their children; they'll tend sheep for forty years![7]

It is here where My Lord released unto me, my first EPHIPHANY! God does not want timid slaves! He wants obedient warriors!

Numbers Lesson! <u>GOD WANTS HIS PEOPLE TO BE OBEDIENT WARRIORS!!</u>

AND WHO ARE GOD'S CHOSEN PEOPLE? Correct! We are! My fellow Christian soldiers, God wants us to be warriors to cleanse America of evil!

America is <u>our</u> Promised Land but it too is inhabited by sinful infidels! Today, I bring you good news! We, who have been too timid to destroy the evil heathens occupying our lands now know what God commands us to do! Only sheepish fear prevents us from crushing the wicked in our cities, just as sheepish fear kept Israel living as slaves in Egypt instead of conquering their Promised Land! And so it is with us, my children; our fear is keeping us enslaved!

Ah, forgive me, but my enthusiasm cannot be restrained as I recall my intoxicating days of spiritual enlightenment at the Buckroe Beach Consulate Suites off exit 27. To find God's Truth, sealed as in clay jars for three thousand years, now opening like a scroll before me! Yes, even then I saw what lay ahead for the wicked: A terrible swift sword!

God led me out of meek confusion! I followed Him into the desert and saw that His way leads to victory. By

---

[7] *Numbers 14:22-34*

The Seventh Illusion

the time I reached Numbers 15:32-36[8] I knew my awakened understanding of scripture was right. _Obedience_ is all! Tears of joy streamed down my cheeks upon reading those five wonderful verses. You must understand the significance of this passage my chosen ones. A man was found gathering wood on the Sabbath, a direct violation of God's law! God told Moses "The man must die" and he was taken outside the camp and stoned to death. Do you understand? DO...YOU...UNDERSTAND? We must be _obedient_ and not shirk our responsibility of slaughtering those who break God's Law. This man had broken the Fourth Commandment. Dennis Mazzani and my wife had forsaken the Seventh!!! All heretics must be slaughtered!!

Oh, I see a stir in the audience again, does this make you squeamish? We have much ground to cover and no time for feminine passivity! You, fraulien in the third row. Sit down! SIT DOWN!! I will not have your leaving distract us at this critical juncture!

You sir, on the front row, step forward. What does this tattoo on my left breast say? That's right; "NUMBERS 31". When I was cast into jail awaiting arraignment for one of my murders (I can't recall which) I had a fellow inmate carve this genuine "prison tattoo" into my flesh. A very nice keloid is it not? It itches to

---

[8] _Numbers 15:32-36 - While the Israelites were in the desert, a man was found gathering wood on the Sabbath day. Those who found him gathering wood brought him to Moses and Aaron and the whole assembly, and they kept him in custody because it was not clear what should be done to him. Then the Lord said to Moses, "This man must die. The whole assembly must stone him outside the camp." So the assembly took him outside the camp and stoned him to death, as the Lord commanded Moses._

this day! Do you recall this chapter from Sunday school? No? Oh, allow me the privilege, for it was in this passage that I learned that God's *obedient* conquerors shall reap a great reward!

"Take vengeance on the Midianites!" Spake the Lord, and Moses sent 12,000 men into battle. His warriors murdered every man but took the Midianite women, children, and livestock as plunder back to their camp. Moses saw them approaching and angrily went out to confront his returning men.

"Have you allowed all these women to live?!" He asked. "Now kill all the boys. And kill every woman who has slept with a man, but <u>save for yourselves the virgins!</u>"

Oh, my great joy of learning that virgins will be allowable booty for our upcoming campaigns!! I had those five wonderful words tattooed in a place where it would be imprudent of me to identify at this time but... I TOLD YOU TO SIT DOWN!!!

Now, I shall cover much ground quickly so you must stay alert. Now watch this, because it is important, irrefutable evidence that we must cleanse America of heathens. Turn to Joshua chapter one.

OH, IMAGINE MY GREAT JOY DEAR STUDENTS AS I DISCOVERED GOD'S DESIRES ACCOMPLISHED IN JOSHUA!!! For there I found a new generation of Israel that were no longer slaves but warriors! God gives his final orders before sending them into battle!

> *"Be strong and very courageous. Be careful to obey all the law my servant Moses gave you...<u>Do not let this Book of the Law depart from your mouth; meditate on it day and night..</u>" (Joshua 1:7-8)*

In the twinkling of an eye, I was born again and on the march with God's New Chosen Ones, storming city

The Seventh Illusion

after city and slaughtering infidels! I wish you could have joined me during those first days of spiritual warfare! Awakening to find that we are *conquerors!* It is our sacred duty to slay the idolaters and fornicators in our lands.

"Und schlachtete alles, was in der Stadt war, mit der Schärfe des Schwertes! Mann und Frau! Jung und Alt! Rinder, Schafe und Esel!"[9] *Joshua 6:21 is our rallying cry mien children!!*

Feel the glory of slaughtering every man, woman and child, along with all the cattle, sheep and donkeys of Jericho!! Charge the city of Ai and impale twelve thousand men and women with your swords! OII! The ecstasy of decapitating the polluters of our Promised Land! Take no prisoners!! Bleed out every man, woman, beast and babe!!

So Joshua subdued the whole region, including the hill country, the foothills and the mountain slopes, together with all their kings. <u>He left no survivors. He totally destroyed all who breathed, just as the LORD, the God of Israel, had commanded.</u> Joshua 10:40-43!

A total of thirty-one cities destroyed! Imagine being there as God's warrior, smeared with bloody entrails! Feel the weight of your sharp sword as it pierces the rib cage of an idolater! Do you hear the bones cracking? The warm spray of blood as you finish a filthy barbarian? Hark! Hear them shriek, see their children fruitlessly attempt to flee our swords!! Chase down the women with suckling babes and hack at them until

---

[9] *Joshua 6:21 - They devoted the city to the Lord and destroyed with the sword every living thing in it – men and women, young and old, cattle, sheep and donkeys.*

their screams are silenced! Wipe your bloodied brow knowing that you are about God's work!! Now, cripple the horses! Cut off the thumbs and toes of kings!!!

Why do you squirm in your seats? Who calls me a blasphemer? Are you not familiar with the book of Joshua? Who shouts "sacrilege"? Show yourselves. Be seated! Be seated all of you and hear me out! I offer the following quote from a well-known statesman:

"Natural instincts bid all living human beings to not merely conquer their enemies but also destroy them. In former days it was the victor's prerogative to destroy tribes, entire peoples.[10]*"*

Wait! I will not be misunderstood! God commands us to slaughter all in America that do not worship or obey Him! I am prepared to step forward as God's new Joshua to destroy all infidels! Come follow me as a Christian soldier! Your alternative? To live as sheep, condemned to wander the desert until the end of your lives! Are you wayward slaves or conquerors?

Wait! Please return to your seats! I see I have moved too quickly and you are not yet prepared for the lesson of Joshua. I will return to the theme of Obedience!

Let us jump ahead three books and read that which proves me right! Turn to 1st Samuel 15. The Lord demands **_Obedience!_** And genocide. See what happens when Saul disobeys! God Almighty told him to:

"...attack the Amalekites and totally destroy everything that belongs to them. Do not spare them; <u>put to death men and women, children and infants, cattle and sheep, camels and donkeys.</u>"

---

[10] *Adolf Hitler*

The Seventh Illusion

Saul attacked the Amalekites and murdered all men, women, children and infants with the sword. But Saul's army spared the best of the sheep and cattle, the fat calves and lambs! To God's great disappointment, Saul did not kill <u>all</u> the livestock! Then the LORD said: "I am grieved that I have made Saul king, because he has not carried out my instructions."

DO YOU HEAR? SAUL DISOBEYED!! HE DID NOT KILL ALL LIVESTOCK!

Samuel said, "What is this bleating of sheep in my ears? What is this lowing of cattle I hear?"

Turn your eyes to the large screen behind me. This is a work of art I produced while temporarily institutionalized at a mental health facility in Gainesville Florida. As you can see in the foreground one of Saul's soldiers has an infant infidel impaled on his spear. But look behind him in the blood-spattered pasture! A cow calmly chewing its cud! DO YOU UNDERSTAND? HE WAS COMMANDED TO SLAUGHTER THEM ALL! WE MUST SLAUGHTER THEM ALL!!!

COME BACK! IF YOU LEAVE YOU WILL NOT BE GRANTED READMITTANCE! THERE WILL BE NO REFUNDS!!! WHO HAS POISONED YOUR MINDS? DAS IST DAS WERK DER KOMMUNISTEN![11]

---

[11] *"This is the work of Communists!" – Attributed to Adolf Hitler after the Reichstag fire.*

*The sun will be turned to darkness
And the moon to blood
Before the coming of the great and
dreadful day of the Lord.*
                        Joel 2:31

Two

My first lecture series was disappointing. I stood mystified, as my audience of five hundred and thirty-seven Baptists trickled down to fourteen. I of course could not continue with such a paltry congregation and so packed my slides, books and notes back into my banker's boxes and exited the stage. Hundreds of dissatisfied Christians were still crowded outside in the hallway, and I was forced to thread through them as they sneered despicable words such as "Antichrist", "blasphemer" and "refund". The Red Sea of angry faces parted and I reached the parking lot unmolested.

But as I opened my car trunk to load my boxes, a white van emblazoned with "Jesus Saves" spelled backwards on the hood, screeched to a stop beside me. The van emptied from all portals and for the next ten minutes a sweating, obese youth pastor roughed me up, to the delight of his adolescent charges. During my Come to Jesus beating I learned that they had spent their "Youth Mission" funds to drive all the way down from Mt. Airy North Carolina to hear how a "butcher" like me had been saved. Upon finding that they had been "deceived by Satan" the good pastor became determined to cast out my demons and retrieve his money. He was unsuccessful in both attempts, but managed to bruise my ribs severely.

Somewhere through that beat down, I realized I had misjudged my audience. I'd presumed that Southern Baptists would welcome my conquering message of salvation and therefore placed ads in church bulletins throughout the South for my seminar. Although my "notoriety" from three murder trials was already sufficient to draw a wide audience, I didn't want my lecture series to degenerate into a Carnival Freak Show with the media. For this reason alone, I had narrowed my marketing efforts to the Baptist community.

Yet, they were not prepared to have their eyes opened to Old Testament Truth. I've since learned that most believers haven't read the complete Bible and so their knowledge is confined to childhood lessons and whatever proof texts Pastors used to support their Sunday morning message. Consequently, most of the faithful, when they think about God at all, think of love and lambs and the compassion of Jesus. That is certainly a comforting aspect of Christianity but there's more. I wanted them to have a deeper understanding of the Holy Bible; beyond Sunday school illustrations of lost lambs and children running to Jesus.

Oh, and how invigorated I was to see the room fill with hundreds, hungry for the Word on that first, and only, day of my lectures! I knew they still held only a simple view of faith and didn't yet realize that they could be conquerors. I too had once held only a cursory understanding of my faith and assumed that God is gentle love and in him there is no evil. But as I absorbed the Bible in the Buckroe Beach Consulate Suites I learned that God was quite comfortable with evil and dispensed it often in His conquest for righteousness on earth. His evil included but was not limited to plagues, incineration, dismemberment, genocide, infanticide, animal cruelty and virgins as plunder.

"But it is not evil!" The Mt. Airy Youth minister screamed as he kicked me in my ribs.

"It's not?" I gasped.

"NO, you idiot, because it was ordained by God! Those slaughtered people in the desert were idolaters! Every man, women and child had to be sacrificed because they worshipped false gods and partook in horrendous acts like murder and incest and child sacrifice!"

"Don't you get it?" He demanded while digging through my pockets. "Don't you see that God destroyed Sodom and Gomorrah because it was full of queers and blasphemers like you? How dare you curse a righteous man like Lot!" They left me slumped between parked cars after I lost consciousness. I awakened to find my banker's box overturned and papers flapping by in the wind of a gathering storm. I peeled a sheet from my chest and held it up with trembling fingers. It was one of the five hundred copies of my Manifesto I'd planned to distribute during our first bathroom break.

"I'm not quitting..." I groaned, "until America conquers the wicked with God's Truth."

* * * * *

I found "Truth" two weeks after leaving Margaret. I discovered it at the Buckroe Beach Consulate Suites as I sat at the feet of Patriarchs and Prophets in suite 341. They spake unto me constantly; commanding me to "take up and read", exhorting me to "pay heed" to every word of the Bible. I read each passage aloud slowly, sometimes repeating the verses until I grasped the meaning of each page. I kept copious notes in a spiral notebook that had formerly been used for accounting issues. But now, they recorded Truth as it revealed itself, one chapter at a time.

In the early hours of January 7, 1992, I witnessed two bright orbs, beam through my pulled drapes and hover above me. They illuminated a pockmarked landscape possessing words, written in ancient, indecipherable text.

"Take up and write!" Commanded a voice and I obeyed. I turned to a fresh page and looked up, gripping my mechanical pencil.

"I...I can't read the words." I said.

"TAKE UP AND WRITE!" Said the voice again and I was so terrified that I lost consciousness. When I awoke, "The Manifesto of Truth" lay before me, written in my own hand:

The Manifesto of Truth
As given to Leonard Boseki

God abandoned us because of our <u>disobedience</u>!

1. *In the beginning, God talked directly to us. He walked with Adam and Eve in the Garden of Eden, like a Father. But Adam & Eve <u>disobeyed</u> God and they were thrown out of paradise.*

2. *Mankind multiplied and God grew disgusted with their <u>disobedience</u>: "I am going to put an end to all people, for the earth is full of violence because of them." (Genesis 6:13) God drowned everyone except Noah and his family because they were obedient.*

3. *Yet even after killing everyone and starting anew, <u>mankind remained disobedient</u> because by working together they built the Tower of Babel without consulting God. This angered God so he confused their language and scattered them across the earth. (Genesis 11)*

The Seventh Illusion

4. *God decided to give up on everyone except a select few. He found Abraham in the desert and said, "Leave your country... I will make you into a great nation..." Abraham obeyed and was led to Egypt. (Genesis 12)*

5. *Pharaoh enslaved God's chosen in Egypt. God's people are not born to be slaves, but conquerors. God sent plagues and death upon Egypt until Pharaoh released them.*

6. *Thus began the Golden Age of God's physical presence and interaction on earth. He met Moses "face to face" and dictated specific laws (Exodus 20-31, Leviticus, Deuteronomy) ranging from The Ten Commandments to treating mildew (Lev. 14:33). God traveled with His chosen people in the desert and went ahead of them in a cloud to find good places to camp out. He pitched His tent with them. God spoke and the people were frightened. But He cared for them and was an excellent Host. Moses and 73 others saw and ate with God (Ex. 24:9-11)*

7. *The Chosen Ones became <u>obedient conquerors</u>. At God's command His people attacked and slaughtered city after city and thousands of infidels (men, women, children, babies, livestock) until they won their Promised Land. (Joshua)*

8. *But after conquering their Promised Land the Chosen Ones became wicked. <u>They disobeyed God's Laws</u>, which angered Him greatly. God allowed His Chosen Ones to be conquered and enslaved by Midianites, Philistines, Assyrians, Babylonians, and Romans.*

9. *God became discouraged because His people were so <u>stubbornly disobedient</u>. God made fewer public appearances. He talked less. Eventually, when He spoke at all it was through Prophets and always with the same message:* **You are slaves because you disobeyed Me! Stop Sinning! Obey My Law and become conquerors again!**

10. *God's people continued their disobedience and therefore remained slaves. And so it is today. God has stopped talking altogether.*

Conclusion: WE MUST RETURN TO OBEYING ALL OF GOD'S LAWS GIVEN TO MOSES. ONLY THEN WILL WE BECOME CONQUERORS AGAIN!!!

How overjoyed I was that God opened my mind to finally comprehend Truth! My life's purpose now lay before me! I was God's chosen one to lead America back to obedience! I wept with uncontrollable joy before the bathroom mirror, knowing I was gazing into the piercing eyes of a Prophet. I found my salvation in God. Whereas only days before I'd verged of suicide; had tortured myself with weak minded "how's": *how* could Margaret destroy our family? *How* could my best friend destroy my life's work like this? *How* could God let this happen?

Oh, but now, now I had God's Truth and a future. Although it would be another year before I became acquainted with the writings of another German Prophet, he was already standing in the bathroom that morning, whispering into my ear:

He who has a strong enough why can bear almost any how. -Friedrich Nietzsche

* * * * * *

At 3:33 a.m. on January 9th, 1992, while midway through the book of Jeremiah, I heard the Lord call my name. He instructed me to leave Consulate Suites and drive south. I obeyed and possibly traveled at the speed of light, for I recall nothing of the Carolinas, Georgia or north Florida. I am told I was arrested at the University of Florida campus, waving Gideon's Bible and screaming

The Seventh Illusion

"Jeremiah 48:10!![12]" as students made their way to morning classes. You'll find in *Appendix A* my mug shot taken by the Gainesville Police Department. You may recognize it from the book cover of my biography written by the cirrhotic Roger Barnhart. I've never liked the photo but provide it now so that you may better understand my state of mind at the time of arrest. One can't help but note lucidity burning as a pure blue flame in my eyes.

After my incarceration, I was institutionalized for ten months at the Chattahoochee Mental Health Care facility. All my talk of "cleansing with the sword" and "I am His war club!!" alarmed both law enforcement and psychological counselors. I was kept from the general population as they tried various drugs and counseling sessions to calm me, all to no avail. Finally, someone suggested oil painting to sooth my "frenzied" state and, to their surprise, discovered I had artistic ability. I confess that the therapy worked so well that I lost much of my righteous zeal while producing dozens of paintings. I took great interest in my art and had a proclivity for impasto and dark colors, especially for larger works. All the pieces were Biblically inspired. My doctor, though troubled by the themes, encouraged me to continue.

Years later, I displayed my Chattahoochee collection at the "Jesus 95 Faith Festival" in Birmingham Alabama. Like many artistic geniuses, I was

---

[12] *Jeremiah 48:10 - A curse on him who is lax in doing the Lord's work! A curse on him who keeps his sword from bloodshed!*

misunderstood, vilified and badly beaten with my own director's chair as I stood surrounded by my works. It was only after Police arrived that the murderous redneck finally ceased.

Later that evening, while being interviewed on local news, my attacker defended his actions. One of my larger oils (six feet wide by four feet high) entitled "2 Kings 2: 23-24" [13] had greatly offended him. This surprised me because I felt I had perfectly captured Elisha smiling as bears mauled the forty-two boys. Unfortunately, the wailing red headed boy in the foreground with the chewed off arm looked remarkably like my attacker's son.

But I'm digressing from my Chattahoochee story. I made a rapid recovery there after I began painting and Doctor Rhodes took interest in my case. We spent hours walking the grounds and discussing my personal history and religious values. How refreshing it was for him to understand my Biblical point of view – that we were not slaves but conquerors.

"My god Lenny, what's frightening is that you almost make sense!" The doctor said once over coffee.

I was flabbergasted. Of course, I made sense! It was America that was insane!

"You know what all your ranting about conquering our slave-morality reminds me of Lenny? Nietzsche."

"Who?"

"Nietzsche; Friedrich Nietzsche. Ever heard of him?"

---

[13] *2 Kings 2:23-24 - As (Elisha) was walking along the road some youths came out of the town and jeered at him. "Go on up you baldhead!" they said. He turned around, looked at them and called down a curse on them in the name of the Lord. Then two bears came out of the wood and mauled forty-two of the youths.*

The Seventh Illusion

"No."

"He was a German philosopher that lived about a hundred years ago. He advocated that we should follow a conqueror mentality rather than a herd mentality."

"Yes!" I said, leaning forward. "Can you bring me his writings?"

"No, Lenny. Don't waste your time. He died insane."

* * * * * *

After almost seven months at the mental institution, I was pronounced cured. Upon gaining my freedom I was shocked to learn that the impound fee for my automobile exceeded its fair market value. The proprietor announced the cost with such casual disdain that I suffered another religious vision and had to be re-institutionalized at Chattahoochee for another twelve weeks. I was seething with such indignation that the owner of the towing service argued that I was unsafe for society. He did not prevail, but his "legal rights" prevented me from liberating my car upon my release on Thanksgiving Day 1992. I abandoned my car, caught a cab to the Greyhound bus terminal and secured passage to Orlando; the cheapest fare slated on the menu board.

I arrived into Orlando midafternoon; clad in State issued clothes and a backpack containing the Bible, *Golden Poems,* notebooks, and art scrolls. A besotted fellow traveler coaxed me to the Salvation Army for a sumptuous turkey dinner. It was there, amidst the downtrodden, that I began writing my meditations that would eventually be published as *And while you sang a Dirge...I Danced! - The Aphorisms of Leonard Boseki.* My first aphorism of course:

Doyle Black

We give thanks on Thanksgiving, yet forget that millions of Turkeys must be slaughtered for the sake of our Great Day!

I was sketching a barren field of decapitated birds under graphite clouds when a Salvation Officer approached. He introduced himself as Captain Fontaine and asked if I'd like to be a bell-ringer the following day. The job paid $3.75 per hour and guaranteed a meal and bed at The Salvation Army Mission. It was my first work in almost a year and I quickly accepted. The next morning, I was transported via van to a grocery store within the affluent city of Winter Park. My first day was encouraging. I welcomed all as they approached, ringing my bell and hoping to thaw the frozen smiles of wealthy wives. At the end of my shift, we counted $424.67 in collections and a Salvation Army officer complimented me regarding my fundraising abilities. I lay in my cot that night ruminating on how to improve performance the following morning. I reasoned that I could increase revenues 20% if I greeted patrons more urgently as they passed. I executed my plan upon arrival the following morning, but missed my revenue goals due to a supernatural occurrence that still mystifies me. At approximately midafternoon on my second day of employment I had, what is now referred to as my "Christmas Vision of Slaughter". The "incident" has since been so distorted by press, pundits, and police that I will now provide the actual facts of the event.

First, my physical condition. In my zeal to work two shifts I had left early for work that morning without taking breakfast. When lunch break came, I sought spiritual, rather than physical nourishment and so spent my thirty-minutes studying Jeremiah. I'd become quite obsessed with that pessimist's writings and had reread his book several times. While seated at the curb devouring his prophecy once more, I suddenly saw that his jeremiads existed beyond space and time. They lived! His warnings against Babylon applied to Winter Park! These idolaters in their black Mercedes and chic clothes would soon be destroyed if they did not cease their decadent ways and horrid practices of child sacrifice! Oh yes, they were slaughtering their seed with superfluous riches and apostacy! And now, the fetid fruit of their wombs seeped with the rancid juice of soft riches!

"He doesn't look like Santa to me..." whined a plump pear in soccer clothes.

"Mommy he looks angry..."

"Why is he ringing so hard?"

And all the while, emaciated mothers ignored their children and charitable duty, with their stiff assed walks and averted eyes, while browsing lavender shopping lists with swirling script, demanding fine wines, milk, and honey. Oh, but I read their minds! They hated me; wanted to slay me just as they had wanted to slay Jeremiah. I looked into their cold mascaraed eyes and surgically stretched skin as they plotted evil! They heard my bell and feared its message. They wanted to remain asleep in their sins without suffering the exhortation of a prophet! They intended to silence my bell by leading me to slaughter! A cart boy pointed at me while helping Jezebel to her car and said:

Let us destroy the tree and its fruit;
Let us cut him off from the land of the living,
That his name be remembered no more.

The stench of his words wafted over the parking lot and seduced the Babylonian bitches. They smiled with tanned botox cheeks and bleached teeth. Was this how I would be martyred? Was I to fall clutching the Glory Bell amidst forewarned whores? Forbid it ALMIGHTY GOD! I stepped off the curb ringing my bell in supplication to God as Jeremiah 12 spake through my lips:

Why does the way of the wicked prosper?
Why do all the faithless live at ease?
You have planted them, and they have taken root;
They grow and bear fruit
You are always on their lips
but far from their hearts.
Drag them off like sheep to be butchered!

Oh, how my enemies froze at those righteous words! Their luxuriant wool trembled atop bony shoulders! I smelled their fear and felt the mood turning, turning in God's favor.

Now, to my spiritual condition. With the passage of years, I'm no longer certain that what happened that afternoon occurred within the realm of "reality". But at the time I was sure it was the End of Days. For Lo! Jeremiah and a heavenly host of white robed horsemen appeared in the clouds and swept down into the Gaddings Grocery store parking lot on the corner of Mills and Minnesota Avenue. Many warriors had bows, others spears, but all held weapons honed for destruction. Great was my joy at the sight of them, for now conquerors committed to God's work surrounded me! I charged forth with Jeremiah 51 as my battle cry!

"YOU, WHO LIVE BY MANY WATERS...AND ARE RICH IN TREASURES... YOUR END HAS COME!!"

God's Archers cheered those righteous words. They drew their arrows from quivers and galloped onto the lot toward the unholy harlots. I saw Jeremiah, wild eyed and mud matted, raise his sword and scream!

This is the word of the Lord
Take up your positions around Babylon
All you who draw the bow

The Seventh Illusion

Shoot at her! Spare no arrows,
For she has sinned against the Lord...

Oh, the magnificence of a thousand arrows arching through the sky toward infidels! The first volley clattered onto cartops and pavement as Babylonians ducked behind parked Mercedes, carts, and their own children. And as God's foot soldiers ran in with swords, spears, and axes I shouted Jeremiah's sacred encouragement!

You are my war club
My weapon for battle –
With you I shatter man and woman
With you I shatter old man and youth
With you I shatter young man and maiden!!

But just as the first boney bitch was about to be clubbed, I was ambushed from behind by a portly Winter Park police officer. I battled valiantly against his steel cuffs but was eventually wrestled to the ground and treated shabbily by him and his partner. Jeremiah and his warriors receded as I was unceremoniously stuffed into a police cruiser and driven away from Gaddings parking lot.

The local media took great pleasure reporting the following morn that "Santa" was arrested for disturbing the peace in Winter Park. In what would prove to be typical over the upcoming years, the press and police greatly misrepresented the truth. According to an "Eyewitness News" piece, which featured numerous witnesses and the police report, I began "acting irrationally" while working as a bell-ringer.

"I was heading into the store with my kids" a woman stated, "when this guy in a Santa suit started screaming about 'butchering' everyone!"

"He was babbling about slaughtering women and children." Said another. "It really scared me!"

"If the cops hadn't arrived when they did, he might have killed someone..." reported a third.

The police report stated an employee dialed 911 after a customer complained, and the officers responded within three minutes. I resisted arrest and was difficult to restrain until I collapsed from exhaustion in the back of the cruiser.

Upon reading the article days after my arrest, I was appalled that no mention was made of God's warriors from the skies.

"Do yourself, your faith, and the entire community a favor, Lenny." Captain Fontaine said after getting my charges dropped. "Don't spend so much time in the Word."

I was surprised by his admonition and instinctively reached for my Bible. It was gone! Had it been torn from my hands during the ambush at Gaddings? Or was God in fact speaking through Captain Fontaine? I walked away from the Salvation Army that afternoon, lost without the Word to direct my path. Still, I believed God would guide me toward destiny.

When already the moon's sickle, Green between purpled reds
And envious creeps forth:
So, I sank once, out of my madness of truth,
Out of my longing of days
Weary of day, sick from light,
With one truth scorched and thirsty:
Do you remember hot heart?
How you then thirsted?
                Friedrich Nietzsche
                The Song of Melancholy

Three

I did not eat for three days after deserting the Salvation Army. I found shelter under a bridge spanning Lake Ivanhoe and slept on abandoned cardboard. I laid for days upon the embankment, staring into the waters as cumulus clouds rippled by. On the morning of the fourth day, I left my concrete cave to scavenge for food. While rifling through a trash bin on Harrison Lane, I spied a red and white sign, taped to a casement window:

For Rent : 1 bedroom furnished
$295 per mo.
648 - 6585

I rapped at the door. A sullen, elderly woman appeared. She did not like me. Perhaps even then she sensed my destiny; saw the line of the curious in cars, crawling down Harrison to stare at the former lair of Leonard Boeski. Yet, despite her suspicions, she let a second-floor unit of her College Park quad to me.

I immediately began organizing my life after securing the room. I walked to the grocery store and found soaps and dishtowels for my shower; bread and canned goods for my kitchen and notebooks for my table. I located a bank, opened an account, and deposited my cashier's check. I spent the next month sketching, brooding, and planning my ministry. In the evenings, I trudged along the shores of Lake Ivanhoe, searching the surface of the waters for direction, but found none. I was a stranger in a strange land.

Christmas came. Bagged luminaries guided my nightly walks down to the lake. Trimmed trees shimmered through living room windows. Smiling faces greeted one another on the yards and sidewalks. Love, friendship and community evaded me. I sank into despair.

In January, I began walking to the Orlando Public Library daily, for I thirsted for society and intellectual stimulation. I spoke to transients loitering on the steps, but their schizophrenic minds could not comprehend God's Truth and the impending slaughter of the Great American Whore. They invariably sat slack jawed or spoke nonsense as I prophesied. I soon deduced that I was casting pearls at swine and so quit the moral lepers for the upper rooms. I was greatly tempted to reach for the Bible, but heeded Captain Fontaine's exhortation and abstained. I wandered the aisles instead, reading the spines of books as I slowly passed, searching for a title to feed my quest. Then, on a lazy afternoon in mid-January, as I sat mulling over Margaret, I recalled my Chattahoochee doctor's words:

"Friedrich Nietzsche. Ever heard of him?"

At the time I had only the phonetics of his name, and not the spelling. But the raised eyebrows of the Librarian told me that his books were on property.

"That Fascist? You'll find him on the fourth floor." Sniffed an effete assistant.

On the fourth floor, I slowly scanned down a long, deserted aisle before finally plucking _Thus Spake Zarathustra_ from his lonely tomb. I did not know who

The Seventh Illusion

Zarathustra was and so looked it up in the dictionary. "See Zoroaster" it demanded and I did. It read:

Zoroaster (also known as Zarathustra), 628 BC – 551 BC, religious prophet of ancient Persia; founder of Zoroastrianism. His youthful studies were crowned at the age of 30 by revelations of a new religion.

My spirit stirred. Was I not approaching thirty years of age? Was I not a prophet of God with the revelation of Truth? Was it possible that God had led me to Zarathustra so that I might see I was not alone? I opened Nietzsche's book and read the opening sentence:

When Zarathustra was thirty years old, he left his home and the lake of his home and went into the mountains.

Great God! Had I not also left my home off Lake Ivanhoe to rise unto this six-floor mountain to seek Truth? I found a small table by the window and read on. Zarathustra had lived for years in solitude on the mountain until he became enlightened. When leaving the mountain in search of disciples, he came upon a saint, collecting roots in the woods. The saint urged Zarathustra not to return to mankind, but remain in the forest as he did. "Now, I love God" said the saint, "Man, I do not love." Zarathustra asked the holy man what he did in the forest and was told:

"With singing, weeping, laughing and humming I praise the god who is my god. When Zarathustra had heard these words, he bowed to the saint. But, when Zarathustra was alone, he spoke thus to his heart: "Could it then be possible? This old saint in his forest has not yet heard, that God is dead!"

God is dead!? Is that his revelation? No! But this is madness!

But wait...wait Leonard, would this not explain His silence?

No! No, I will not hear of it! God is alive! He is leading me to cleanse the earth of the Adulterers of Truth!

Yes, Leonard but don't you see? They killed Him with evil neglect. They disobeyed and ignored his commandments for so long that it killed Him! You must clear away the wicked filth so that He may be resurrected and lead the righteous to Paradise on Earth!

I slammed the book closed and turned toward the window. I did not want another reader to see my tears of rage and despair. Was I so completely alone? I had lost everything: my parents, love, friendship, career and now this? God, dead?

It was more than I could bear. I decided to kill myself. I would take my chair, shatter the window before me and hurtle into the street below. Yes, that was what I was going to do. I rose, clasped the back of the chair, and... my heart stopped. For there, on the back cover of the book jacket was a photo of me with a walrus mustache!

And yet it wasn't me. It was Friedrich Nietzsche, resting his head in his hand precisely as I had moments before while pondering suicide. His combed back hair, piercing eyes and Salvation Army Coat mirrored my appearance precisely! It was a message from God's grave! I was The Prophet who would raise God from the dead!

And so began my seven-month delusion of believing I was Zarathustra, (or Friedrich Nietzsche, I've never been sure). From that first moment on the fourth floor until late summer I studied Nietzsche, while grasping little. But that didn't stop me from thinking I had. I began writing his aphorisms in a composition notebook that I constantly carried. Somewhere during those frenzied

The Seventh Illusion

studies, I began recording my own aphorisms besides his and since at the time I considered my work his and his mine I never bothered to label whose was whose. During my third murder trial some industrious entrepreneur retrieved copies of my Nietzsche period notebooks from the public record, disentangled Nietzsche's quotes from mine and published mine as: <u>And while you sang a Dirge...I Danced! - The Aphorisms of Leonard Boseki.</u> It was quite an undertaking and for the most part I believe he achieved his goal. However, I still maintain that aphorisms 24, 67, and 108 are Nietzsche's and not mine. Or are they mine and not Boseki's? Or Zarathustra's and.... aw fuck it.

Suffice it to say that I was influenced by and commingled with Nietzsche. For example, below is an excerpt of an unpublished portion of my Composition notebook #2:

I have had quite enough of this <u>slave morality</u> in which the "virtuous" meekly turn the other cheek while their masters rape their wives, and smother God! NO! It is far past the time to cast off self-pitying passivity and sail our warships into uncharted waters! Let us move our Man 'o Wars broadside against the wicked and slaughter them as they slouch at silly computers and primp in foreign cars. That which doesn't kill me makes me want to KILL!! I teach you der Ubermensch (Superman)! You must become der Ubermensch!

I filled four notebooks with such musings that became inextricably tied with Nietzsche's. I grew a thick mustache and took to striding with head thrust forward. I had no time for society during those months and lived entirely in my mind. In addition to essays, my notebooks were alive with sketches of a wild haired, mustached Ubermensch beheading enemies with the sword, as black blood falls thick and rutted on the page.

And mid-way through my writings, sketches, and studies; while reading Nietzsche's opinion of priests in *The Antichrist*, a repressed memory arose:

Pastor Hearty, yes, I remember him.

But do you remember that night he drove you home Friedrich, um? Do you recall that frightening night of thunder and wind? He insisted on packing your bicycle into the trunk of his car, do you recall?

No, no I don't.

YOU DO! YOU DO RECALL!! DO NOT BE A COWARD! He drove you home from Wednesday night fellowship and asked about your calling!

Do you mean the time he asked what I planned to study in college?

Yes, that's it, now it's returning to you, eh?

Yes, I told him I liked math.

And what did he say?!!

Errr, he said I was special?

YES! YES! AND THEN WHAT?

Uhhh, I'm trying to remember...

Why, after coming in contact with a religious man do you always feel that you must wash your hands?

Errr...I do?

YOU IDIOT!!!

As I strained to lift the veil, that blustery night slowly came into focus. A quiet conversation, as Johnny Mathis whined erotica on the car stereo.

"Tell me Leonard, what will you major in at college?"

Yes, I remember. The thrill of riding alone with Pastor Hearty, his profile aglow from streetlights passing in the rain.

"I love geometry," I said. "maybe I'll be a math major."

"You're special Leonard, do you know that?" He smiled and scanned the intersection. "You'll succeed at anything you set your mind to."

My heart beat faster. Anything! Wow!

"I want you to know this, Leonard. I see an aura around you…"

Raindrops falling on the windshield; trickling red under a stoplight. Strange, I don't recall what happened after that…

DUMKOFF!! You do remember! You do!!

Wait…wait a minute, I remember now! He put his hand on my knee and stared into my soul as a Tarantula crept up my thigh. WHAT THE HELL!!!

This much I assure you, gentle reader: Nothing happened that night, nor any night thereafter, other than innocent adolescent confusion. I was dropped at my house as a torrent skated down the driveway in thick iridescent sheets. Ah, oil and water. Oil and water.

That repressed memory spurred me back to my notebooks, where I reacquainted myself with Sodom and Gomorrah as well as Leviticus 20:13[14]. I knew then that I'd received my first calling: I had to slaughter Pastor Hearty.

* * * * * *

Despite my new found conviction, I delayed hunting Hearty for months. I had become weary of my wisdom, like a bee that had gathered too much honey, and longed for society.

Shouldn't you find work Friedrich? Climb down the mountain and find a job.

---

[14] *Leviticus 20:13 - If a man lies with a man as one like with a woman, both of them have done what is detestable. They must be put to death; their blood is on their own heads.*

"Never! I will not return to the idiocy of 'career' and the herd!"

Look, Friedrich, the classifieds...

Thus, I hounded me, insisting I peruse the help wanted ads in the afternoons. I wanted none of the responsibilities of the business world, and so eventually circled a classified for a lifeguard position available at a waterpark. I won't tarnish the company's reputation by mentioning their name here, for I have fond memories from my time there. I hopped a bus to the park, found Human Resources, and asked for an application. After completing the necessary paperwork and returning it to the clerk, I stood at the counter waiting for approval. She eyed me suspiciously while comparing my application to my driver's license and Social Security card.

"Uhh, Friedrich, your name on the application doesn't match your drivers license..."

She handed me my license and I stared at the laminated stranger. *My God – who is this Man?*

But upon discovering I had a degree in accounting, her demeanor improved.

"Would you be interested in working in the Cash Control room Mr. Boseki? It pays more than a life guard position..."

Two days later I was counting wet cash dropped off by teenage cashiers. Initially, I was quite sullen, having been forced to remove my mustache and trim my hair. Yet, the shave and trim had the unexpected benefit of making me look years younger. I caught the admiring eyes of gift shop cashiers cashing out nightly and became the center of attention amidst excitable Hispanic girls easily five to ten years my junior. The cutest one started staying behind after the others left.

Within a month Isabel was living with me in my Lake Ivanhoe flat.

Oh, and with tear swelled eyes, she would have you believe, as she had talk show hosts and American housewives believing, that for a summer her love saved me from my depravity. For one brief season of beaches, theme parks, and candle lit dinners, we *were* Latin romance. Bel, I am sorry, but it's simply not true, despite your sophomoric insistence through twenty-three minutes of jejune national television. Never for a day did our love affair diminish my task before me! I loved you my sweet Puerto Rican princess but, placed beside the crescendo of my holy crusade, you were extraneous noise.

Still, we tried, despite our age difference, language barrier and wide chasm of intelligence. Bel would leave barely decipherable notes for me in her cashier's bag, on my windshield and inside my pants pockets:

"I hear always"

or

"I love you long time"

or

"I love you horney.."

Her tender, illiterate missives reminded me more of a Vietnamese prostitute than the passionate, simple beauty that she was. Still, I understood the heart of her message and for a while I too felt the pangs of new love. Our first kiss on the Empress Lil, as we cruised the St. Johns River, is among my treasured memories of life. The taste of champagne in Bel's mouth; her smile as I drew away, green eyes holding mine, as sunlit strands of hair, floated behind her in the wake.

"Oh Freddy, let's go to St. Augustine this weekend. We make love all day..."

And off we'd go for unrestful nights of lovemaking and days of her sniping playfully in broken sixth grade English.

"Freddy, I never see Disney! Take me Poppy! We kiss on Hunted Manson!"

But such euphoria could not last. Soon, I was back at my work again; reading, writing, sketching and planning my mission to clean the path of righteousness for God's resurrection.

"What you read and write about all the time Freddy?" She asked one night while watching Wheel of Fortune. I offered little, knowing she'd never grasp that a prophet sat beside her on the sofa.

"Just a to do list..."

"To do list?" She asked, and grabbed my book from my lap.

"Thus Speak Sarah-th-th-us-us-tra? What this about Freddy?"

"Give me that!"

"You so mean!" She screamed, and threw the book across the room.

"What the hell!!" I yelled, rising after it. When I turned back to the sofa, she was clutching notebook #4, staring aghast at page 33. It contained the sketch of a mustached man holding a sword aloft while under his hobnailed boot squirms a bespectacled coward gripping an adding machine. The caption under the sketch is now known as Aphorism #51:

When stepping on a cockroach, exert enough pressure to hear it pop.

"Freddy! What is this!" She cried.

"Errr, a road map..."

"Is no road map...is...is...dirty!"

She flipped back a few pages and gasped at page 29. Fortunately, the prosecutors of my first trial failed to

The Seventh Illusion

discover it or I'd likely be on death row writing these words. It featured a man clad in black with a priest collar, clutching a crucifix and grimacing as a sword impales his ass and exits through his abdomen. Over his head is jotted:
Hearty Harr Harr!
And below his buckling legs, surrounded by a shower of black blood are Nietzsche's words...

So long as the priest, that professional slanderer and poisoner of life, is regarded as a superior type of human being, there cannot be any answer to the question: What is truth?

She of course, could not comprehend the words, but the sketch articulated enough to send her into a frenzy.

"Aieeeee, you evil Freddy! Evil!" She ripped the page from my composition book and crumpled it.

"Give me that!" I screamed and lunged but she slipped my grasp and was in our bedroom behind locked doors within seconds. I pounded on the door, demanding the return of my work, but she refused to come out. For the next two hours, as I lay fuming on the couch, she screamed in Spanish staccato through the thin composite door:

"Aieeee yi yi, Fredrico! You crazy!!....."

"...you evil Fredrico! You scare me!!"

"...Diablo! You no good! Diablo!!"

Until I could take it no longer. I left our "love nest" and wandered the lake shore, brooding for hours over her mental instability and low intelligence. And as I stared over the dark horizon, I saw that I had made a mistake taking her in. I felt as Lee felt that night at Gettysburg when JEB Stuart proudly presented a herd of captured Yankee horses.

"Sir," Lee said, "I have no use for them, they're an impediment to me now."

And so was she, on the eve of my great battle. She was part of the vast herd that wanted nothing more than to punch the clock, collect a paycheck and retire to their stalls to watch Wheel of Fortune. She was hobbled and could not ride swiftly with me on my righteous journey.

Still, I loved her. The next morning, as I slurped Cuban coffee to stave off exhaustion, Bel emerged in the same clothes she'd disappeared in.

"You go to church with me Sunday!" She pointed.

"Oh, Bel, what are you talking about?"

"You need Hay-Sus! You need to be saved!"

"I was saved before you were born!"

"You need to be saved again!" She insisted.

And so, for the next three Sundays we went to a Spanish Evangelical Church located in a seedy strip center on Curry Ford Road. The services habitually started forty-five minutes late and rambled aimlessly into midafternoon. I understood not a word of the sermons but smiled pleasantly while feigning interest. On the third Sunday I was escorted down to the front of the congregation to "be saved again" as Bel put it but, I knew it was some kind of exorcism. The minister scowled as I approached and pointed to me:

"¡Males de ojo!" He screamed and a hot wave of moans from the crowd surrounded me. I reached the minister and he gripped my shoulders.

"¡Pura Mal!" He screamed as his saliva sprayed my cheeks. A folding chair appeared and the minister forced me down on it.

"¡Jesús Salva!"

The crowd erupted. There was much howling and sweating and squirming and at any minute I expected roosters to run down the aisle for sacrificial slaughter. The room was close, the minister's hand now pressed tight over my forehead as he beseeched the false, nicotine-stained ceiling. Three men slowly circled my chair, studying me, and yelling while, from the corner of my eye, I saw Bel in the front row flanked by two morbidly obese women. They held her arms as she wailed at the freak show before her. And as the crowd grew louder and the air thickened with urgency, I thought:

You see Friedrich, Isabel shall be that fat before she's thirty.

But nothing else. Despite their screams, rants and demands of my demons, I felt only vague ennui and mild embarrassment. Really, I didn't want to be an imposition. But the minister and congregation insisted; spitting and screaming louder with their entreaties, upsetting Bel, and further frustrating the minister. It was obvious he'd keep at it all afternoon if necessary to purge my unclean spirits. I eventually tried to stand but his men slammed me back into my seat with such force that the chair tipped, taking me and the elders with it. I saw then, as they pinned my cheek to dank, well-worn carpet, that they weren't stopping until they rid my soul of evil. I had no choice. I'd like to say that I did it for Bel but it's possible I was simply concerned for my personal safety. Regardless of my motivation, I must now confess my sin: I faked a kind of weird seizure for five minutes or so.

I could hear the collective gasp of the congregation as I began my charade. The minister responded with gusto, straddling his legs over me, and sitting on my stomach. It knocked the wind out of me. He had my demon in the open now and was determined to shoot it on the fly. With great force he brought the palm of his hand down onto the bridge of my nose and proclaimed: "¡Salga a Demonio!!"

And from the pews a cacophony of tongues:
"¡Satanás blanco!"
"¡Mirada! ¡El es poseído!"
"¡No me gusta este demonio!"

The congregation writhed and screamed like a great satanic centipede and as my head rolled toward them and away, toward them and away, I saw collective calves and cheap scuffed shoes jumping and dancing. I felt something warm trickling down my cheeks in through my lips. It was my own blood seeping out my nostrils from the minister's blow. That's when I decided to just go limp.

When it ended and they brought me to my feet there was much joyful crying, praising and singing as I nodded politely while being steadied by my new friends. I did my best to project the beatific look of the newly cleansed, but my blood smeared face and shirt kept many from approaching. I was quickly released into Bel's custody and, thank God, she led me into the parking lot to leave. She was in such nervous euphoria that she couldn't unlock the car. I took the keys from her trembling fingers and drove us home.

Later that afternoon, as she slept beside me, I brooded. What the hell just happened? Why had I been so weak as to allow myself to mislead the congregation with my theatrics? What tormented me more was that I had felt nothing at Church. Part of me would have preferred demons to howl and exit my orifices, for then I would have known that what has been told to us from childhood, and told to our ancestors for thousands of years was true. But the fact that nothing happened but my trickery troubled me. Perhaps God really was dead. I got out of bed and found my Pastor Hearty sketch that I'd scotched taped after Bel's outburst.

"You. People like you killed Him, Pastor Hearty." I whispered. And as I stared at that dark assassin a voice whispered:

"You are my war club, my weapon for battle."

I felt honored. A great sense of pride welled inside me.

"No, I'm not worthy." I smiled.

"A curse on him who is lax in doing the Lord's work! A curse on him who keeps his sword from bloodshed!"

So, I picked up Bel's car keys and went shopping.

* * * * * *

I spent two hours that afternoon hunting for swords and war clubs at pawnshops and sporting goods stores to no avail. I finally located a samurai sword in a seedy little Oriental import store on the corner of Colonial and Mills. Oh, I know what you're thinking: "Leonard, you're too literal", but it conveys my state of mind at the time. I wanted to remain traditional and use the same mode to dispatch infidels as Joshua, Jephthah, and Jehu used.

"Is this the sharpest sword you've got?" I asked the obsequious chain-smoking proprietor.

"Oh yes, yes, very sharp."

"But is this the sharpest one you have?"

"Hi, very sharp." He said bowing repeatedly.

"Do you have one that's sharper?"

"Yes, yes, sharp…"

"Oh shit, forget it. Listen, this needs to do the Lord's work. Will this sever bones?"

"One hundred forty-five dollar."

"I'll give you one thirty."

We settled on one thirty-five. I had it wrapped, slid it under the mat in Bel's trunk and drove home.

I sit here sniffing the best air,
Truly the air of paradise,
Bright buoyant air, streaked with gold,
As good air as ever
Fell from the moon.
     Friedrich Nietzsche

Four

Gary Larson, the court appointed public defender for my first murder trial, thought that the two most damning facts of my case were the raincoat and seventeen documented phone calls I'd placed in search of Pastor Hearty.

"Can you explain why you were so determined to track down the good Pastor, Leonard?" He asked.

"Yes."

He stared as I calmly smoked a cigarette across the table from him. (I took up the habit for three months at the Savannah correctional facility because it helped curb the doldrums).

"Well then, let's hear it!"

"Hear what?"

"Damn it, boy! Why were you determined to find Pastor Hearty?"

"Because God told me to. Or Jeremiah? Nietzsche maybe?"

"That's it boy. You're not taking the stand."

I never understood why Gary settled with just being a public defender. He was an excellent lawyer and could have made a fortune in Atlanta or Nashville working as a criminal defense attorney. At the time, I reasoned that

God had placed him in Savannah for me. Gary was my guardian angel and right about so many things; right about not letting me take the stand, right about the raincoat problem and particularly right about the seventeen phone calls that almost cost me my freedom. But when I was placing those calls, I wasn't concerned about how a jury might view them.

* * * * * *

I called in sick the morning after my exorcism and started working the phone, as soon as Bel left.

"Lenny Boseki! My gosh how have you been…"

"…Pastor Hearty's address? How would I know?"

"…call Tad Harrington, I bet he'd know…"

"… I heard he moved down to Charlotte…"

It took about two weeks, talking first with openly nostalgic friends, then reticent pastors and finally an irritated lay minister before I tracked Hearty from Hampton to Fayetteville to Augusta to Live Oak Florida, where I was told he'd taken the pastor position just a year before. I got the phone number and called the church. A cantankerous man answered.

"Good afternoon, I'd like to speak to Pastor Hearty."

"There's only one pastor here and it's me." He said.

"Ok. I was told that Pastor Hearty was the minister there. Ever heard of him?"

"Yes, of course I've heard of him! We kicked him out after he stole four thousand dollars from our capital fund. And then the thief got an attorney to sue us for past wages!"

"Do you know where he is now?" I asked.

"Yes, I do! I just had to mail a severance check to that hypocrite!"

"May I have his address?"

The Seventh Illusion

"Now, who is this?"
"This is Leonard Boseki. I have a message for him."
"A message for him?"
"Yes, a message from God."
"A message from God? You don't sound right in the head young man."
"God would greatly appreciate it if you could tell us where he lives."

He hesitated at first, asking me if I was "touched" and wanting to know why I'd want to contact "a no-good thief". I kept repeating myself until he finally gave up Hearty's forwarding address in Savannah, Georgia. I walked up to the gas station and got a map of the Eastern states. Hmm. Looked like a day trip to me.

* * * * * *

"Ladies and gentlemen, throughout the entire three days of this trial you have not been presented with a shred of physical evidence that my client committed murder. Now, the prosecution would have you say, 'Yes, but what about that raincoat found at the scene that came from the water park where he worked!?' Yeah, they held up that raincoat as if it was the murder weapon didn't they?! But we showed you just how flimsy that evidence was didn't we? Do you remember the numbers? I'll run through them again. That particular style of raincoat has been available at the Park's gift shop for the last seven years, during which time over seven million guests have crossed its turnstiles. Seven million! Due to the Park's poor record keeping we have no idea how many rain coats were sold during that time period but let's be conservative and assume only one in ten guests purchased a raincoat at the gift shop. That's still seven...hundred...thousand raincoats in existence!"

It's funny, but that little snippet of Gary's closing argument is among the few memories of my first trial. I recall looking up from my doodling and thinking: *But wait a minute. That was an employee issued raincoat. They never sold them at the gift shop.*

Gary was like that; always shifting truth for my benefit. From my perspective I didn't see the need, for I was sure that whatever happened was as it should be. The Apostles had also been imprisoned and killed for their ministries. If my fate was crucifixion, then so be it. I spent my three-day trial sketching the bloody memory of a night that would not leave. It always pissed off Gary when he'd return to our table after cross-examination to find blue blood spraying through my yellow world.

"'OK Mr. Larson', you may say, 'we understand about the raincoat but why did your client make all those phone calls looking for Pastor Hearty?' Ladies and gentlemen of the jury, haven't we all searched for old friends of our past? Haven't we all sought the warmth of friendship during trying times? And what better friend than a minister? Pastor Hearty had been a beacon of hope for Mr. Boseki during his high school years! Yes, we've heard witnesses testify that Leonard was 'extremely interested to find Pastor Hearty', as if to imply foul play was afoot, but where is the witness to testify that his motive was murder? Where is the testimony that Leonard ever even argued with Pastor Hearty? Where is it? I'll tell you where. Nowhere! It doesn't exist. Only Christian fellowship and kind words ever passed between them, so why would Mr. Boseki murder Pastor Hearty so brutally? No, the prosecution's flimsy evidence tastes foul does it not? Foul! No murder weapon. Not a single eyewitness to the murder and not a single witness to testify to motive. But we've provided a witness to testify why Leonard couldn't have committed the crime haven't we? We've provided a witness to testify that Mr. Boseki was not even in Georgia during the time period of the murder..."

Ah Bel, why? Why would you turn your back on truth for the sake of our sickly love? You knew that night I returned something was wrong. My pale, clammy face. The distance in my eyes. You were sure I had cheated on you, sure I was in love with that pockmarked girl you were jealous of in Cash Control. If only it was true, then you would have something tangible to contend with. But what swept me away to Savannah, and swept me away from you forever, was stronger than lust. I was sure I was following God's word Bel, as dictated to Moses on Mt. Sinai. I was listening and acting on His Law, one man at a time. And had you ever asked, I would have told you Truth. But neither you, nor most women want Truth. You want moon lit cruises, soft St Augustine Sundays, illusions of joy, and will lie to yourself and a heavenly host of witnesses to have them. But you miscalculated Bel, for I could never condone your willingness to bear false witness.

"... In summary ladies and gentlemen of the jury, we shouldn't be here today! There is nothing of any substance that ties my client to this murder. Yet the prosecution has chosen to drag an innocent man into court and make him stand trial! An upstanding man, unfairly charged and now tainted by the accusation of a violent, evil slaying!"

* * * * * *

Gary Larson was correct. Executing God's Law was a violent act. But evil? I struggled with that word for days after the slaughter, confused as to whether my action was of God or Satan. God said clearly in Leviticus 20:13 that homosexuals must die but, after the murder, I suffered with much physical and spiritual retching on the drive home. I wasn't doubled minded on the drive up, though. No, for portents exhorted me along the highway.

It was a warm, moist Tuesday morning in August. I had the day off and asked Bel for her car to visit an old church friend from high school. After learning the friend was male she readily agreed, pleased that I was associating with a Christian. I dropped Bel at the Park, filled the tank, and merged onto Interstate 4 for my four-hour mission trip to Savannah. Within an hour into my drive, signs from God exhorted me on. As I passed the Palm Coast exit a billboard in black demanded:

Do you know where you're going? - God

"Yes, Savannah!" I said. Miles later, just south of Jacksonville, another board (left hand read) shouted:

Don't make me come down there! - God

Finally, just north of Brunswick a third threat emerged above twenty-foot Oleanders ...

You think it's hot here? - God

I needed no further admonishments, for I knew the odds of three direct messages from God was not a statistical anomaly.

I reached Savannah midafternoon and stopped for gas and a map. Fifteen minutes later, I was sitting in Pastor Hearty's parking lot. Considering all the money allegedly embezzled, he resided in a modest place; a gray little two-story apartment house mildewing under Live oaks. I exited the car and found the mailboxes. "*Hearty*" was penned in black marker over slot six. I ascended the stairs and knocked on his door. Despite the long drive I had not planned on what to say or when to smite him with the sword. I don't recall what went through my mind as I stood peering through his window.

He wasn't there. Thoughts of failure entered my mind. What if he was out of town? What if he didn't return for weeks? What if he heard I was coming and fled? To think of Hearty escaping God's wrath stirred such intense agitation in me that I began pacing back and forth along the second-floor walkway, trying to wring out my next move. I settled on driving to McDonald's for takeout, and then for the next five hours sat behind the wheel, waiting for the pastor. I made a vow as I drained the dregs of my super big gulp that I would wait five weeks if necessary to accomplish God's will.

My resolve proved unnecessary. At 7:17pm, Pastor Hearty pulled into the parking lot in a late model Saturn. I recognized him immediately as he emerged from the car and minced up the stairs to apartment six. The sight of him brought forth a strange, unexpected sensation. Rather than righteous indignation, I felt…comfort. Comfort to see a familiar face that brought back memories of halcyon days. For the next half hour, I sat staring at Bel's cracked maroon dashboard, thinking of high school… of fellowship on blue shag carpeting… the scent of Pastor Hearty's cologne… a samurai sword wrapped in newspaper in the trunk. I now wrestled with my cause, torn between good and evil. But what was good? What was evil? Was I mad? How could I think that I had to kill Pastor Hearty? Because the Bible told me so?

"Because you are a prophet, Friedrich." I whispered. "You are among those most esteemed: You are with Moses and Joshua; Elisha and Elijah; Ezekiel and Jeremiah." A late summer storm advanced across the sky; low gray clouds crawling above a dense canopy of green. And as distant thunder groaned, I searched for Truth. I closed my eyes and laid my brow against the steering wheel. My mother appeared, carrying a tray of tomato soup and grilled cheese sandwiches.

"This will make you feel comfy Lenny. And after you've eaten, I want you to take a nice nap..."

Mother's love enveloped me. Oh, nestled in the safe sanctuary of the second floor. Nestled within her clean fragrance and blue, daffodil patterned walls.

Suddenly thunder and lightning shocked the night and thus spoke Zarathustra:

"To you I advise not peace but victory! Let your work be a battle, let your peace be a victory!"

"...but Joseph, the poor boy is suffering a nervous breakdown!" Mother cried.

"These Preachers of Death! They would like to be dead and we should welcome their wish!"

"Lenny No! You're a good boy!"

"'What is good?' you ask? To be brave is good. Let the little girls say: 'To be good is what is both pretty and touching.'"

And as the rain overran the car in loud sheets, I began taking strength in Zarathustra.

"...the world is beautiful, but has a disease called Man!"

Yes, I see. Pastor Hearty, preaching love and renunciation of flesh while sharing a hand job with a confused young man in the front seat of his powder blue Ford; "Friends in Love" playing loud. Pastor Hearty, renouncing material things while embezzling the widows due. Quoting scripture, living lies. Yes, the good pastor was a murderer. He killed innocence and God.

And behold! A glorious lightning bolt from the heavens, smiting a transformer and killing light for blocks. Dogs barking, car alarms in the distance, rain, blowing harder!

"Behold!" Spake Zarathustra, *"I teach you the Ubermensch: He is that lightning! He is that frenzy!"*

I opened the door into driving rain. The trunk opened before me and lo, sent from heaven, a company issued blue, hooded raincoat. I pulled it on, threw back the trunk carpet and found my Japanese comrade bundled safely beside the spare. I unraveled him from his newspaper blanket, slid him through my belt under the raincoat and sloshed across the puddled lot toward sacred vengeance. Yea, I climbed stairs of death, knees bending the blue sheen of my coat, slick with heavenly rain as wet words collided onto the rooftops of cars below:

KillHimKillHimKillHimKillllHimmm!

Nausea, trying to pull me from a soft glowing window. A silhouette, lighting candles clustered at a low table.

Yea, it is I. Rapping, gently rapping, rapping on his chamber door.

Deep into that darkness peering, long he stood there wondering, fearing,
Doubting, dreaming dreams,
no mortal ever dared to dream before;
But the silence was unbroken,
and the stillness gave no token,
And the only word there spoken was the whispered word,

"Leonard?"

He pulled me by the arm into his yellow, trembling cavern.

"Lenny, my lord, what are you doing here?" He chirped nervously as my war angel whispered sacred thoughts:

A curse on him who is lax in doing the Lord's work!

"...still as handsome as ever..."

A curse on him who keeps his sword from bloodshed!

"...oh, my you're dripping all over the floor! Let's take off your coat ..."

Nevermore!

I could not speak. All my strength was consumed in anticipation of holy duty. I stood just inside the door; his words muffled by my knotted hood.

...the cat got your tongue Lenny? You look like Pallas Athena standing there! Here..."

Pastor Hearty tugged at the string on my hood and pulled apart the velcro of my raincoat. His sudden closeness, the familiar smell of Brut animated my limbs with righteousness.

"...I was just reading Luke by candlelight. This nasty storm knocked the power out..."

I sidestepped, pulled the samurai from my belt and brought it down hard over his extended hand. He was faster than I anticipated and my blow only severed the first three fingers to his second knuckle. He shrieked and fell backwards to the floor, blood pumping through his tightly gripped fingers.

"MY GOD! WHAT ARE YOU DOING?" He screamed, as he rubbed his ass backward toward the couch.

"I have been called, as Moses, Joshua and Elijah were called: to slaughter infidels!"

He found support for his elbow on the couch and stood to beseech me.

"Lenny no! Dear God no!"

I raised the samurai over my head.

The Seventh Illusion

"No, Dear God save me! Please God! Dear God NO!" His eyes rose to the ceiling as I spake the last words he would hear on earth:

"Could it be possible? This old saint in his forest has not yet heard that God is dead?!"

The sword swung so hard that it wedged into his collarbone. Blood sprayed. I suddenly recalled a high-pressure garden hose Father hit with a lawn edger long ago. I tasted Hearty's life on my lips, warm and metallic. The samurai handle slipped through my hands as he walked stiffly backward, sword lodged deep, eyes rolling up into his skull. The couch caught his calves and he fell heavily onto the cushions, the back of the couch hitting the blade and twisting Pastor Hearty's head like a marionette. His eyes fluttered open and stared blankly at me, gurgling words that bubbled up with his passing life.

So, this is Moses and the Golden Calf, Joshua at Jericho; Elijah in Kishon. I didn't have their zeal for the Lord.

And his eyes had all the seeming,
of a demon's that is dreaming,
And the lamp light over him streaming,
throws his shadow on the floor;
And my soul from out that shadow,
that lies flouting on the floor
Shall be lifted... nevermore.

When I snuff you out, I will cover the heavens,
And darken their stars;
I will cover the sun with a cloud,
And the moon will not give its light.
                              Ezekiel 32:7

Five

I could not stop crying after devoting Pastor Hearty to the Lord. Something inside me had torn loose, and throbbed without ceasing.

"Please, tell me what is wrong? What is wrong Leeny?" Isabel pleaded, but I answered not. I lay in bed for days facing the wall, refusing to eat, refusing to explain, refusing to rise. The only thing she could drag out of me was my insistence that she call me by my Christian name, Leonard.

In an attempt to keep me employed, Isabel called work twice on my behalf offering implausible excuses.

"Freddy is very, very sick. He is going in for operation today but I hope he can go to work tomorrow. Eh, cancer operation. Yes, he has cancer. Brain cancer..."

After two days of such nonsense the Director of Finance called one morning just as Bel was leaving for work.

"Freddy can't come to the phone, he is recovering from his operation. I am telling the truth. He has brain cancer! Today I will bring the doctor's note!"

She was hysterical after the call, shrieking that unless I got out of bed and returned to work, I would lose my job, her car, and our apartment. "Where we live Leeennny?" She slapped my hip hard through the covers for emphasis, but I simply could not bring myself to care. I heard her rip a sheet of paper from my notebook and stab out a note on the kitchen counter.

"Check my spelling Leeny! Is good?" She held the note over my face.

> *Exuse Fredrich Lenard Boseki for week. He had bran surgary.*
> *Gracias.*
> *Dr. Smith*

I don't care." I said.

"You better care Leeny! You loose your job and I leave you! I move in with Yolanda!"

I was fired that day in absentia. Isabel was almost terminated too, for forgery. It was only her exemplary employment record and the Director of Human Resources that saved her job. Later, somewhere in the middle of darkness, Bel called and left a rambling message on our answering machine; crying that I had been fired, that I was crazy, that she wasn't coming home because I'd broken her heart. I got up, took a leak, and unplugged the phone.

It was a dark night for my soul; my first great struggle with the Seventh Illusion. Although I thought I had grasped onto Truth, it evanesced. Was it really Him? What if He wasn't who I believed He was? What if He was something else, or nothing at all? Who was speaking to me? What did He expect of me? And how could I be sure that what I believed He expected of me was really what He expected of me? Such questions rendered employment a trivial distraction and Bel extraneous noise. And amidst my questions lay the ubiquitous, Pastor Hearty slumped on his couch; in my dreams, my days, nights, breath and bones - blue filmed eyes, staring at the floor. Was I walking with Elijah, or Beelzebub?

Eventually, I arose and took sustenance. Cold pizza from the refrigerator and water. Afterwards, I felt good enough to walk to the grocery store and buy a cheese steak sandwich at the deli. The stroll, coupled with the meat, strengthened me. I assessed my situation. I had cast aside the shackles of a job and roommate, freeing me to seek only Truth.

I sought Truth through reading and meditation. I decided to discard Nietzsche, finally admitting to myself that I wasn't him and he wasn't me. My heart sought calm, and gravitated to *Golden Poems*. The words, coupled with memories of innocent days with my parents, brought forth unbearable nostalgia. I ached to see Father again and, after reading William Blake one evening, abruptly called his house. The temple prostitute answered and quickly condemned me for calling at such a late hour. She then coolly and clinically outlined his health history that had led Father to now reside in a nursing home. I wasted no time. I took a cab to Yolanda's and stole Bel's car.

It was during the twelve-hour drive back to Virginia that I began to recover. I was heading home, to see Father! I ruminated about our reunion; how we'd forgive one another and sink back into the comfortable love we felt years before. And though our first encounter upon my return did not go as intended, I still visited him most nights for the remainder of his days.

As for living arrangements, I returned to Buckroe Beach Consulate Suites, and spent most of the first days lying in bed staring at the ceiling. The idle hours brought forth memories of childhood, my parents, and of course, Margaret. I started a routine of driving by our marital home, hoping and fearing for a glimpse of her. I noted strange cars in our driveway and toys strewn on the lawn that suggested she'd vacated, but I persisted. Finally, after watching the house for hours one Saturday morning, the garage door opened. A man emerged pushing a bike with training wheels, as a woman and child trailed behind. It wasn't Margaret. Clearly, she was gone.

So, I shifted attention the following Monday morning to my old CPA firm. I noticed upon pulling into the lot that Dennis had changed the firm's sign to "Mazzani and Company". I parked several rows back from the door and waited for him until midafternoon, to no avail. I repeated surveilling his office for days, from 8 a.m. to 1 p.m., without success. I shifted my hours. Eventually, on the evening after Father died, he appeared.

Yes, I remember the event clearly. It was 5:37 p.m., with the parking lot almost emptied. I was wearing Father's checked linen shirt, pulled from a bag a nurse handed me after his death. I was studying a large stain on the right cuff; wondering how it came to be. Had Father tried to manage coffee but his tremors denied him? My musings vanished upon hearing Mazzini's distinct laugh, drifting across the lot.

I sank in my seat and stared through the steering wheel to find him strolling and gesticulating to two smiling girls carrying files. I was enraged to discover he was still cocksure and happy, despite having destroyed me. There he strutted, flirting and exploiting naive girls for billable hours, while probably fucking them to boot! They rounded the corner toward cars. I started mine and drove back to Consulate Suites.

******

The Seventh Illusion

Upon entering my room, I immediately grabbed Gideon's Bible, like a tremoring sot, grasping for drink. And though it had been two years since I'd last read the Word, I knew full well where I'd left off. I turned to Jeremiah and began again. His words triggered indignation. I rose and dug through my bag until I found my Bible notes after Margaret's betrayal. Within them, I rediscovered the *Manifesto of Truth* that God dictated to me in January, 1992. My passion climbed. I finished Jeremiah, Lamentations, and started Ezekiel. There, in chapter 9, verse 3, I received God's divine message:

> *And He called to the man clothed with linen,*
> *which had the writer's inkhorn by his side...*

I reread the passage slowly. *I was clothed in Father's linen shirt!!* The "inkhorn" clearly meant the ball point pen I was taking notes with! *God was speaking to me again!*

I immediately drove to Mercury Mall and found a Study Bible, concordance, and notebooks. It was while standing in the "religion" aisle of Logan's book store that I read the remainder of Ezekiel 9:5-11:

> *...kill, without showing pity or compassion. Slaughter*
> *Old men, young men and maidens, women, and children...*
> *Begin at my Sanctuary...*
> *Then the man in linen with the writing kit at his side*
> *Brought back word, saying, I have done as you commanded.*

God, commanding me from his grave, to slaughter the disobedient! "Begin at my sanctuary" was clear acknowledgement of His appreciation for my devoting Pastor Hearty to the Lord! I returned to my room and studied many hours without food or sleep. God spoke to me throughout the night via passages such as Ezekiel chapter 21:

> *This is what the Lord says:*
> *"A sword... sharpened and polished –*
> *sharpened for the slaughter..."*
> *Cry out and wail, son of man, for it is against my people;*
> *Let the sword strike twice, even three times.*
> *It is a sword for slaughter-*
> *Oh! It is made to flash like lightning,*
> *It is grasped for slaughter,*
> *O sword slash to the right, then to the left,*
> *Wherever your blade is turned.*

By mid-morning I was convinced that God wanted me to destroy everyone in America that ignored His statutes. But there were two immediate problems: (a) I had abandoned my samurai sword and (b) I didn't have the stomach to sever flesh and bone in that manner again. God told me not to worry - I could use a pistol if I preferred. And, I knew just where to get one. The clock read 11:43 a.m. If I left immediately, I could lift Father's 38 snub-nose from his bedroom closet and be back by 1pm. I drank some coffee and headed out.

******

Have you ever considered how mere seconds can change one's destiny? Had I left Consulate Suites ninety seconds earlier, or driven five miles per hour faster, our fates would have been entirely different. But it was not to be.

I was almost to Father's; idling with window down at a red light, when he pulled alongside me.

"Hey, Boseki!"

I turned to find a bloated face under a black baseball cap, smiling in a loud pickup truck. I'd seen that face before.... Oh....My...GOD!

"Boseki! How you doing puss boy? Hey pull over, I wanna talk!"

I promise you, I wanted only to ignore him. But either timidity or politeness forced me into a 7-11 parking lot to converse with Randy Head for the first time since I'd shattered a beer stein across his face. I was nervous and kept the engine running as he pulled up behind me and blocked me in. He opened his door and stepped out. I scanned his hands through my side-view mirror, expecting a tire iron or bat to be dangling from one, but he approached unarmed and bent down to my open window.

"Lenny Boseki, you old faggot!"

"Randy, how have you been?"

"I'm doing great, man. Hey, check this out." He lifted his cap and pushed back oiled locks to reveal a jagged pink scar on his right temple.

"Listen, Randy I'm sorry about that night. I've regretted it for years..."

"Shut up Boseki, it's ancient history. Hell, I barely notice it anymore."

"Well, still, it was uncalled for..."

"Yeah, especially when it turned out I was right about that bitch huh?"

"I suppose you were." I said.

"You suppose? Are you kidding? Everyone knows what happened."

I stared at his stained teeth.

"Listen, Randy, I'm in town because my father passed away and I have to make arrangements..."

"OK, man." He said, unfazed by Father's death. "I just had something to tell you about your old partner and wife."

"Oh? What?"

"It's a long story, Boseki. Listen, I took a half-day off and bought some new irons. I'm gonna hit a few into Blue Sink. You remember the place?"

"Yes."

"I've got a six pack in the igloo, come have a beer with me and I'll tell you all about the Magnificent Mazzinis."

"Randy, I really need to be going..." I said. But I was curious.

"Believe me, Boseki! You'll love this story."

So, I followed him to Blue Sink, a place I wasn't fond of. I'd been there several times after church to swim with Pastor Hearty and some other boys. Unfortunately, it was a popular place with ruffians. They liked riding dirt bikes and pickup trucks down there to raise hell and smoke marijuana. What a shame to see that clear pond assaulted by noise and vices. One serene Sunday, as we laid under the pines, a truckload of partiers arrived with cases of beers and loud music. Within an hour they were throwing stones at us, driving us toward our church van. Had Randy been among the attackers?

I followed him along the hard packed dirt road toward Blue Sink until it turned to sand. I pulled over, knowing Bel's Honda would never make it. I got out and walked the final quarter mile down to the water's edge to find Randy driving balls over the pond. Two Budweiser's rested atop a small cooler.

"I thought maybe you pussy'd out." He said as I approached.

He swung and the ball flew a perfect arc into the blue.

"Nice shot." I offered.

The Seventh Illusion

"Big Bertha driver. Wife bought it for my birthday."

He hit more; complementing each drive, haughty as always. I watched politely, thinking about Father's pistol and how perhaps tomorrow would be a better day for retrieval. Yes, it could wait, for God had not yet told me who specifically to smite first. But as Randy kept talking, I started thinking He was already telling me.

"I tell you Lenny, it's like God had a hand in us meeting today…"

"Yeah?"

He swung again and looked at me. "Your old boss has been a busy boy. And your wife? Oh, yeah, she's still a slut…"

Could it be?!

He strutted to the igloo, popped another beer, and took a long draw.

"Anyway, I'm getting ready to send that asshole buddy of yours to state prison. Thought maybe you'd like to help out by telling me about all his stealing. Besides Margaret I mean…"

Son of a bitch, COULD IT BE?!!

He spewed his story between swings; how Dennis started building spec homes on lots at his country club and made a killing. He soon expanded into other neighborhoods and quickly prospered enough to seek additional opportunities.

"About six months ago, Mazzani bought the Title Company I work for." Randy said. "It took only two months before he was stealing funds from escrow. Thought he was too smart for anyone to notice but I did. I'm telling ya Lenny that prick's a douche! I mean, how much money and pussy does he have to steal to be happy?"

I stared at Randy. He popped a third beer and held out the driver.

"Here, try this club."

I stared at the out stretched club.

You are my war club...

"What's the matter Boseki, you look weird."

"Nothing. I mean, why do you care if he's stealing from his own company?" I asked.

"Because the prick's gonna fire me! Shit, he told me himself. Said if I don't produce twice what I did last year I'm out. He's itching to get rid of me. Fuck him!"

"Do you have a glove? Thanks." I pulled it on and took up a stance.

"Shit. You address the ball like a fairy, Boseki."

I took a swing. The ball skipped forty feet and dribbled into the Sink.

"I don't know what you want from me." I said, placing another ball on a tee.

"You worked for with him for years. I bet you saw him do some fucked up things - besides fucking your wife."

I swung and missed. "I didn't see him steal anything, Randy."

"Sure, you didn't puss boy. Why would you cover for that piece of shit?"

My weapon for battle...

I swung hard again and watched the ball shank over the pond.

"Especially after he started butt fucking your wife in your own bed?"

My trembling fingers reached for a lime ball floating atop a tuft of dead grass.

With you I shatter nations ...

"...I'm sure she was sucking him off too under your own roof while you were making him rich..."

With you I destroy kingdoms...

"You've always been a pussy, Boseki. Bad judge of people too. Shit, I told you when you met Marg Mouthful she was a slut, but did you listen?"

I swung and whiffed.

"No!" Randy said, answering his question. "All you did was sucker punch me with a goddamned beer mug!"

With you I shatter chariot and driver...

"Yeah, I bet you don't know anything, Boeski. I bet you don't know whether her kid is yours. I bet you don't know...

With you I shatter man and woman...

"...I was still banging your slut wife after we kicked you two out of the Frat hou..."

"Arrrgghh!" I pivoted and swung Bertha hard against his jaw, fracturing it on first blow. He staggered back and wheezed, stunned by the impact. I raised the club over my head and struck again, but the shaft had too much flex and warped badly over his shoulder blade. Randy fell to his knees and spit out what were likely teeth, but I was far more interested in his golf bag. I pulled out a new three iron on him but my accuracy was off. I drew a seven and an eight before finally settling in with a Sand Wedge. Oh! And it flashed like lightning! I grasped it for slaughter and it slashed to the right, then to the left, wherever my blade was turned.

* * * * * *

I was in somewhat of a frenzy after golf with Randy Head at Blue Sink. Contrary to published reports, Randy was still alive when I left him. He was belly crawling along the shore, groaning much the same as anyone would who had been pummeled with a complete set of Ping Titanium irons. I was in bad shape too, gasping from exertion and soiled with my sweat and his blood. I pulled his "Hampton Roads GC" towel off the bag and wiped my brow. To my surprise, blood was smeared on the white terry cloth as I pulled it away. Blood glistened on my arms, shirt and pants as well. For several minutes, I stood cleaning up at the water's edge, as Randy slithered like a sluggish alligator toward the road. I called after him, alternately apologizing and quoting Ezekiel. After I cleansed his clubs and placed them neatly back in the bag, I started packing up for Randy. I poured out our half-finished beers and dropped the empty cans into a nearby trash receptacle, then placed the ice chest and golf bag back into the truck bed. Why was I so meticulous? I'm not quite sure. Perhaps I suspected it was the wrath of Leonard Boseki, rather than God, that was unleashed on Randy Head, and so I was trying to correct the error. If that's true then of course my actions were fruitless because a legion of Virginia's finest surgeons couldn't have put Humpty Dumpty back together again. I apologized a final time as I passed him, but I don't think he heard me. There was really nothing left for me to do but leave.

I do not remember making the conscious decision to continue on to Father's house after leaving Blue Sink. I only recall standing at the front door, finding my key still worked, and climbing the stairs to the master bedroom. I've often wondered what I would have done had Father's whore been home. I think I know.

I found the pistol in the same place it had rested for decades; plucked it up, box and all and made my way back downstairs. How Randy's bloodied country club towel ended up on the third step from the bottom is beyond me. County prosecutor Blaine Gilbert opined that I left it intentionally as a message to "the newly widowed Mrs. Boseki", but I assure you that was not my intent. It simply must have slipped from my pocket and therefore planted the seed for my third trial.

But I'm getting ahead of myself. As for the remainder of that day, I drove back to Consulate Suites, gathered my things, and left Virginia. Unlike my trip home from Savannah, in which I cried non-stop and felt great remorse, my drive from Hampton was fraught with heated arguments with unseen entities. I entreated ancient Judaic prophets, whoever, whatever they were, to understand the justification of my actions. Was not Randolph Head an idolater? Had he not been stiff necked from his youth? Had not Ms. Tinkler sent him to the office multiple times? Did he not rebel against parents and authority? Did he not lead innocents astray with his wicked, slothful ways? Oh, he needed to face God's wrath! He, and all fornicators needed to face God's wrath!

And all the while as I ranted, a dark eel writhed through my bowels.

Yes, Lenny, but...

"Nay! Nay! This is what the Sovereign Lord says; I will carry out great vengeance on them and punish them in my wrath!"

Do you not see? It was not Randy Head ...

"Will such a man live? He will not! Because he has done all these detestable things!"

It was not Pastor Hearty ...

"He will surely be put to death and his blood will be on his own head!"

It is Dennis Mazzani!

"He defiles his neighbor's wife! He commits robbery! He does detestable things!"

It is your adulterous wife!

"Ezekiel 16:32!!!!! You adulterous wife! You prefer strangers to your own husband! Every prostitute receives a fee, but you give gifts to all your lovers! Aieeeeeee!"

...and after the adulterers are slain, thou shalt gather many swords for the Lord. Thou shalt gather an army for righteousness!

Unfortunately, by the time God disclosed my destiny I was parked in front of my apartment on Harrison. It occurred to me to return immediately to Hampton and take the Lord's vengeance. But calmer heads prevailed and convinced me to get a good night's sleep in my own bed before taking up my Crusade again.

Part III: I Am Slain

The stench of unseen corpses,
rises from the gutter,
along this winding path called Truth.
And lo! Hanging from the poplars ahead,
I see them! Swaying stiffly,
Beneath a barren moon.
                The Aphorisms of Leonard Boseki. (#21)

One

Guest Sermon: My Mission to bring The Word to Somalia
Location: St Paul's Catholic Church: Winter Park Florida
January 8, 1995

Good morning, and thank you for allowing me to address your blessed congregation on this beautiful Sunday morning. How fortunate I am to be in the presence of true believers of the Catholic faith, and how gracious of you to allow a man of my sullied reputation to stand before you today. Father Finnegan tells me that you've agreed to receive me despite my past, for you are anxious to hear of how I've now devoted my life to doing God's work. It is obvious that you believe forgiveness is an essential part of the Catholic faith. I hope then that you'll forgive me, as I discard today's announced sermon and replace it with one more fitting. It is entitled: "*How history has and will justify my actions: The Holy Crusade of Leonard Boseki*". If you'll grant me patience for twenty minutes, I think you will find that this theme is far more illuminating to our faith than a simple regurgitation of a rather jejune trip of handing out Bibles to the illiterate of Mogadishu.

Doyle Black

I will begin with a question. By show of hands, how many here consider yourselves good Catholics? Excellent. And how many believe that ours is the true faith? Amen. Now consider the sinful condition of our world today; consider the Godless direction of America and the evil in our neighborhoods. Are we not surrounded by the faithless and wicked? Are we not a holy minority threatened with extinction? Do not adulterers, robbers and rapists walk our very streets? Where are our leaders to save us from this unchecked evil? Our government you say? Wasn't it our government that allowed prayer to be purged from our public schools and city halls? Do they not still impotently debate whether God himself should be mentioned on our coinage? Yes, they are willing to silence God but who is willing to silence evil? Who is purging drugs, prostitution, and violence from our streets? Who is willing to silence blasphemy, pornography and every form of filth secreting through the airwaves into our children's eyes and ears? Certainly not the government. We are being overrun with infidels my friends. Infidels who are insidiously destroying the very core of our Holy Land, by coveting our neighbor's wives, committing adultery and laughing at God's statutes. What is anyone doing about it? More importantly, what can we do about it?

Do not despair gentle flock, for Catholic history provides our answer. A Holy man of God faced a similar crisis nine hundred years ago when Jerusalem was overrun with infidels! Ruthless Islamic Turks had suddenly overthrown the Fatimids, a passive Moslem people who had ruled Palestine peacefully for years. But now, these new conquering Turks hated our Catholic pilgrims traveling to Jerusalem and beat and plundered

The Seventh Illusion

them without mercy. They even had the audacity to levy a tax on everyone entering our Holy City!

Oh, this wickedness from the faithless could not be allowed to stand! When Pope Urban heard these reports, he was filled with righteous indignation! Our Pope immediately traveled throughout Europe to tell Catholics of the treacherous Turks and raised support for a Holy War against them! Listen to Pope Urban, in the year 1095, as he delivers the most powerful sermon in Catholic history!

> *O beloved, chosen by God! From Jerusalem an accursed race, wholly alienated from God, has violently invaded the lands of Christians. They have led away captives into their own country and killed some by torture. They destroy our altars!*
>
> *You, who have the true faith... You, whose ancestors have been the prop of Christendom and have put a barrier against the progress of the infidel, <u>I call upon you to wipe off these impurities from the face of the earth!</u>*
>
> *Go, then, in expiation of your sins; and go assured that after this world shall have passed away, imperishable glory shall be yours in the world which is to come!*

Listen to those holy words again. *"I call upon you to wipe off these impurities from the face of the earth!!!"*

Now you are beginning to grasp our Holy calling are you not? You see our true mission now, do you not? Err, I see a few blank looks in the pews, so allow me to unpack this a bit more. . .

We agree that America has been invaded by an accursed race alienated from God. The race of nonbelievers that ignore God's Statutes. We see these accursed infidels soiling our Country with sin that is destroying the very altars of our faith. We hear Pope Urban, calling to us across nine hundred years that we of the true faith must *wipe off these impurities from the face of the earth!* Plus, as an added bonus, *expiation of our sins and imperishable glory shall be ours!*

Now do you understand? Now do you see what I saw the night I was called for a Holy Crusade! Yes, I who stand before you, was called! Oh, state prosecutors would have you believe that I've committed great crimes, but you see now that I was simply toiling at God's work; which Pope Urban would certainly endorse! If slaughtering the... What's that, Father Finnegan? Please just a moment and I shall wrap this up...

Yes, I was a one-man Crusade, wiping impurities off this earth. And up until my last acquittal I chose to go alone because I did not want to take responsibility for the actions of disciples that may follow me. Those of you familiar with the first Crusade recall that, as our faithful Catholics marched on their way to liberating Jerusalem, they raped, plundered, and slaughtered many Hungarian Jews. I didn't want similar complications on my Crusade. But you dear parishioners, you seem more disciplined than your ancestors. Consider me then as your new Pope Urban! Will you take up the sword and follow me to slaughter infidels? Will you?

Oh, I see it now, the horror in your eyes. I know what you're thinking. "Who made you judge, jury and executioner Mr. Boseki?" You know who did my little sheep, you know! "Oh, but those poor people you murdered" I can hear you whine, "wasn't one of them a peaceful minister that died beside his open Bible?" Yes, he was and yes, he did. But he was an INFIDEL! He did not follow the True faith and therefore deserved to be slaughtered! Are you not familiar with the outcome of the First Crusades? Do you not know that when our Christian soldiers finally reached Jerusalem, they found that the peaceful Fatimids had already overthrown the bloodthirsty Turks? The Fatimids gladly offered our catholic knights peace and guaranteed safety for all future Christian pilgrims to Jerusalem. And did we accept this generous guarantee from these peaceful Moslems? NO, BECAUSE THEY WERE INFIDELS!!

Oh, the ecstasy of our righteous slaughter! If only we could have been there when our Christian Soldiers hacked 70,000 Moslems and Jews with the sword! Men, women, and children! Listen to the words of our Catholic priest, Raymond of Agiles, who had the good fortune of being an eyewitness!!

Wonderful things were to be seen!! Numbers of them were beheaded... others were shot with arrows or forced to jump from the towers; others were tortured for days and then burned in flames. In the streets were piles of heads and hands and feet. One rode about everywhere amid the corpses of men and horses and...

Wait! Wait! OK, OK I'm talk about Somalia! I'll talk about Somalia!!

(Sermon terminated)

* * * * *

How strange to listen to that Sunday sermon again, seven years after its delivery. I was still holding a firm conviction that my actions were justified; still hanging onto the illusion of absolute good vying against absolute evil. But, after the rough handling I received at St Paul's that morning, particularly once they discovered I'd never set foot into Mogadishu, I felt low. I returned to my hotel room and stood at the bathroom sink staring into the mirror. Those words the congregation had called me as police escorted me out; were they true? Was I "insane", "evil" and "of the Devil"? I struggled with the Great

Indefinable again, trying to pierce Truth, but It kept slipping away. What did It want of me? Was not Truth and duty clearly written by the prophets of old?

"We must look one another in the face and be truthful." Spake a handsome man, framed in silver. He wept. I wept with him. "Oh, what a long sad dream this is!" He choked, and the words echoed cold across pale tiles. Where is solid ground?

"*What is truth? Pilate asked the correct question two thousand years ago Lenny, and it must be answered!*"

Oh, how I wanted to embrace that sad, brave man but he could not be held. And so, I turned to <u>Golden Poems</u>, now tattered from my endless wanderings.

> *Ah, love let us be true*
> *To one another! For the world, which seems*
> *To lie before us like a land of dreams,*
> *So various, so beautiful, so new*
> *Hath really neither joy, nor love, nor light,*
> *Nor certitude, nor peace, nor help for pain;*
> *And we are here as on a darkling plain*
> *Swept with confused alarms of struggle and flight*
> *Where ignorant armies clash by night.*
>   Matthew Arnold

We stood face to face until the pale fire of day dimmed the room. We faded from each other as we drifted into dark waters without direction. Where am I going?

"Patience," He spake, "patience and I shall bring you to the sea of calm."

I will not violate my covenant,
Or alter what my lips have uttered.
It will be established forever like the moon,
The faithful witness in the sky.
  Psalm 89: 31-37

I have become world-famous for slaughtering infidels. I believe there's a good chance I'll eventually be sainted.
  - The Aphorisms of Leonard Boseki. (#34)

Two

My plans to slaughter the Mazzanis stalled after I returned to Orlando and found Bel in my apartment.

"Leeny! Where have you bean? You steal my car dinn'it you?"

I was in no mood for illiterate accusations. I tried to push toward the bathroom but she wouldn't have it.

"The police have been calling Leeny! The Police! What have you done Leeny? WHAT HAVE YOU DONE?"

A sword, drawn for the slaughter...

"Leeny, what is wrong with you? You luke crazy!"

...polished to consume...

"Leeny! I smell it on you!

...and flash like lightning!

"Diablo!"

It will be laid on the necks of the wicked who are to be slain,

"Talk to me Leeny! Say something!"

whose time of punishment has reached its climax!!

For those of you familiar with my "biography" by the feckless Roger Barnhart, you'll recall that Bel allegedly told him that I "exuded a deranged aura" that night. I doubt he ever spoke to my poor vacuous princess. But if he did in fact conduct an interview, I'm sure he was disappointed with her deformed thoughts and mangled

English and thus decided to shape her words into what he wanted for his shitty little book of lies. I guarantee you she never said a word of what that asshole passed off as her comments. He knew she'd never read his worthless tripe and so he simply inserted his own flaccid thoughts into his fucking little... ah shit, here's an excerpt of Bel's "interview" according to Barnhart:

> *After several weeks without a clue as to his whereabouts, I was stunned to find Leonard barging through my front door around 1am. One look in his eyes and the hairs on my back stood up. They were the eyes of a demon! His face was filmed in milky sweat and his lips mouthed silent words. He personified evil. I screamed in horror and begged him to leave. He silently moved passed me, heading for the bathroom. I barred his way and demanded he leave immediately. He just stared straight through me. I told him the police were looking for him and that I was going to call 911 Even that didn't draw a response. He just kept staring with mad dog eyes. It frightened me. Somewhere deep in my soul I could hear Randy Head and Pastor Hearty moaning, crying, begging me to bring peace to their souls. I could smell their murders emanating from Lenny's very pores...*[15]

OH...MY...GOD! First, how could she feel Hearty and Head deep in her soul when they were already on the highway to hell? Second, if Bel ever heard the word "emanate" she'd think it meant, "he already ate" or something equally barbaric. Third and most importantly, if she was so convinced that I was a mad murderer why then did she later testify on my behalf at my first trial? Oh, sure Barnhart puts the question to her in his typical half-assed style on page 132 and immediately provides his own lazy opinion. He surmises

---

[15] *From Getting Away With Murder: Inside the Twisted Mind of Leonard Boseki – By Roger Barnhart*

that I had a "Rasputten-like effect on her". *Rasputten*? It's <u>Rasputin</u> you subliterate dipsomaniac!! And how about trying "influence", rather than "effect"? Go back to writing wedding announcements and funeral notices for the Fayetteville Star thou great slaughterer of the English language!

Look, here's what happened. I was a little distracted when I returned home from devoting Randy Head to the Lord. It had been a long day and a long drive and I was ill prepared to find a possessed Puerto Rican, spasming around *my* apartment. I bid her good evening, excused myself like a gentleman and retired to the bathroom for a long soothing shower. My muscles were taut from the activities of the day and the warm gyrations emanating from the showerhead were wonderfully calming. Upon reemerging, I discovered Isabel had locked herself in *my* bedroom and left a nasty note penned in pathetic second grade English that insisted I leave *my* apartment immediately. I found the demand rather mystifying given that it was after all, *my* money paying the rent. I shrugged and looked around for the car keys. It was only 2 a.m., I felt refreshed and, if I left immediately, I could make Virginia by early afternoon. But the keys were nowhere to be found. Had Bel hidden them? Could it be my deluded little demon had aligned herself with Satan? Perhaps a Spanish Inquisition was in order! I knocked politely on the bedroom door to ask about the car keys but the only response I received were unintelligible Latino shrieks. As I stood with ear pressed to the door; testing the doorknob, I suddenly recalled I'd left the pistol under the driver's seat. I pulled on my pants and went outside, hoping that I'd forgotten to lock the doors. No such luck. I walked around back to the Landlord's shed and retrieved a shovel, then lanced the driver's window with the handle end and unlocked the door. I gathered the pistol & case, wrapped it in a plastic trash bag and buried it in the back yard. Then I returned the shovel to the shed, retrieved my books and writings from Bel's car and spent the remainder of the night reading on the couch. When I awoke the following afternoon, Isabel was gone. But the police were on the phone calling from Savannah.

* * * * * *

I have neither the strength nor interest to recount the entire ordeal of my first murder trial. The arrest, interrogation and subsequent trial spanned only three months start to finish, during which time I grew pale, shed twenty pounds, and suffered slow death at the Savannah Jail. The police there hated me, probably because of their own failed efforts at telephonic interrogation. I offer an excerpt from that initial interview:

Officer Hanson: ...we have a few questions regarding the murder of a Laurence Hearty that occurred here in Savannah a few months ago. You knew him, is that correct?

Boseki: Pastor Hearty? Yes sir, I knew him.

Hanson: We spent some time tracking down Pastor Hearty's friends and associates and discovered that you called several of them shortly before his death, is that true?

Boseki: Yes sir.

Hanson: And why did you call them?

Boseki: I was trying to find Pastor Hearty.

Hanson: OK, why were you trying to locate Pastor Hearty?

Boseki: I had a message from God.

Hanson: A message from God?
Boseki: Yes sir.
Hanson: And what exactly did God want you to say to Pastor Hearty?
Boseki: He didn't want me to say anything.
Hanson: He didn't want you to say anything? Then what was the message?
Boseki: He wanted me to grasp my sword for slaughter and slash it to the right, then to the left, wherever the blade is turned.
Hanson: ....He....He...come again?
Boseki: He wanted me to grasp my sword for slaughter and slash it to the right, then to the left, wherever the blade is turned.
Hanson: Uh, God wanted you to grasp your sword?
Boseki: Yes sir.
Hanson: And uh, slaughter Pastor Hearty?
Boseki: Precisely.

Unfortunately, they hadn't read me my Miranda rights so the entire interrogation was inadmissible. Of course, I was ready to offer the same testimony again after I was extradited to Savannah but by then Gary Larson had been assigned as my public defender and he wouldn't let me. I think Gary's obstinacy was another reason the Savannah Police treated me so shabbily. Why else would they confine me to a cell for months with "Tee-Bone", the most brutal man I've ever known. He was a common criminal of low intelligence, awaiting trial for beating another man to death with a broken pool cue. He hated me immediately, partially because I was white but mainly because the jailers told him I'd "butchered a preacher".

"Gat Damn boy! Yo's EEvul!" He'd announce from nowhere and slam his anvil fist into my face. The jailers thought it was funny as shit. After seeing my facial bruises Gary Larson demanded that I be moved to another cell. Request denied. The jailers must have counseled Tee-Bone though, because he stopped swinging for my head and moved down to kidney punches and various body blows that showed less bruising. I took the first such beatings stoically, figuring that Saints Peter and James had suffered similar persecution. But after a particularly nasty pummeling from a pillowcase packed with soap bars, I figured God was trying to tell me something.

"Perhaps he's meant to be your first soldier for the Lord." I moaned, while Tee-Bone snored in his bunk above me. I rolled out of bed and composed what would be my first communiqué for my new ministry. I was so sure of its historical significance that I duplicated my note by hand and folded it carefully in my Bible for posterity. I offer the full text below:

September 30, 1993
Dear Mr. Tee Bone,

Do you ever wonder why God quit talking to his people like He used to do in Old Testament times? Think about it. He spoke with Adam, Abraham and Isaac. He wrestled with Jacob and met face to face with Moses on Mt. Sinai. He led the Chosen Ones through the desert and even camped out with them. So why, after years of walking and talking on earth did he suddenly vanish? I'll tell you why. He got sick of our disobedience.

God used to hang out with us 3500 years ago when we obeyed his Laws as laid out in Exodus, Leviticus, and Deuteronomy. We did what he told us to do and he blessed us. He told us to slaughter every man, women, child, baby, and goat standing in the way of our Promised Land (See Joshua) and we did it. But do you know what happened after we accomplished His Holy Holocaust? We forgot about Him. We abandoned the Law and worshipped idols. Our apostasy angered God and so He allowed infidels to defeat us and strip us of our Promised Land. God made fewer appearances but sometimes sent prophets like Jeremiah and Ezekiel to tell us to slaughter the invading idolaters. We didn't kill them so God quit talking and infidels remained in power. So, it remains today.

But there is hope. God has sent another prophet by the name of Leonard Boseki. God has shown Leonard that we must return to obeying His Laws as dictated to Moses on Mt. Sinai and recorded in Exodus, Leviticus and Deuteronomy. We must also slay all those that do not worship Him and follow His Laws. I am God's prophet sent to return America to God's Law and to slay those that violate His statutes. I have been sent to cleanse the earth with the sword. The harvest is plentiful but the workers are few. God is leading me to recruit you as my first soldier of the Lord, but you must first cleanse yourself and return to following God's Law. Stop taking the Lord's name in vain and cease your indiscriminate killing. From now on you are only to kill for God as laid out in the Bible. You're going to need to be circumcised too. Oh yeah and one more thing; although I can't find specific reference in Scripture, I'm pretty sure God doesn't want you masturbating as much as you do.

Sincerely,
Leonard Boseki.
Prophet of God.

My epistle didn't produce the response I intended. I didn't realize he was illiterate and so when he found my letter in his boots the following morning, he thought I was being an "uppity bitch". I insisted I wasn't and immediately read the letter aloud to him.

"Gat Damn Boy! You is crazy And eevul!" He gave me another "Ivory Soap Bath".

I abandoned all attempts of communication with him after that. I lay in my bunk facing the wall for days afterward, refusing to eat or speak. My ribs were cracked but that wasn't the focus of my pain. No, my aching was from a spiritual fracture that occurred as Tee-Bone swung the pillowcase time and time again across my writhing torso. I knew that I'd see and feel similar reactions again by other Christians who were complacent and ignorant of their faith. They would not believe that I was speaking God's directives because they had not read the Bible.

"Who am I, to deliver the children from Egypt?" I moaned.

But I knew it was me.

* * * * *

By the time Isabel arrived, two months into my incarceration, I had little to say. She wept bitterly, promising that she still loved me enough to do anything I asked.

"Tell me Leeny! Tell me what you want me to do?" She pleaded as they announced visitation was over.

"I want you to remember Job 13:15 when you think of me. 'Though he slay me, yet will I hope in him; I will surely defend my ways to his face.'"

"WHAT DO I DO LEEENY? TELL MEEEE!"

"Remember me, Isabel. And know that I am innocent."

By innocent I didn't mean to convey that I didn't devote Pastor Hearty to the Lord, nor that I wanted her to lie to get me freed. But apparently, she misconstrued my message.

The Savannah Police and district attorney also misconstrued me. They saw me as another "crazy", guilty of an open and shut case of murder. With typical lazy public servant bravado, they spent little time preparing for trial, believing that witness testimony of me hunting for Hearty, coupled with my abandoned raincoat at the murder scene, would be enough for conviction. They were wrong of course. They underestimated Gary Larson, and appeared slow witted against his razor-sharp mind.

The Seventh Illusion

"Has the jury reached a verdict?" The judge asked at the end of the three-day trial.

"Yes, your honor. We find the defendant, Leonard J Boseki, not guilty of murder in the first degree."

Gary Larson showed more enthusiasm than I did upon hearing the verdict. He pounded his fist in the air and hugged me like a brother. I stared dully over his shoulder into the lifeless eyes of my prosecutors. They knew I'd slaughtered Hearty. I felt lifeless too because I now saw my duty until the End of the Age.

I did not rejoice. I did not rejoice.

Isabel greeted me with great tears outside the courtroom. She drove us back to Orlando and babbled incessantly of how we would start again, how we'd find a home and get married. I knew it was not to be. Nietzsche once wrote, "A married philosopher is a comic character." It was also true for a prophet of God. My destiny was not conducive to marriage.

As we passed the New Brunswick exit I came upon an unsettling realization. I placed my hand over my heart and could not feel its beat. I placed my fingers on my jugular, then lowered them to my wrist. Nothing. There was no doubt about it. I was a dead man, floating amidst the marshes of Georgia.

Remember your Creator in the days of your youth,
Before the days of trouble come
and the years approach when you will say,
"I find no pleasure in them."
Before the sun and the light
and the moon and the stars grow dark,
And the clouds return after the rain.
                    Ecclesiastes 12:1-2

I had to go Old Testament on her.
              -   The Aphorisms of Leonard Boseki. #67)

Three

The first week after my 1st murder acquittal had all the illusions of happiness. I'd awaken each morning to find Isabel's luxuriant hair enveloping my face as she licked at my ears. Sleeping together again after months of separation aroused our passion into an insatiable hunger and there wasn't a morning during our final days that she did not ride me like a stallion. I'd drift back off to sleep afterwards only to have her nuzzle me awake again as she was leaving for work.

"I'm so happy you're back Leeeny. Now, you relax. I see you tonight."

I'd stare blankly for hours, then rise from bed midafternoon and pour a cup of Bel's coffee, still cooking on the burner. It tasted like popcorn. After sitting at the kitchen table for a while I'd walk to the lake and feed stale bread to the resident goose. It was all I could do to force a few slices on him, he was that apathetic.

I felt the same way. I just couldn't pull out of lethargy or depression or whatever was dully throbbing like a phantom limb. I'd sit damp assed on the lake bank, rolling up white bread into tight balls and popping them into my mouth, trying to slow anger that intensified with each passing day. I couldn't admit it at first but, I knew it was her.

On the second week of my new found freedom I walked to the library and returned to my studies. I retrieved Hall's Bible Concordance and found forty references under "adultery", five under "adulteress" and twenty-two under "whoredom". I read each passage carefully and studied each cross-reference and footnote. By the end of my third day of research I'd gathered enough to write a 1st draft of my mission statement:

Holy Mission of Leonard Boseki:
December 22,1993

To murder Margaret, the Queen of Whoredom and her whore mongering husband Dennis Mazzani. Justification for their deaths have been found in the following passages:
1. *Thou shalt not commit adultery. Exodus –20:14*
2. *If a man commits adultery with another man's wife <u>both the adulterer and the adulteress must be put to death</u> – Leviticus 20:10*
3. *If a man is found sleeping with another man's wife, <u>both the man who slept with her and the woman must die.</u> Deuteronomy 22:22.*
4. ~~*Because he's a fucking lying bastard that can't keep his dick out of anything that moves!*~~
5. *Go thou to a woman? <u>Don't forget the whip!</u> - Friedrich Nietzsche*

To Do:
    a. Drive to Hampton, Virginia & locate their address.
    b. Drive to their house.
    c. Kill them both.

Upon accomplishing thy <u>Holy Mission,</u> thou shalt pray to be led to the next sinner to be slain. Let the Bible be your guide. You are authorized to use secular references to locate infidels also. A good source could be your high school Year Book. Try to locate them while in Hampton.

The Seventh Illusion

Unfortunately, I left my notebook opened on the kitchen table while I took a short nap. Little did I realize that Bel was literate enough to comprehend some of my writings. I jumped from the couch after she shrieked and came waving my notebook like a sword.

"Leeny! You a killer! You a sick, ASESINOOOO AIEEEEEEE..."

So off we went to Puerto Rican church for another exorcism. And though I tried to stand obediently before the congregation, I simply couldn't bring myself to suffer through the same ignorance I'd experienced months before.

"Demino!" The reverend screamed after I lost patience and backhanded him. (Shit, Bel I'm sorry but it had been almost an hour). His assistants tried half-heartedly to restrain me but, having heard I was a murderer, did not have much zeal for their task. I walked up the aisle past frightened faces, left the church and headed for a bus stop.

When I got back to the apartment Isabel was already there, hurling my worldly possessions onto the yard. I owned little more than Mahatma Gandhi had at his death. I gathered two pairs of pants, three shirts, a pair of shoes, some socks and underwear and calmly stacked them at the curb for the garbage men. I placed my notebooks, Bible and *Golden Poems* on the back stoop and dug up the pistol from the back yard. I slipped my books and pistol in a plastic garbage bag retrieved from the shed and walked out of Bel's life forever.

* * * * * *

It took two days to get to Hampton, Virginia via Greyhound but much longer to finally act upon God's will. I rented a furnished efficiency near the Riverdale

Plaza and spent the intervening months struggling against my calling to be His sword. My time spent at Riverdale apartments has been the source of much speculation by police, prosecutors, and "biographers". They've all offered "expert" opinions on what was crawling through my "sick mind" based on their notes gleaned from sloppy investigations. Like wooden puppets, they all marched lockstep with the identical theory that all my murders were motivated by a hatred of Margaret and Dennis. Bullshit! The truth is that even then I still loved my wife and forgave her.

The *only* motivation for my murders was because I *had* to obey God's Law. I spent every day during those Riverdale months studying Scripture and trying to live Holy; something those sophomoric "experts" never pursued. Had any of them read Leviticus they'd have understood that God demanded the killings. They were too stupid to grasp that they were putting God on trial, not me. If they'd been competent enough to know this then I would have gladly served as God's attorney and easily gained His acquittal! Allow me to present my case:

1) Fact: God personally gave the Law directly to Moses. It covers not just the 10 Commandments but many chapters in Exodus (20-31), all of Leviticus and much of Deuteronomy.

   a) *And God spoke all these words: (Exodus 20:1)*
   b) *The Lord Called to Moses and spoke to him from the Tent of Meeting (Leviticus 1:1).*
   c) *These are the commands the Lord gave Moses of Mt. Sinai for the Israelites.* (Leviticus 27:34, Final chapter, final verse).

The Seventh Illusion

2) <u>Fact:</u> God wants us to follow the Law *forever*!

   a) *Know therefore that the Lord thy God, he is God, the faithful God, which keepeth covenant and mercy with them that love him and <u>keep his commandments to a thousand generations</u>. (Deuteronomy 7:9)*
   b) *Be ye mindful always of his covenant, the word which he commanded to <u>a thousand generations</u>. (1 Chronicles 16:15)*
   c) *Thy word is true from the beginning: and every one of <u>thy righteous judgements endures forever</u>. (Psalms 119:160)*

3) <u>Fact:</u> Adultery is against God's Covenants! Anyone committing adultery must be executed!

   a) *Thou shalt not commit adultery. (Ex. 20:14)*
   b) *If a man commits adultery with another man's wife both the adulterer and the adulteress <u>must be put to death</u> (Lev. 20:10)*
   c) *If a man is found sleeping with another man's wife, both the man who slept with her and the woman <u>must die</u>. You must purge the evil from Israel. (Deuteronomy 22:22)*

I rest my case. Even a state prosecutor can calculate that the Law applies for another 800 generations or so. "Forever" is even longer. I learned once and for all during my Riverdale studies what slothful authorities never bothered to investigate: I had to do what God clearly commands in The Old Testament. Still, I tried to shirk duty...

"But why isn't anyone else obeying the Law?" I pleaded. And I heard a quiet voice in the wind:

That is why you have been called, that is why you have been freed...

So, with great remorse I did as He instructed. But I must tread carefully now, for I have no desire to suffer yet another trial. Where shall I begin? How about with our public servants?

Shortly after my return to Virginia, the Hampton Police became embroiled in a public relations crisis after an elderly woman was abducted and murdered. The Hampton Police Chief immediately went before the cameras to announce they had a prime suspect and expected an arrest "within hours". He was wrong, and six months passed without an arrest. The press and citizenry began to insult the competence of the police department with such vehemence that the mayor stepped into the fray to demand the murders be solved. The chief allegedly went to his detectives and ordered the murder to be pinned on someone ASAP. The two detectives assigned to the case quickly convinced themselves that I was their man and reached almost religious fervor the day they called on me concerning Sophia Bantera's murder. I wept silently for poor Sophia as her incompetent champions grilled me with simple good cop/bad cop tactics for almost two hours.

"Come on Lenny, Ronny wants to see you fry." The pock mocked officer whispered while "Ronny" left in a huff for coffee. "He's a bull dog for digging up evidence. He's been on the force for twenty years and's the best detective in the city..."

Yawn. Oh, excuse me. All right, I'll admit I was slightly concerned at the time because I thought they might keep me from my duty. But I took comfort knowing that there were plenty of infidels in jail to

The Seventh Illusion

slaughter if things went south. Anyway, the facially scarred officer kept droning on until he finally summarized by offering me vague assurances if I'd only agree to confess to the murder of Sophia Bantera. I demurred, partially out of boredom, but mainly because I just wanted to go back to my cell and get some sleep. Ronny had a major hissy fit when they failed to extract a confession.

Poor Ronny. He was a lazy policeman with a 95 IQ (at best) and spent most of his career responding to domestic disputes. Once during his twenty-one years of pounding on mobile home doors he discovered a corpse inside. Ronny quickly discovered that the surviving spouse had drunkenly thrown the murder weapon in a nearby dumpster. That's pretty much the high point of his stellar reputation in Homicide.

And so, when the police chief threw the Bantera file on his desk and said "Find the asshole that did this!" Ronny felt his throat tighten. The chief had that same disgusted look that Ronny's wife often had on weekends. He didn't like his wife; she was too plump and criticized him way too much about his drinking and personal hygiene. She didn't appreciate the kind of stress he lived under daily! He didn't appreciate the kind of profanity she hurled at him either: "dickless wonder" and "limpy" were way out of line, WAY OUT OF LINE, BITCH!

He needed to calm down. Thinking about the chief and his wife this close together made him anxious. Shit! He didn't need this kind of pressure! Four years away from pension! He tried to concentrate. He opened the Bantera file and gasped at the crime scene photos lying loose inside.

"My God! What kind of animal..." He checked his emotions. *Must stay calm...fight nausea! {dickless} You're tough Ronny boy! {limpy} Tough!*

Ronny closed the file. He had to do something to solve the case. Go to the crime scene? No, too much trouble. Interview Mr. Bantera? Sounds dull. Review the file? God no! Donuts? Sure! But wait, he had to do something or else the chief would have his ass! But what? He started poring over the police blotter to see who'd been arrested recently for violent crimes. Someone on the list's gonna take the fall by God! Huh, what's this? A Leonard Boseki living within a quarter mile of Sophia's establishment and now awaiting trial for two murders?

The thrust of Ronny's charge revealed flaccid thinking and an impotent imagination. He had no firm evidence to back up his premature accusations but it didn't stop him from yanking it out and exposing it to us anyway.

According to his theory, I passed Sophia's place often while walking from my apartment across the field to Big Ben's Groceries. Shortly before the murder, I must have gone in to get my fortune told and didn't like what I heard. I later returned, kidnapped and violently murdered Madame Sophia at the same place as Randy Head, a remote location less than three miles from my apartment!

"Interesting. Is that all you have on him?" Asked the district attorney.

"Isn't that enough? He's our fucking guy!" Ronny yelled, hoping high volume would strengthen low logic.

"Do you have any physical evidence?"

"He's our fucking guy! He stood trial for murder in Savannah and got away with it! I've seen photos of the Savannah crime scene and it's brutal just like Head's and Sophia's. I'm telling you he..."

"Do...you...have...physical...evidence?'

"No, but..." Ronny whined.

The Seventh Illusion

Poor Ronny, if only he'd tried an enseey-weensy bit harder he'd have found something. A decent detective would have gotten off his fat ass, poured through my writings and found buried on page 56 of Notebook 3, something that would have drawn the DA's interest. Perhaps waving my hand written notes in front of the district attorney would've given credence to Ronny's claims. Perhaps despite Ronny's ignorance he was onto something. What if I really did pass Madame's place of business often? Perhaps I would have seen her sign posted in the plate glass window and slowly read it aloud:

> *Psychic Readings by Madame Sophia*
> *Spiritual Healing*
> *Palm Reading*
> *Advice on Love, Marriage & Business*
> *See the future*

Perhaps the words would have resonated with me. Perhaps I was spiritually ill and hoped Madame Sophia could heal whatever was eating my soul. And was not love, marriage and business the cause of this overwhelming sickness? Perhaps I walked in, hoping to find a way back and found Madame Sophia to be a kind woman with the true gift. Perhaps my reading was so unusual that upon returning home that night Madame Sophia told her husband of a "strange young man with wild, troubled eyes". And perhaps if Mr. Sophia had not been half drunk and completely disinterested by her tale then Madame Sophia would have told of the reading she gave to the soulless man. Perhaps she would have told of taking her soft hand into his and saying:

"I see it in your eyes, young man. You have the Sadness."

Perhaps the man said nothing. Perhaps for the first time in many a month he felt a touch of peace in her hand because finally, finally someone recognized him. Perhaps they saw in each other's eyes that they were kindred spirits that understood this great illusion.... This great, sad illusion.

"How do I lose it?" Perhaps I asked.

"Oh, but that is very, very hard. For the Sadness is a stain on the soul. This world has tainted you young man and there is only one way to cleanse yourself. Now tell me, do you have a picture of you with your loved ones?"

"No," perhaps I responded. "Oh, wait, I do have this..." And perhaps I pulled out my ancient delaminated Virginia driver's license.

"Ah, I see that you are not the same person." She may have said. "You were innocent when this photograph was taken. But now... you have fallen."

Perhaps her eyes filled with compassion. Perhaps she took my face into her hands and held it like my loving mother.

"You have a deep purple aura, young man. You are bruised... and deeply confused. You have been misled and now find yourself lost in pathless wilderness. You can find your way back home. Listen to me. You...can...find...your...way...home. To find your way, you must seek love, for it is the only compass that can save you..."

Perhaps at that point I began to cry because I knew that she spake a great truth. Perhaps she held my sad face and spoke soft, soothing words. Yes, that would have calmed me. I would have taken great comfort in her touch. A fragile, tender hope would have surfaced and I would have thought that perhaps it was possible to love and live again. And with my new found hope would have surely asked what the future held for Margaret and me.

"I cannot tell you of your wife without a photograph."

"Well then what about me? What does the future hold for me?"

"For you..." and her voice would have trailed off.

"Please tell me, what does the future hold?"

"I...I see very little. Very little for it is so dark. But I feel.... I feel...."

"What? What do you feel?"

"I feel...fear."

* * * * * *

How strange to strain against the reins of the Lord. How frightening to know what is expected and yet pull against duty. God's great men of the Old Testament, how did they do it? How could Abraham be willing to sacrifice his son? He was Holier than I, for I wailed angrily against God's Commandments. I hated my calling but gradually realized that didn't matter. Did not Moses and Gideon and Jeremiah dread their callings also? I was walking the same dark road.

If in fact I murdered Madame Sophia (and I'm not admitting I did) I would have done it with great reluctance. Madame Sophia reminded me of my mother; she was around the same age with a similar tendency toward plumpness. From everything I read about her after her murder it appears she was kind and gentle. How could I have possibly brought myself to kill such a sweet, matronly woman in such a horrific way? The only rational explanation a competent investigator could have come up with was that I was forced to. It's possible that I may have returned home from Madame Sophia's that afternoon feeling better than I had in years. It's plausible that in celebration I prepared a tossed green salad with fresh tomato and avocado in my tiny kitchen while singing joyful songs of love from the early Beatles...

But then, just as I slipped fresh fish into the oven, perhaps a troubling thought stirred within me. Had I not read something regarding fortunetellers in the Bible? No surely, I was mistaken.

But what if the phantom verse whispered to me as I munched salad while awaiting flounder? Could it be that fortunetellers were evil? No. Yes! But why? Perhaps I arose and began thumbing through the Bible until I came to Exodus 22:18. Perhaps my palms began to sweat as I prayed that I was misinterpreting what I read. Perhaps I turned to a fresh page in my notebook and carefully wrote at the bottom "page 56" before rereading the passage. I still was not sure. I wrote the passage slowly in my notebook:

Exodus 22:18 - Do not allow a sorceress to live.

"She has to die Leonard..." perhaps a voice said.
And perhaps I scrawled under the passage...
NO! NO I WILL NOT DO IT! LOVE!!

Perhaps I continued through the Bible scrambling for justification for my refusal to obey. Perhaps I searched no further than Leviticus when I discovered I was doomed. Perhaps I cursed as I lacerated the page with the passage:

LEVITICUS 20:27 – A MAN OR WOMAN WHO IS A MEDIUM OR SPIRITIST AMONG YOU MUST BE PUT TO DEATH. YOU ARE TO STONE THEM; THEIR BLOOD WILL BE ON THEIR OWN HEADS.
WHY? WHAT THE FUCK HAS SHE DONE WRONG??

The Seventh Illusion

Perhaps my flounder burned. Perhaps I sat reading Leviticus 20 over and over, hoping that perhaps I'd misunderstood, or had a bad translation. Perhaps I walked back to a bookstore at the Riverdale Mall and read the definition of sorcery in a Merriam Webster dictionary. Perhaps I found and read three different Bible translations of the applicable passages. Perhaps the words were different but the message the same. God had spoken. Perhaps as an apology for my action, I bought a Bible and left it on Madame's desk turned to Leviticus 20 on that fateful night.

Yes, I could see where an average detective could have built a solid case. He would have used my notebook to establish motive and with just a little digging could have found the receipt for my Bible purchase; perhaps a bookstore cashier as witness, and certainly my fingerprints on the Book. From there he could allege that the day after my palm reading, I walked into Madame Sophia's just as she was closing for the night (10 p.m.). But Madame Sophia did not have average detectives on the case and therefore suffered a gross distortion of her final hours.

It had been a quiet evening for Madame Sophia, the police deduced from reviewing her receipt book. She gave only two readings the entire night, the last one occurring at 8:30. According to detectives she spent her idle hours reading the Bible. They knew this because when the police arrived to her store the following morning with Mr. Bantera, they found a brown leather Bible lying open on her desk. Mr. Bantera said he found this strange because Madame was not prone to read the Bible nor did he recall her possessing one. The police found Mr. Bantera strange and did not like his strange foreign mannerisms nor his strange reaction to the Holy Bible. When Mrs. Bantera's body was found later that afternoon the police immediately considered Mr. Bantera the prime suspect. Over the next 48 hours Mr. Bantera's background came under intense scrutiny and the Hampton Police Chief held a press conference to announce that they were close to solving the case. A fifteen-thousand dollar life insurance policy with Mr. Bantera listed as beneficiary was the final nail in his coffin! How disappointed the police were to soon discover that Mr. Bantera had been playing poker with four men during the night of the murder. How disappointing that the chief had promised something he could not deliver and now had to rely on "Hampton's best detective" to find another suspect. Oh, and Ronny found his perp all right, but what the motive? Where the evidence?

Madame Sophia, I am sorry that your champion was an idiot. Had I been your advocate I would have located your murderer. I would have pointed to the evidence, looked your assassin in the eyes and explained to the court precisely how and why you met your end. Ladies and gentlemen of the jury, I submit the following for your consideration...

* * * * *

I have a confession to make. I am quite drunk. I do not relish writing in this condition and am therefore sucking down mint green tea between sentences. Spearmint steeped with Sencha in pure spring water. My oriental tea cup makes me feel sophisticated. But I feel more drunk than sophisticated. But not drunk enough, for I still hear her howling in the wilderness. Howls and pleas and screams and the thumping of ripe melons. OH MY GOD! The tea has become tepid. Because you are neither hot nor cold, I shall spew you from my mouth.

The Seventh Illusion

Where is the true believer? Where is the man or woman that truly does the work of the Lord? Where? I am not like the rest of you. Unlike you I did not shirk from duty. Or did I not shirk madness? Fuck this, I'm opening another bottle of White Rabbit wine. Yes, a light crisp Sauvignon Blanc is a fitting complement to such a bitter tale.

We lived in rural Virginia for a few months after Father secured a summer teaching job at a country high school. I was just five or six at the time and can't remember the area; Meadows of Dan perhaps? I recall walking along a dirt road, armed with a slingshot. Some older boy in soiled T-shirt and blue jeans accompanied me. We came to a crossroad to find a vast row of caged pigeons across the ditch from us.

"Shoot them!" My foul friend ordered. I scrounged around for a pebble, placed it in my sling and aimed. But I could not let the stone fly. I stared through one eye at those pigeons, wondering why they were caged, wanting to flip the hasps of their cells and free them into the cool Virginia air.

"Shoot them!" He demanded. But I couldn't.

"Sissy!" He snarled and grabbed my slingshot. It took him many shots, the pebbles clinking off the cages and birds fluttering and me crying.

"Shut up ya little girl!" He said while stooping for pebbles. A soft thud and a bird quivering at the bottom of the cage finally satisfied him. I let him keep the slingshot and pretty much stayed inside after that.

Oh, but I can hear your vacuous voices: "Cease your drunken babbling and tell us what we've paid our ten shillings for! Give us our story then!" Woe to you, thou wicked and adulterous generation! Woe to you that seeks amusement and shirks duty! Woe to this generation, this self-righteous horde of harlots that hath neither courage nor will to do what God commands! But for that one in a million men that does God's will, what becomes of him? He is a freak, an aberration, a circus geek to gawk at while you stuff popcorn down thy fat, sagging gullet. You are not worthy of the Lord's wrath. You are a soft generation of imagined experiences.

And so, imagine this my weak ones. Imagine the Sadness bearing down on you like a juggernaut and a pistol tucked under your blue stripped Polo shirt. Shirt tail out. Your index finger tapping, tapping, tapping on a brown Bible as a mantra whispers along a dirt path in the night.

"Thou shalt not suffer a witch to live... thou shalt not suffer a witch to live... thou shalt not suffer ..."

The distant lights of the Riverdale Plaza bobbing closer. You reach her store front; the gold gild edge of the Good Book gleams under her fluorescent sign. Ah, there she is through the plate glass window. She sees you. A weak smile. Does she know?

You apologize for the late hour. You come bearing a gift. She bids you in and you follow her back to her wood table behind the curtain. But you are not there for a reading. Then what? Will she please turn to Leviticus? She fumbles through the pages, embarrassed that she knows not where to find it. You turn the pages for her as she nervously smiles. She's too polite to show concern for your stiff behavior and asks what she can do for you. You lift your shirt tail to expose Father's pistol.

Oh, the sad drive in her car. The fragrance of ripe bananas, do you recall? She said they were on sale at Big Ben's and Mr. Bantera loved them. And her eyes, as she looked back at you in her rear-view mirror; will they ever fade? Or the rutted, Blue Sink Road, white headlights bouncing over the shore line where Randy Head had fallen months before. But you were not there to mourn Randy; No, you had more important work at hand.

Yea, how you both wept.

By the waters of Blue Sink,
We wept when we remembered Zion.
There on the poplars I hung her arms
But how can we sing the songs of the Lord
While in this foreign land?

She was tied to a tree with yellow nautical rope acquired from the hardware store several doors down from Madame's. She cried for help as she strained against the ropes, her arms pulled over her head under the glare of headlights. This small rock quarry along the shore of Blue Sink; are there houses near? You must be about God's work and be off.

Those first jagged chunks of quartz flew wide. You drew closer. You wept. The sound of a coconut struck by stone. Gurgling screams. Promises to abandon fortune telling, promises to forgive and pleadings of forgiveness. An evil spirit, hanging low and stagnant in the air; strange voices crying, moaning, chanting "Leviticus, Leviticus". How long, shall I suffer the wickedness of Earth? Oh, and the stumbling for more stones, for larger stones as she moaned incoherently; the sounds of stone against flesh and bone, the groans of death, the torturous Holy task of obedience.

Oh, daughter of Babylon,
doomed to destruction,
Happy is he who repays you,
for what you have done...

How then can a man be righteous before God?
How can one born of woman be pure?
If even the moon is not bright and the stars not pure in his eyes,
How much less man, who is but a maggot-
A son of man, who is only a worm!
          Job 25: 4-6

Four

It was front-page news. The city was appalled to read that a second horrific murder had occurred at Blue Sink in under six months. Everyone wanted to know what the police were doing to solve the crimes. The Hampton Police Chief assured the citizenry they had a "prime suspect" and that soon an arrest would be made. I harbored such great hope that I'd soon be arrested that I did not sleep for three days after Madame's murder. I had found a radio in the back seat of a car and played it loud in my apartment to block terrible thoughts. An imagined vision of Madame, under the headlights of a Buick, her bloodied corpse listing at forty-five degrees from the ground, yellow rope holding arms aloft in supplication to the bowers.

Why? Why did she have to die that way? Her passing was bad enough, but why such an excruciating death? Why not a quick bullet through the head or sword through the heart? Why did God want such a slow painful murder? I meditated on the question at length; thought of the thousands of stonings that must have occurred through thousands of years.

"I will not go on! I will not go on!" I screamed.

On the Saturday after Madame's death, I put my things in order and cleaned the apartment. I washed and folded my clothes. I made a simple will, leaving my Bible, *Golden Poems* and notebooks for Margaret neatly stacked on the kitchen table. Then I wrote my suicide note:

> *February 26, 1994*
> *To Whom It May Concern:*
>
> *All my life I listened to my elders and obeyed.*
> *I was a good boy.*
> *When I was young, I believed life was full of love.*
> *I believed that God was Love.*
>
> *When I became a man, I found that life was full of evil.*
> *I found that God hates evil.*
> *God told me through the Holy Bible to destroy evil.*
> *I was a good man and obeyed.*
>
> *I don't want to be good any more.*
> *It sickens me.*
> *Please forgive me.*
> *Bury me next to Mother and Father.*
>
> *Thank you,*
> *Leonard Boseki*

I did not want to inconvenience the landlord with a messy clean up nor wake the neighbors so I eschewed the pistol. Instead, I tied yellow nautical rope to the hinge of the closet door, tied a knot around my neck and strangled myself. And as I hovered over drab shag carpeting at forty-five degrees, I protested: *this is suicide! You will rot in hell for this!* But I was already there. Better to gamble on an unknown hell than accept a known one. I gasped involuntarily for air into starved lungs as panic surged. But I was brave. I hung on until I died.

Part IV: I Am Reborn

But oh! That deep romantic chasm which slanted
Down the green hill athwart a cedarn cover!
A savage place! As holy and enchanted
As ever beneath a waning moon was haunted
By woman wailing for her demon lover!
                    -Samuel Taylor Coleridge

"Sword" appears 104 times more than "love" in the Holy Bible.
                    - The Aphorisms of Leonard Boseki. (#42)

One

In the fall of 1994, shortly after I was acquitted from my third murder, I took "Bible Truth" on the road. I was certain my three acquittals were confirmation that I was on the right spiritual path and the next step was to spread Truth throughout America. Although by then I could have reached the entire Nation by granting interviews to the endless newspapers, magazines and networks clamoring for my views, I shunned them all. I feared that they would distort my words in the interest of ratings and knew that if I wanted pure "Truth" conveyed I needed to take a grass roots approach. I first sought fundamental believers and reached them by teaching at various Christian Conferences. It did not go well. The organizers and attendees assumed my "How I found strength in the Bible" lectures would be a confession of a new found faith which renounced my prior life of "butchery" They were wrong of course. And as they absorbed Truth via my speaking engagements, art exhibits and coffee klatches they were appalled. Within three months after taking the role of prophet, I was so brutally ostracized that I couldn't even gain admittance to the annual Jackson Mississippi Revival. I thereafter adjusted my message to a more sophisticated audience (Catholics) but suffered the same ignominy with their congregations.

I was therefore quite encouraged when, after months of persecution, I received a package from Mr. Nolan R White Esq. of Fort Smith Arkansas, which contained a note and VHS tape:

Mr. Leonard Boseki
7319 Thomas Eastern Rd. Apt. 207
Hampton, Virginia

March 10, 1995
Re: Murder Trial of Wendell Holmes

Mr. Boseki,

I had the great misfortune of representing Mr. Wendell Holmes during his murder trial in Russellville, Arkansas recently. I resided in Russellville for many years. I went to school with Wendell's father and once dated the former Mary Hope; the mother of the young man that Wendell was convicted of murdering. Wendell's trial did not gain much attention in the national press (as your last one did) and I'm sure you've never heard of Russellville or Wendell Holmes. Unfortunately, we've heard of you, and the impact of your pathetic, evil beliefs have forever stained this quiet Christian (yes Christian you bastard!) community. May you rot in hell!

Sincerely,
Mr. Nolan R White, Esquire
Dictated but not read

He was right, I'd never heard of Russellville or Wendell Holmes and I certainly had no idea what he was referring to. Curious, I popped in the VHS tape. The film opens with the camera trained on an obese red headed teen being sworn in at the witness stand. The young man takes his seat and looks slowly around the room while, who I presume to be the prosecuting attorney stands before him. The testimony is transcribed below:

Prosec: Please state your name and age.
Smith: Buddy Smith.
Pros: And your age?
Smith: Eighteen
Prosec: Do you know the defendant, Wendell Holmes?
Smith: Yass sir.
Prosec: And how long have you known Mr. Holmes?
Smith: Wendell?
Prosec: Yes.
Smith: All mah life.
Prosec: And did you know Buford Dyer?
Smith: Buford?
Prosec: Buford Dyer.
Smith: No sir.
Prosec: Is it your testimony that you <u>did not</u> know Buford Dyer, the young man that Mr. Holmes is accused of murdering?
Smith: Oh! You mean Porky? Yass Sir, I knew him! I knew him real well.
Prosec: Porky? You called Buford Dyer, Porky?
Smith: Yass sir. Everybody did.
Prosec: And why did you call Buford, "Porky"?
Smith: Cuz he like to fuck pigs.
Prosec: Objection! This is an outrage!!
(Stirring in the audience, jostling of the camera, someone muttering "Tsk. Can you believe this here trash?")
Judge: ORDER! ORDER! YOUNG MAN I WILL NOT HAVE PROFANITY IN THIS COURT! DO YOU UNDERSTAND ME?!
Smith: Yass sir.
(The room settles and testimony resumes.)

Prosec: Do you recall a conversation you had with Wendell regarding Buford?
Smith: Buford?
Prosec: Porky! Er, Mr. Dyer...
Smith: Uhhh...
Prosec: Do you remember when Wendell told you that he murdered Porky?
White: Objection! He's leading the witness!
Judge: OVER RULED!
Smith: Ah don't like this...
Judge: Young man, I don't give a good goddamn whether you like it or not! Now answer the question!!
Smith: Uhhh...
Prosec: Allow me to repeat the question. Do you remember Wendell telling you of how he murdered Porky?
White: OBJECTION!
Judge: OVER RULED! Answer the question!
Smith: Yass sir.
Prosec: Tell the court, to the best of your recollection, what Wendell told you about murdering Porky.
White: OB
Judge: OVER RULED!!
White: jection
Smith: Well, Wendell and me waz setting on his porch drinking ice tea when all sudden he just spits it out.
Prosec: Spits what out?
Smith: That Bible verse. Levetercus something...

"Leviticus 20:15 my poor inbred illiterate." I said to the screen.

Prosec: Leviticus 20:15 Perhaps?
White: Your Honor...
Judge: SHUT UP!
Smith: Sounds Right.

Prosec: I'll read the passage: "If a man has sexual relations with an animal, he must be put to death, and you must kill the animal." Is this what Wendell told you that night on his porch?

Smith: That's it. Yass sir.

Prosec: Ok. And, as best you can recall, what else?

Smith: Well, after he quote scripture, he say 'I did what God told me to do last night. I did the right thing.' I said, Wendell what're you talking about? And he said, 'You know it ain't right what Porky's been doing.

Prosec: And what had Porky been allegedly doing?

Smith: Fuc...er...having sex with pigs. Way on back to sixth grade.

(Screaming from women out of frame. It takes the judge and bailiff several minutes to bring order. Trial resumes.)

Prosec: What else did Wendell tell you about Porky's pigs?

Smith: Well, I was just laughing and Wendell got all mad. Told me to shut up. Said 'We know it ain't right when we catch Porky rooting with sows! All that grunting and squealing!' Then Wendell starts yelling 'It's unnatural!' and 'It's against scripture! But ain't nobody doing anything bout it! Nah, they just laugh like it some joke. Thass what's wrong with America, nobody doing nothing to fight evil ' He was all pissed off.

Prosec: Anything else?

Smith: Oh, yeah. He start saying how Lenny Boseki is right. Said he knew it from the first time he heard him in Little Rock. Wendell says he's a prophet. Wendell said Mr. Boseki got him to read the Bible and damned if he didn't find Porky when he hit Leverticus. Said he always knew it was wrong and now he saw in black and white it was against scripture.

Prosec: Now, tell the court exactly what you recall Wendell say about the night of the murder.

Smith. Uhhh, he say 'I was brave enough to follow what God told me to do! I shot Porky with my shotgun last night round sundown, when I caught him with the hogs again. That damn sow tried to make off too but I got er! I drug em both down to the crick and left em. You wanna go see em? They all bloated...'

Prosec: Wendell took you down to look at the bodies?

Smith: Yass sir. It was horrible. Wendell just kept saying it was scripture. I finally asked him what got him all crazy like that, cuz killing Porky just seemed wrong. Wendell yelled 'It ain't wrong! It's in the Bible you Idijit. We gotta kill the unclean so we can take back the earth. Yo need to read Bible Notes of Lenny Boseki!'

Prosec: No further questions.

Thus concluded the first documentation attesting to the success of my itinerant Truth crusade. Over the next months I received additional letters from others testifying that they had heeded my words, read the Bible and killed as God instructed. There were the Simon brothers who entered a gay bar in New Braunfels Texas and opened fire with semi-automatics, killing seven and wounding twelve. Shortly thereafter a mother residing in Mobile Alabama stabbed her teenage son to death inside the Cattle Baron's Steak House, offering Leviticus 20:9[16] as her reason. Weeks later, I received an anonymous letter postmarked Bithlo Florida that contained an 8x10 close-up of the battered, lifeless face of a teenaged girl. Her once blond hair matted with dried blood, her

---

[16] *Leviticus 20:9 - If anyone curses his father or mother he must be put to death.*

purpled cheeks the texture of raw hamburger. On the back of the photo was scrawled "Deuteronomy 22:20![17] – She weren't no virgin Mr. Boseki."

But by far my most fervent disciple was Douglas R. Harrington of Chattanooga, Tennessee. Mr. Harrington kept a running, one way correspondence with me from April until July 1995 when he was finally institutionalized in Nashville and his mental health counselors prohibited further communications with me (Thank God). But during his four active months, Mr. Harrington averaged three communiques a week, some spanning over ten pages, all professing his undying devotion to "Truth".

"You have opened my eyes to God's Truth Mr. Boseki," He confessed in his letter of 4/4/95 "and for that I owe you, my soul. I was going nowhere after my wife left me but you showed me that I can devote my life to fighting evil."

And devote his life he did. His initial letters confessed of four separate slayings of adulterous couples within the Chattanooga area. But he soon strayed from his niche to pursue more arcane sins. Perhaps the catalyst was another romantic relationship that went sour for him. His writings became more erratic, starting with his letter of 5/19/95, which confessed to strangling a Vietnamese girl he'd casually dated for two weeks.

"I really liked her Mr. Boseki. We'd hit it off well and she'd listen attentively as I told her all about "Truth" and

---

[17] *Deuteronomy 22:20-21 - If, however the charge is true and no proof of the girl's virginity can be found, she shall be brought to the door of her father's house and there the men of her town shall stone her to death.*

you. In hindsight it's possible she didn't comprehend much because her English was so poor. Anyway, one night after a movie, she asked if I wanted to see her apartment. I agreed and before I knew it, I was using her bathroom while she boiled water for tea. But to my great horror when I emerged, I found her kneeling before a small Buddhist shrine in the corner of her living room. I'd walked right by without noticing it when we came in! I stared aghast as she lit incense in a bowl at Buddha's feet. 'Exodus 22:20[18]!' I screamed so loudly that she jumped. 'Wha poppa san?' She asked. Those were the last words that infidel breathed before I sent her gasping into hell!"

He seemed to become a bit unhinged after that. I received several letters from various addresses out west promising "something big" that he was working on. It took him only three weeks, far less time than he'd projected, before I received a manila envelope post marked Pleasant Dale, Utah. His enclosed letter brimmed with euphoria:

...and now I've finally accomplished what I never thought possible! Oh, but believe me Mr. Boseki, this was thoroughly researched and verified before I performed God's will. I know that they were guilty because they confessed at gunpoint! Can you believe I found them? Leviticus 20:14 is indeed a rare flower!!

I could not recall the passage. Anticipating my lapse in memory, Mr. Harrington had penned very neatly on a sealed envelope.

---

[18] *Exodus 22:20 - Whoever sacrifices to any god other than the Lord must be destroyed.*

The Seventh Illusion

Leviticus 20:14 – If a man marries both a woman and her mother, it is wicked. Both he and they must be burned in the fire, so that no wickedness will be among you.

I didn't like the tone of his letter. Didn't like it at all. With trepidation I opened an interior envelope to find six Polaroids of a man and two women tied back-to-back in the desert at dusk. The first shows them illuminated by a camera flash, their eyes red with anger and fear. The second photo showed them protesting/crying after apparently being drenched with gasoline (three five-gallon cans are placed neatly in the lower left corner of the picture). The third photo captures the first rush of blue flames licking over their bodies. The fourth through sixth are too horrific to describe.

"I owe this all to you Mr. Boseki. I will always be grateful for freeing me through God's righteousness." He concluded.

His freedom didn't last long. Federal prosecutors subsequently subpoenaed Mr. Harrington's letters to me. Those documents became the most important evidence in obtaining a guilty verdict from his murder trial.

* * * * * *

Had I known on February 26, 1994 (the day I returned to earth a second time) of the tribulation that would soon lay ahead, I would have taken Father's pistol, put it in my mouth, and fired. But as life slowly seeped back into my lungs after my suicide, I knew that God wasn't finished with me. My tired soul reentered the corpse as it slumped beside the closet door, a yellow umbilical cord pulled so tight around the neck that it felt as if I was breathing through a flattened straw. Panic gripped me as I rose and clawed uselessly at my throat. The noose would not loosen. I managed to rip the door off the upper jam and work the rope over the hinge. I stumbled into the kitchen for a knife, slipped it between the rope and neck and breathed again.

My throat felt like it was crushed. I rushed to the bathroom mirror. It was horrible. Horrible to see the deep purple welt wrapped round my neck, horrible to stare into blood shot yellowed eyes, horrible to know that I was not to depart until my sacred mission was through. Swollen lips hoarsely whispered:

"Ye shalt not escape duty.
Ye shalt not flee the lord.
Sword. Sword.
Sword of the Lord."

And so, I went forth. I went forth to lose my life in order to save it. I went forth to save my life in order to lose it.

* * * * * *

I got serious after my second coming, for there was much to accomplish. I now approached my calling as a career and began working in businesslike manner. I purchased a used Volvo, shopped JC Penney for business attire and visited a barber. Thus, groomed and attired, I sat at my dining room table and developed a plan for my first day of employment. I arose at 5 am the following morning and reread the agenda:

5:00 – Rise, light exercise
5:30 – Breakfast: Oatmeal
5:45 – Prepare bag lunch: PBJ sandwich/ jug of water
6:00 - Shower, shave, dress for work

6:30 – Study the Bible for one hour
7:30 – Leave for work. Study Bible during downtime.

I arrived into the Mazzani & Co parking lot at 8:17am. I planned to document Dennis's arrivals and departures, tail him whenever he left the office and follow him home at day's end. Upon discovering his residence, I'd conduct reconnaissance to: a) confirm Margaret resided there, b) identify terrain characteristics and c) determine the best escape route after devoting them both to the Lord. If mission success appeared promising, I'd rap on their door and announce that all was forgiven. They would invite me in for a glass of wine. Five minutes later, while sipping chardonnay, I'd calmly quote Leviticus 20:10 and dispatch a bullet into each of their confused foreheads.

But things did not proceed as intended. Although I successfully recorded Dennis's day (arrived 9:17 a.m., lunch at Bodega's 11:45 a.m.-1:40 p.m., Vintage Cellars 5:35 p.m.), the plan unraveled as I watched him turn into a gated community at 6:03 p.m.. I pulled onto the shoulder across the street from the security gate and studied a guard, waving residents through for the next hour. Frustrated from not locating Dennis's address nor knowing whether Margaret was there, I gave up for the night.

I returned to the parking lot at 8 am the next day with a new plan: to continue surveilling Dennis until he eventually met Margaret somewhere outside their gated walls. The new approach remained fruitless for weeks, and I filled many stagnant hours studying my Bible.

My botched biographer opines that by now I was "at the height of a blood thirsty frenzy", and obsessed with "murdering his best friend that had robbed him of friendship, wife and wealth". He further insists that "while stalking the Mazzanis, Boeski fomented violent psychotic delusions of Old Testament scripture to serve as justification for murdering them."[19]

This is simply mean spirited and unfair. In fact, by this time my studies had taken me beyond the Old Testament and through the Gospels. And, while Jesus seemed to confirm my duty,[20] His overall theme was clearly more passive than His Father's. I now hesitated with my mission and questioned whether Jesus advocated slaughtering the Mazzanis. I vaguely recalled Paul's teachings; that the Law no longer applied, after Christ's crucifixion. Was this true? I hadn't found Jesus stating that. Did Jesus teach this to Paul and other Apostles during His earthly ministry? Amidst great doubt, I prayed for scriptural clarity and Truth.

God answered as I studied Acts. There, the Lord showed me that Paul wasn't one of the original twelve Apostles as I'd thought. In fact, Paul never met Jesus when He lived, nor witnessed the resurrected Chris

---

[19] *Footnote for Roger Barnhart, "biographer". You are by far the worst author I've ever had the misfortune to read. Your ineptitude as a writer is only surpassed by your spectacular failure as an "investigative reporter". How do you know what I was thinking in Mazzani's parking lot, you fermented toad? I'll tell you what's "pathological": The fact that you've made north of a million dollars butchering my life's story.*

[20] *Matthew 10:34 – Do not suppose that I have come to bring peace to the earth. I did not come to bring peace, but a sword.*
Luke 12:49-51 – I have come to bring fire on the earth...Do you think I came to bring peace on earth? No, I tell you, but division.

teaching the Apostles for forty days before ascending to heaven. Paul wasn't even at Pentecost, when tongues of fire descended on the Apostles; filling them with the Holy Spirit.

"So," I asked aloud, "if Paul never met Jesus, never received the Holy Spirit at Pentecost, and Jesus passed over Paul as the new Apostle to replace Judas[21], what qualifies Paul to speak for Jesus?"

Further into Acts, Paul tells of meeting Jesus near Damascus. Paul recounts the encounter twice more in Acts; each with new, conflicting descriptions. Was Paul confabulating?

But it wasn't until I was well into Romans; reading Paul's diatribe about faith and his strange new theology, that I comprehended what God was telling me: *Paul had gone insane!!* Of course! I'd met dozens of such men while institutionalized in Gainesville. Paul's mood swings and hallucinations clearly indicated schizophrenia and bipolar disorder. Had he lived today, a psychiatrist and a daily regime of Thorazine would have stabilized Paul and prevented him from corrupting God's words! The Lord's message was now clear: *Paul was one of the greatest misfortunes of history.*

Discovering this Truth convinced me that I was to stay on task. And, since weeks of reconnaissance had failed to find Dennis and Margaret together, I now shifted to a "divide and conquer" strategy. I'd simply shoot Dennis the following evening, which would prompt a funeral that Margaret would attend. I'd follow her after the service until God showed where to execute His statutes.

---

[21] *Acts 1:12-26*

* * * * * *

I learned from weeks of tailing Dennis that his only predictable travel pattern was to stop nightly after work for wine at Vintage Cellars. I was so confident with his routine that I drove to the store thirty minutes early that final Thursday. I parked a few rows away from Vintage Cellars, wrapped Father's snub-nose in a bath towel and waited.

My intended method of killing Dennis vacillated between a drive by shooting and a Jack Ruby Special. I finally opted for the latter. I'd wait until he exited the wine shop, follow him to his car; approach as he opened it and:

"Hey - Dennis!" He'd turn to find me eight feet away, towel wrapped tightly over extended fist and pistol.

Businessman with broken hand wants to shake mine? would be his final thought as I thrust the gun into his gut and cleansed him from the earth. I played the scene in my mind enough times to be confident of the task, but was not prepared for what occurred.

"Lenny!" I was standing by my Volvo, putting on a jacket when he appeared twenty minutes earlier than expected. I turned to find him rushing me from ten feet away, arms extended.

"Lenny, my God!" His bear hug straight-jacketed me. It was our first embrace in years and for some bewildering reason my heart filled and I broke into tears.

"I'm so sorry Lenny...I'm so sorry." He kept saying as we rocked and cried in the parking lot. His love and remorse soaked into me and in that moment, I felt such overwhelming compassion for Dennis that I knew I couldn't... just couldn't.

"My God, I think about you every day!" He said, loosening his grip and staring deeply into me. "Where have you been?"

I told him I'd moved to Florida for a career in tourism and was in town on business. It sounded weird but he didn't notice.

"Tell me! Tell me you're moving back to town!"

I said I wasn't, but simply looking for a potential water park site near Williamsburg.

"No, Lenny, you've got to move back! You've got to come back to work with me, I need you man!"

He was euphoric over finding me again and his mood so infectious that I knew I couldn't kill him and saw how insane it was to think so. Had he split from Margaret? Clearly, he wouldn't be acting like this if they were still together.

"Look, let me grab some wine and we can catch up." Dennis said. I demurred. It was moving too fast.

"Lenny, I'm not taking no for an answer, man. I have dreams about us all the time buddy. I'm not letting you get away. Just wait here while I get a couple of bottles from the Cellar…"

Twenty minutes later we were heading out of town in his Mercedes with a Styrofoam cup of champagne between my legs. It was disorienting. Was I dreaming? Where were we going? Why had I tucked the snub-nose under my coat in his back seat?

"…We've a lot to talk about my friend." He smiled. "Look Lenny, I know at the time it must have crushed you but believe me; it was the best thing that coulda happened for you…"

We were winding along a quiet two-lane road; soft jazz and the fragrance of car leather enveloping us. I sipped at the champagne and felt my shoulders relax against the seat. His familiar voice and mannerisms soothed me. Maybe I could come back home again.

We turned onto a black top lane and threaded through cedars along the river. The waning sun shimmered on the waters. We slowed at a mailbox with "Mazzani" stenciled in white, and crept down a crushed shell driveway.

"My little retreat from the world." He smiled.

We parked beside the wood skeleton of a house; the river flowing in the distance behind it. Dennis grabbed the open bottle and I followed him out and into the house. Room by un-walled room we toured; the study, the kitchen, the master overlooking the water. He proclaimed it had all been done "for Margaret" but as we stepped over stacks of sodden wood and corroding rebar, I figured the plan had been abandoned.

We drained the first bottle on the back stoop as the sun sank. Dennis' ebullience waned. I sensed despondency creeping in.

"I'm sorry Lenny. I really fucked up. There's not a day goes by that I don't regret what happened."

"Forget it." I said and for the first time believed I forgave him. I was exhausted, tired of the hate that had drained me since I'd last seen him.

"No, I fucked up both our lives. He said. "I've fucked it up so bad I'm not sure I can recover. And it all started with Margaret..."

Dennis said that she'd moved in with him shortly after I left. She was pregnant and claimed it was his. She gave birth to a baby girl which they named Jennifer, after his mother. A few months later they hired an attorney, who dissolved my marriage to Margaret on grounds of desertion. They married and purchased a lot in one of the most prestigious neighborhoods in Norfolk.

"She's got expensive taste" he sighed, "I just wanted her to be happy..."

He confided that he'd pulled profits from his CPA firm to fund construction of their new home by the country club. He struck up a friendship with his builder and they partnered on several speculation homes on the golf course. The houses sold so quickly that he made fifty thousand dollars in six months. He purchased his and her Mercedes and the lake house lot with the proceeds.

A few months later the builder approached Dennis regarding an opportunity to buy a Title Insurance firm. Dennis purchased it, making the down payment with cash borrowed from his CPA firm. He soon discovered that he'd been lazy in his due diligence and overpaid for the Title Company. The business couldn't cover its expenses so Dennis constantly diverted cash from his accounting firm, which in turn precluded him from drawing his accustomed salary. In order to meet his ever-increasing personal expenses; car payments, mortgage payments, country club fees, new family etc., he started raiding the Title Company client escrow accounts, intending to repay them once business improved. But now the Title Company was bankrupt and an investigation into his books was underway. Rumors now ran so rampant through the country club, that Margaret and he were pariahs. To make matters worse, his CPA firm was now failing too.

"I may have to serve time, Lenny." He said, finishing his cup. "And you know what? All my problems started after Margaret moved in. You don't know how lucky you are that it's over between you two..." and then, on cue, Margaret called his cell phone.

"Oh, hey" he said with feigned happiness. "Yeah, sorry I didn't call. I'm out with an old friend at the river house. You'll never guess who."

I raised up my hand and shook my head.

"Uh, I'll tell you later, Honey. No, I'll tell you later. Go ahead and eat, I won't be home for a few hours. Tell Jenny I love her. Ok. Bye." He hung up. We didn't speak for a long time.

"I'm sorry, Lenny." He finally whispered.

"Forget it."

"You haven't. I can see it in your eyes."

"I've moved on." I lied.

"I promise you this, Lenny. She came on to me. I never planned it. I just responded the way most men would when a beautiful woman makes a pass."

An ominous breeze lifted over us. Mad dogs, baying across the river.

"I'm still paying for it too." He continued. "And you know what the real joke is? She's seeing another guy. Can you believe it? Seeing some fat turd at the Club. She thinks I don't know but she's too stupid to be a good liar and too scared to stay with me now that the walls are caving. You're lucky to be free of her, Lenny."

I knew he was lying about Margaret. I just couldn't figure out why.

"She's nothing but a selfish slut, Lenny. That's all she's ever been. All she'll ever be."

I stared at his fading profile.

"Lenny. We've both been fucked by a whore. Listen, do us a favor and get that last bottle huh? It's in the back seat. We'll commiserate about her over champagne."

It wasn't the bottle I brought back. The first shot entered the rear of his skull and exited through his forehead. I've never been able to explain why I fired the remaining five into a dead man.

Crazed through much child bearing,
The moon is staggering in the sky;
Moon struck by the despairing
Glances of her wandering eye.
We grope, and grope in vain,
For children born of her pain.
      W.B. Yeats

Two

"Hello?"

"Leonard Boseki?"

"Yes?"

"This is Detective Steven Cayce with the Chesapeake Police Department. We're investigating the murder of Dennis Mazzani and would like to ask you a few questions. Do you have some time this afternoon to come to the station?"

That phone call, days after Dennis' death, had the same tone as the one placed by the Savannah Police after Pastor Hearty's murder. I hung up, surprised that they'd found me so quickly and knowing that I'd soon be facing my second murder trial.

It felt invigorating! I'd been praying to be tried again because only then would the American legal system understand that I was obeying the highest law in the land: God's Law. For years our Nation's courts instructed us to swear on the Bible but now they would finally be forced to open and read its Statutes! Within its sacred pages, the finest legal minds would find justification to set me free. My acquittal would then trigger the biggest religious revival in American history and prompt God's return to earth!

I needed a brilliant attorney to plead my landmark case and scanned the Yellow Pages until I found:

Doyle Black

In Trouble? Let me fight for you!
Todd Hanson Attorney
Experienced Former Prosecutor

I liked the aggressive banner but his photograph didn't exude the same pugnacity. Todd had weak, rich boy eyes and looked too young to handle a historical case. I was about to turn the page but noticed the Christian Agape symbol in the lower right-hand corner of the ad. I took it as a sign from God and called Mr. Hanson. He agreed to meet me at the Chesapeake Police station at 2pm.

I spent the remainder of the morning organizing my notebooks and inserting bookmarks in the Bible for easy reference. With my papers and Bible tucked in a newly purchased brief case, I drove over to the Police Station twenty minutes early, anxious to start. I was prepared to spend the entire afternoon quoting scripture and laying out my case to the police but to my great disappointment, Todd advised me in the elevator to remain silent. I spent that first meeting quietly taking notes while Todd did all the talking. Below is an excerpt of my notes from the initial meeting:

March 28, 1994

Meeting with Todd Hanson and two Chesapeake Police Detectives: Steven Cayce and (name?) regarding the murder of Dennis Mazzani:

Charge Pending - Murder in the first degree

Motive – "Jealous Husband" - Revenge.

Evidence - A written statement from a Village Cellar cashier stating that Dennis Mazzani was in the store on the evening of his murder to purchase champagne. "I just ran into an old buddy I haven't seen in years!" Dennis said at the register.

The Seventh Illusion

Testimony of Margaret Mazzani stating that she talked via cell phone to Dennis Mazzani hours before his death. Dennis was at the river house with an old friend and said: "Guess who I'm having drinks with? Lenny Bos

"Liar!" I screamed.

Todd told me to keep quiet. I did, but I was pissed. I knew Margaret would never lie like that. Suddenly it was clear: the detectives were Satanic.

"What physical evidence do you have?" Todd asked.

"Oh, we're working on it as we speak." Said Cayce. "We're dusting wine bottles and the car for prints. It's just a matter of time Lenny, boy. And ya know what else? Ballistics tell us Dennis was killed by a thirty-eight-caliber pistol, the same type Lenny's dad had before it went missing. We also have a search warrant and officers at Boseki's apartment as we speak..."

"Get behind me, Satan!"

"Shut up Leonard!" Todd advised.

"Oh, we've got a real nut case here. You guys gonna plead insanity?"

"Based on what you have now this won't even make it to trial." Todd said. "Look, Mazzani could have been a victim of a robbery gone bad..."

"Oh, sure Hanson. And I presume the robber just shot Mazzani in the balls five times for kicks after already blowing his head off? And then he drops the Mercedes back off in the Village Cellars parking lot after the murder? You're a fucking genius..."

"How do you know Mazzani's car was at the murder scene?" Todd asked.

"A neighbor saw it pulling onto his lot."

"Did he give a description of anyone in the car with him?"

"We're working on that, don't worry."

"You guys are grasping at air. If you're not arresting my client we're leaving."

"Oh, but wait, there's more." Cayce leaned toward me with a sneer, his bad Beelzebub breath wafting across the table.

"We're coming after you for the murder of Randy Head too. Yeah, you're heading for the Big Chair."

Todd agog. Satan's dwarves exhaling coffee breath glee. Oh, how giddily they sang of a bloody rag that had mysteriously appeared on the stairs of Father's house. The blood had now been tested and traced back to Randy Head, a former employee of Mazzani's Title Company. An investigation into our respective lives uncovered my assault of Randy during college.

"It's all coming together nicely, don't ya think Lenny? Yeah, we've solved a couple of nasty little murders. And ya know what Lenny? You're not gonna get away with it like you did in Savannah."

"Look, sounds like you have some interesting coincidences that don't make sense laid out together." Todd retorted. But his voice was shaky.

"Let me lay it out for you then, Hanson. Lenny beat Randy to death with golf clubs because he hated him for fucking his wife. It won't be hard for the jury to buy it; Lenny had already beaten the shit out of him once before with a beer mug for the same thing..."

"LIAR!!! DON'T YOU DARE SPEAK OF MY WIFE IN THAT MANNER!!"

"Easy Boseki, easy. Save it for the jury, ok?" Demon Two whispered.

"That's it, we're leaving" Todd said.

"No, this will just take a minute." Cayce cooed. "Hmm, where was I? Oh yeah, so after our boy here beats Randy to death, he cleans up the murder scene and drives over to daddy's house to steal his 38 special and accidentally leaves the bloody rag behind."

"Or he leaves it as a message for his step mommy," Says Demon Two, "She says he's threatened to kill her before. Hey, she'll be a great witness at the trial."

"Anyway," Cayce continues, "Lenny boy takes the pistol and waits for his chance at Mazzani. He's patient, willing to wait months for the right opportunity. That's premeditated murder Lenny; cold, premeditated murder. Cowardly too because you slink up to Mazzani like a friend. Probably tell him 'All is forgiven and gosh let's have a drink for old times' sake.' He's a trusting soul so you guys go for a drive down to his river house. Then, like a cowardly pussy you pull out the 38 and shoot him in the back of the head. But that's not good enough for you. You gotta desecrate the body by emptying the chamber into his crotch."

By the end of our first sit down Todd acted like a defeated wimp. He whined in the parking lot over the risks of the Mazzani case based on Margaret's statement. He whined about potential fingerprints that could be pulled from the wine bottles. He whined about my prior history with Randy and the bloody rag in fathers house...

I cut him off and walked away before I lost my temper. The point wasn't whether I killed Dennis and Randy. The real issue was whether the US legal system was righteous enough to accept God's Law as supreme. It was God, not Leonard Boseki that would be facing trial. I was simply acting under direct orders from God via Bible commandments. As stated in Aphorism #4:

The Bible is inerrant. God said it. I believe it. That settles it.

* * * * * *

Two days after my interview with the detectives, I was arrested for the murders of Dennis Mazzani and Randy Head. I was to stand trial first for Dennis which was scheduled just sixty days away. During our second consultation Todd Hanson asked for all the facts and wanted to know whether I was "guilty".

"Of course, I'm not guilty!" I exploded. "But I killed them both."

That didn't sit well with him despite my eloquent and detailed scriptural based justification for the murders.

"Mr. Boseki." Todd said, interrupting me five minutes into my legal brief, "Mr. Boseki, it's just not pertinent."

Not pertinent!? Clearly, he wasn't a true believer. Todd insisted that we strike a deal by pleading insanity and perhaps with luck I'd be out in ten years. I was highly insulted and let him know it. He offered to resign. I declined, still believing that God had led me to Todd.

I'm not sure I was right. Anybody could have represented me as well as the slothful, frightened Mr Hanson did. His defense work was uninspired and the only legitimate argument he came up with during the course of my three-day trial was that Dennis Mazzani had many enemies with motive to murder him. That wasn't enough to save me. No, had Truth not stepped forward I'm sure I'd be on death row today. "The People of Virginia" were simply hell bent on proclaiming I was a psycho killer and Blaine Gilbert, County Prosecutor was their leading zealot. He had delusions of becoming attorney general and I'm sure that's why he contacted the national press about the trial. Blaine pitched it to them as a classic case of good vs. evil and cast himself as the white knight fighting a villain that had butchered his youth minister and gotten away with it. Now the bloodthirsty killer had come home and murdered his wife's illicit lovers! "The State of Virginia's not going to tolerate a murderer roaming our streets." He proclaimed to the cameras a few weeks before trial. The press loved Blaine Gilbert. They loved him because he was handsome, eloquent, and leaked like a sieve. He leaked to the press that the police had found my fingerprints on a beer can at the scene of Randy's murder. Two days later Gilbert leaked that detectives were investigating a third murder and expected that I would be charged within days. "We may be dealing with a serial killer" he blurted one afternoon as he left the courthouse surrounded by local camera crews. The comment quickly drew all the major news organizations to Norfolk. On the night before the trial began, Gilbert gave numerous interviews with various TV, radio and newspaper reporters. He looked and sounded great.

He looked and sounded great on the first day of trial too. He was regal, standing beside Todd, as they conferenced with the judge before proceedings began. But although Gilbert was an attractive man, he did not have an attractive case against me for the murder of Dennis Mazzani. They had never found the murder weapon, never located eyewitnesses, and never lifted any pertinent fingerprints from the scene. Gilbert's case primarily relied on motive and Margaret's and the cashier's testimony. Blaine milked what little he had for all it was worth. He brought my Salvation Bell Ringing Vision into evidence to establish my "violent state of mind". He took testimony from some Frat boy that was present the night I struck Randy, in order to establish my "violent, jealous temper". He was even low enough to parade Father's heavily perfumed harlot before the court, and called her my "stepmother". Despite Todd's objections, she was allowed to besmirch my name by lying about my threats and "odd behavior" she'd witnessed for years.

With each extraneous witness and irrelevant scrap of evidence I grew angrier. *That's not pertinent, you idiot! Let's open our Bibles to Leviticus and get to the heart of this case!*

"Shhh! They'll hear you." Todd scowled.

"I want them to hear me! I want to take the stand for God's Law! He clearly demands in Leviticus 20:10 that..."

"Shut up!"

Todd was pissing me off. The friction between us only grew worse after his cross-examination of the wine shop cashier:

Todd: So, it's your testimony that Mr. Mazzani said, and I quote 'I just ran into an old friend in the parking lot that I haven't seen in years.' Is this correct?

Cashier: Yes sir.

Todd: Did he tell you his friend's name?

Cashier: No sir.

Todd: Did he offer a description of his friend?

Cashier: No sir.

Todd: Did he even say whether the friend was a man or a woman?

Cashier: No sir.

Todd: Did he say that he was going to take his friend for a drive?

Cashier: No sir.

Todd: Did he say he was going to have a drink with him?

Cashier: No sir.

Todd: No further questions.

I just didn't like Todd's tone. While I could accept it with the cashier, I told him I would not accept his handling Margaret in similar manner.

"Are you nuts?" Todd asked.

"Look, just don't bother cross examining her if you're going to be rude."

She looked beautiful. Auburn hair in a bun, pearl necklace, black dress, hosiery and pumps. She was a glamorous widow and I ached for her to look at me. She did not. She approached the stand, swore on the Bible and took her seat. I heard little of what transpired because I was enraptured by her presence. How far we were from innocent days at Sandy Point. I loved her, worshipped her and prayed with all my heart against God's will for her.

"I can't. I can't kill her."

"What? Will you please shut up." Todd whispered.

And then slowly, I became aware of her deceitful words. My God! She was violating the Ninth Commandment! Bearing false witness:

Gilbert: So, you were concerned about your husband's whereabouts and called his cell phone on the night of his murder?

Margaret: Yes.

Gilbert: And what time did you call him?

Margaret: I called him at 7PM. I remember because I had dinner waiting for him.

Gilbert: Were you able to get through to him?

Margaret: Yes.

Gilbert: And what did he say?

Margaret: He said he was at our river house drinking champagne with Leonard Boseki.

Gilbert: So, Dennis Mazzani told you, shortly before he was killed at your river house, that he was drinking champagne with Leonard Boseki at your river house?

Margaret: Yes sir.

Gilbert: Did you speak to Leonard?

Margaret: No sir, but I heard his voice.
Gilbert: What did he say?
Margaret: I couldn't make out what he said, but I heard him laugh.
Gilbert: You heard Leonard Boseki laugh. Are you sure it was him?
Margaret: Yes sir. I lived with him for years. I would have recognized his voice and laugh anywhere.
Gilbert: No further questions.

* * * * * *

The week before Father's death I saw it approaching in his eyes; they became filmed in milky yellow. His face took on a sallow cast and all the broken blood vessels on his cheekbones bloomed vivid red. I'd enter his room and take his hand each evening to learn of a new delusion.

"Listen to me." He'd whisper with a flapping tongue. "I want you to tell the doctor that she spit in my face three times today."

"Who did Dad?"

"That woman. That fat nurse."

"What was her name?"

"I don't remember."

"Give me a better description. What's her hair color, how old is she?"

He sank back in the bed and closed his eyes. "Never mind." He said.

I opened the window to clear the foul air and combed his white hair.

"The other way." He said and so I changed his part.

"You can stand there all day long," he said to no one by the far wall. "You can stand there and spit in my face

The Seventh Illusion

and laugh at me but I will not stand for it. Do you hear me? I will not stand for it!"

"Are you talking to me?" I asked. But he didn't need to answer. He was already off on a diatribe against some other invisible being beside the window, and then another before the TV. He was working around the room, fighting delusions that antagonized him every waking moment of that final week. I hoped that they'd vanish or turn friendly so that his anxiety would ease. They never did. He battled those spirits to the end.

In contrast, I felt entirely alone during his final days. Alone in Father's room, reading poetry to him, while he fought unseen principalities. Alone in Bel's car, hoping for a glimpse of Margaret. Alone in my darkened room, trembling over the weightlessness of life, nothing to grasp. And, while I lay atop a floral comforter screaming into my pillow, Father was two miles away, fighting the evil that surrounded him.

* * * * * *

On the evening after the first day of my second murder trial, an extraordinary event occurred that changed the course of history. The event spawned a world-famous book, countless articles, and gave birth to such well-worn phrases as "Leonardite Dogs" and "Just ask Bruno". The incident had such a powerful effect on Thomas Conlin when I subsequently spoke of it at a Fayetteville Kiwanis Club luncheon in late 1994 that he immediately quit his job to follow "Truth". By early 1995, Mr. Conlin had established a church in Hayton North Carolina that would soon become known as "Swords for the Lord Assemblies" (SFTL). But I'm getting ahead of myself.

I returned to my jail cell around 6pm after hearing Margaret's testimony. I was feeling so low that I just sat on the floor with my back against the cold steel bars. At about 7pm they came with dinner and passed it through the slot. I wasn't hungry and left it untouched on the floor beside me where I lay. I was too despondent to eat after seeing Margaret and witnessing her violate God's commandments again. I stared at the ceiling, brooding over my parents... Margaret... me. I was alone and full of doubt. What happened? Where did I make the wrong turn that led me to this cage? Was I mad? I was wrestling with Satan but, where was he? I confess suicide entered my mind. I probably would have done it too, had Warden Bell not removed my belt when returned from court.

"Nah. I ain't gonna let ya try to hang yaself again. I'm keeping ya alive long enuff to see ya fry."

I did not like thee Warden Bell,
The reason why I cannot tell
But this I know and know full well,
I did not like thee Warden Bell.

He did not like me either. Early into my stay we shared our respective viewpoints of the Bible and it quickly became apparent he'd never read it.

"Ah don't have to read it, ya murderous asshole. Jesus loves me this ah know, for the Bible tells me so."

I told him his arguments were nonsensical. My lack of respect for his mental and spiritual acuity enraged him. To intimidate me, he started leaving his German Shepherd tied on a long leash just outside my cell. But Bruno and I became fast friends; all it took was my willingness to share meals with him. And that's exactly what I was doing on the night of his prophecy.

The Seventh Illusion

I was crying I suppose, when I heard Bruno sniffing around outside the cell. I rolled my head to find his tail wagging slow like a pendulum, nose squeezing through the bars to see what was for dinner. I propped up on an elbow and handed him half a grilled cheese sandwich through the bars. He devoured it in three bites and stared into my eyes. That's when the world changed.

"Hundes des Krieges." He growled.

I gaped, open mouthed.

"Lassen sie Gleiten Die Hunde Des Krieges!" He groaned.

I sat up.

"Your German is rough." I said, holding forth the second half of the sandwich. "Do you know English?"

He tugged the offering from my hand through the bars, chomped a few times and said:

"Cry Havoc and let loose the dogs of war!"

I've since discovered that Bruno was quoting Shakespeare. At the time I thought it was Isaiah, as Bruno began what would become a fifteen-thousand word prophecy. I reached under my cot for my notebook and wrote as quickly as I could to keep pace with his panting paean:

> *...The police, lawmakers and watchmen of America are blind.*
> *They all lack knowledge (just look at my pathetic master).*
> *They are all mute dogs, they cannot bark.*
> *They lie around and dream, they love to sleep.*
> *They are dogs with mighty appetites; they never have enough.*
> *They are stupid Shepherds that lack understanding;*
> *They all turn to their own way, each seeks his own gain.*
> *'Come, let us drink our fill of beer!'*
>
> *But you Lenny, you have the knowledge (I see it in your eyes).*
> *You are a mighty Lion, you roar and spread fear.*
> *You do not dream, but do.*
> *You have a mighty appetite for righteousness,*

But you are alone.
Shepherd those that need understanding.
Take the forgotten message of the Bible to America.
Let the Country see that we must slay unrighteous infidels!
Cry Havoc, and unleash the dogs of war!

Critics have long protested that Bruno's intro smacked of Isaiah 56:10-12. I can't respond as to whether he was influenced by the prophet, for I'm but a humble reporter of his words. And what words, what prophecy! He told me that I was the chosen one to lead the United States of America to a religious renaissance. He revealed that I alone understood "The Truth" that had been so clearly commanded repeatedly in the Bible. Bruno told me that I was to preach Truth to the people of America so that we could "completely destroy the Babylonians" and return to our Promised Land.

"We have been attacked by Assyrians. We have been carried off to Babylon. You must end the Diaspora and return us to righteousness. Selah." He said.

"But how can I spread the Truth when I am standing trial for murder? Surely my wife's testimony will convict me in the eyes of the people."

"This will be a sign for you." Said Bruno "Ye shall be found innocent not once nor twice but thrice for your righteousness. Ye shall be freed to spread Truth to America, that all may see the great danger they face, lest they return to God's Law. You are the new Ezekiel! And like Ezekiel you must warn of the Sword coming against the Land! You are both the warning and the punishment! You must....errr, what's the matter?"

"I miss my wife so much. I want Margaret back. I want things the way they used to be."

"Silence! Ye have a new ministry afoot! A ministry that shall also destroy your great whore of a wife!"

"She is not a whore!" I said.

The Seventh Illusion

"Margaret is America, do you not understand?" Bruno growled, "She is Jerusalem in Ezekiel's day. She is Ezekiel 23:19-20: *'Yet she became more and more promiscuous as she recalled the days of her youth, when she was a prostitute in Egypt. There she lusted after her lovers, whose genitals were like those of donkeys and whose emission was like that of horses...'*"

"NAY! THOU SHALT NOT SPEAK OF MY WIFE THAT WAY!" I screamed.

I flung the tray at Bruno and it clattered against the bars. Warden Bell appeared with other deputies to silence me. The door opened, arms and elbows against my neck, Bruno holding my groin in a vice like grip, righteous suffering shooting through my body. Electrical Current. And as I faded from consciousness, Bruno growling out his last prophetic words...

"This Mother fukas crazy...."

* * * * *

The court took a 24-hour recess per Todd Hanson's request. I slept through the day in a drug induced stupor administered by a court appointed doctor. I was still quite wounded and groggy when court reconvened and so had to be rolled up to the table via wheel chair. I felt nothing but a low throb around my crotch where Bruno had bitten me. I could not think clearly, as the courtroom hummed and a gray pall hung in the air. But Todd was smiling.

"I doubt you're going to like this Lenny, but I think I may just save your life today." He whispered into my ear. And so, he did. And I have never forgiven him.

The morning crawled with a host of insipid witnesses. Testimony establishing that Dennis' businesses were bankrupt, that numerous lawsuits were pending against him, and that he was under investigation for fraud. I nodded off through most of it. Todd brayed afterwards how he'd painted a clear picture of a dishonest man hounded by enemies, any one of whom might have killed him. I grasped none of it at the time and given the ennui in the juror's eyes I doubt that they did either. That would change though, after lunch, when Todd cross-examined Margaret.

He started by asking her how we met, and quickly established that we made love on our first date after a fraternity party. Three questions later Margaret confessed that she became pregnant while we were still in college.

"And was the child Lenny's?" Todd asked.

"Objection!" Blaine Gilbert said and I agreed. But the judge didn't.

"Of course, it was." Margaret said, tears welling up, "But I miscarried."

"Were you not also sexually involved with several other young men during this time?"

"No!"

"Would you be surprised to know I took the deposition of two of your Sorority sisters who swear they saw you in a sex act with a Mr. Randy Head and a Mr. Stewart Mercer while you were living with my client? Would it surprise you to learn that they saw you with Randy Head several times during your pregnancy snorting cocaine?"

"OBJECTION! YOUR HONOR THIS IS AN OUTRAGE!" Blaine screamed. I couldn't move.

A heated discussion ensued before the judge. Margaret wept. I was stone. Todd won and continued, walking her and the jury through our wedding and into our new life and career working for Dennis Mazzani.

"And so, you met Dennis Mazzani for the first time when Leonard was working for him?"

"Yes."

"And you started an affair with Dennis Mazzani while you were still married to Leonard?"

"We fell in love. I didn't want it to happen, but it did. I didn't mean to hurt Leonard."

"So, you left Leonard?"

"No. Leonard left me the night I told him I was pregnant with his child."

"Are you sure it's his child?"

"Objection!"

"I'll withdraw the question your honor." Todd offered.

"How long were you married to Dennis Mazzani before he was killed?" He continued.

"Almost two years."

"And you're the beneficiary of his million-dollar life insurance policy?"

"Yes."

"Wow, a million dollars. That's a lot of money. What are you going to do with it all?"

"Objection! Your honor, not relevant!"

"Withdrawn." Todd conceded. "Mrs. Mazzani, do you know a Mr. Richard Davis?"

"Yes."

"And what is your relationship with him?"

"Dennis and I knew Richard and his wife from our country club. We dined with them often."

"Oh, come now Mrs. Mazzani let's be more specific. Were you having an affair with Mr. Davis?

"OBJECTION! YOUR HONOR, WHO'S ON TRIAL HERE?"

"Overruled. The witness will answer the question."

"No!"

"No what, that you were not having an affair with Richard Davis?"

"I was not having an affair with him!"

"Ok, Mrs. Mazzini, just a few more questions. In your own words, can you share with the court once again the last telephone conversation you had with your husband on the night he was killed?"

Margaret hesitated, as if to collect her thoughts Then, after a sigh:

"Dennis was over an hour late for dinner and so became concerned and called him. He answered and said the reason why he wasn't home yet is that he was drinking with Leonard at our river house..."

"And how did you feel about that news?" Todd asked.

"I was surprised. Neither of us had seen or heard from him in years."

"And although you testified previously that you didn't speak to Leonard that night, you're absolutely certain he was with your husband?"

"Yes, I heard Leonard speaking and laughing in the background.'"

"I have no further questions of this witness your honor. The defense will now call Mrs. Cathy Russell."

For the first time during the trial, Margaret's eyes met mine. Her face suddenly flushed, her eyes, pleading.

Oh, Margaret. How I wanted to take you into my arms and flee this frightening world. It was always far too much for you to bare, my precious love. But it is too late. Far too late.

I had never heard of Mrs. Russell but apparently Margaret knew her well. They had been neighbors for the last year and became best of friends. They played golf together twice a week and often chatted on the phone about the vagaries of being affluent housewives leading country club lives. They held happy hour daily

The Seventh Illusion

from 4:30pm to whenever their husbands pulled into the driveway. During those wine-soaked hours their daughters played in the TV room while Margaret and Mrs. Russell sat in the kitchen gossiping and sharing intimate details of one another's lives. Three months ago, Margaret confided that she was having an affair with Richard Davis.

"OBJECTION! This is hearsay your honor!" The judge allowed her to continue.

Mrs. Russell had also witnessed Mr. Davis pull his corvette into the Mazzani driveway when Dennis was out of town. It remained parked there the entire night. "I told Jenny it was her uncle Dick." Margaret tittered when Mrs. Russell asked how she explained it to her daughter.

Mrs. Russell was also at Margaret's on the evening of Dennis' execution. It was my good fortune, I suppose, that Mr. Russell was out of town and so Mrs. Russell was with Margaret during her final phone call to Dennis. Mrs. Russell had switched to iced tea by then, knowing she still had to feed and bathe her daughter, as Margaret kept drinking her two-liter bottle of Chardonnay and slurring secret stories.

Around 7pm Mrs. Russell recalled asking Margaret where Dennis was.

"Fuck him," Margaret said. "Let's take the girls out for pizza, he'll fend for himself."

But Mrs. Russell hesitated, not wanting to go out in public considering Margaret's condition. She suggested calling Dennis in the hopes that he was on his way home. Margaret called reluctantly and Mrs. Russell was sitting close enough to hear both ends of the conversation.

"He says he's out at the river house with an old friend." Margaret said as she hung up. "Would'n tell me who, like it's some big surprise."

"Who do you think it is?" Mrs. Russell asked.

"Shit, who knows. Knowing him, it's some fucking barfly…"

*In his days the righteous will flourish;
prosperity will abound till the moon is no more.*
            Psalm 72:7

Three

I fired Todd Hanson immediately after my acquittal for the murder of Dennis Mazzani. Todd was livid, insisting that if it weren't for him, I'd be in prison. Perhaps, but the truth is, he was a lazy attorney that only came to life after Mrs. Russell called him regarding Margaret's testimony. She was "simply appalled by Margaret's fabrications" and felt compelled to testify to the true conversation. Todd got lucky, that's all.

It wasn't his laziness that made me fire Todd though, it was the rude, deceptive way he handled Margaret. He cast doubt on her character, making her appear capable of murdering her husband for lust and insurance proceeds. I saw how Todd's cross examination wounded her and I simply couldn't tolerate sitting next to him for another trial. Besides, attorneys were skittering in like cockroaches, offering to handle my third trial "pro bono". I interviewed a few of them; all young lawyers hoping the publicity of my case would make them famous. None of them suited me. I'd escaped conviction twice and knew if God was going to release me again, I'd have to lend a hand by finding a competent defender of Truth. I settled on Reginald Corcoran, the well-known criminal attorney. He turned out to be just another brilliant liar.

The evidence against me for my third murder trial was severely damaged after I was found not guilty of Dennis' murder. Blaine Gilbert had planned on connecting the dots between Head's and Mazzani's murders by placing me in father's house retrieving his pistol to kill Dennis shortly after I beat Head to death. But now that Blaine had lost at trial (and never located the snub-nose) he had to rely on just three key pieces of evidence.

1) A police report of my assault on Randy Head six years prior.
2) A beer can with my fingerprints found in a trash can near to the murder scene.
3) A rag soaked with Head's blood found lying in my father's house.

Reginald was a heavy weight fighting a Boy Scout and quickly dispatched Blaine Gilbert and his evidence.

"Just because my client was arrested for assault, they think he's guilty of murder? Reginald asked the jury. "Mr. Boseki fought with Randy Head while in college almost a decade ago, he does not deny this. But why doesn't the State tell the people the whole truth? Why don't they tell you that the reason for the altercation was Randy Head's vile insults directed to Lenny's soon to be wife and mother of his unborn child? Why don't they confess that Mr. Head, in front of his drunken Frat brothers, called the mother of Leonard's unborn child a common whore? Ladies and gentlemen of the jury I have a confession to make. If any man, ANY MAN, called the mother of my three precious children a whore, I would do much worse to that man than Leonard Boseki did to Randy Head that night. Leonard was fighting for the honor of his wife and child and was right to do so. And Randy Head *knew* that Leonard was right." And here Reginald leaned close to the jury and spoke quietly. "And here's why we know that Randy knew Leonard was right: Because Randy dropped the charges. Think about that for a moment. Randy Head dropped the assault charges against Leonard. Now why would Randy Head drop the charges against my client? I'll tell you what I think. Randy woke up the next morning feeling genuine shame over his drunken and disgusting comments..."

Reginald was brilliant throughout the trial. His high-water point was the method in which he neutralized my fingerprints on the beer can issue. He hired a private investigator to stake out Blue Sink for weeks before the trial in the vague hope of finding something to disparage the State's evidence. He found what he was looking for.

"...you know the Blue Sink must be a pretty interesting place." Reginald said on the second day. "We did a little research there and you know what? We found almost a thousand beer cans and pop bottles lying around on the ground and in trash receptacles..." and here an entourage of clean young men brought in garbage bags of their find to display to the court.

"Almost a thousand cans! And the consumers of all these drinks are potential suspects for murder?!"

"OBJECTION!!"

But it was already too late for Blaine. Reginald had the jury completely under his sway.

"Ya know, Blue Sink is a popular place. Lots of people go there to swim or just enjoy the day. We decided to dust some of the cans for fingerprints and we had a very interesting discovery. Do you know what we found ladies and gentlemen? Do you want an idea of how many people visit Blue Sink? Do you want to know how many people go there to relax, maybe enjoy a beer or a Cola? I'll tell you what we found. We lifted the prints of

Bailiff Rick Johnson off a Coke bottle. The same Bailiff that walks you in and out of court every day..."

"YOUR HONOR! THIS IS OUTRAGEOUS"!

"...should Bailiff Johnson be on trial for this murder too?"

"OBJECTION!"

Blaine was purple with rage and demanded a mistrial. He was denied one but given ample leeway to explain to the jury that Bailiff Johnson had been on a simple reconnaissance trip to Blue Sink to gauge the feasibility of taking the jurors there via bus to view the crime scene. Neither Blaine nor the court were able to establish that Reginald knew this so he was no chastised for his stroke of genius. The jury loved it.

By that point, I knew I'd be acquitted and Reginald did too. That's why there's simply no excuse for the deplorable way he dispatched the third key piece of evidence.

"Oh my, the bloody rag found at Lenny's father house. A house that Lenny had not set foot in for years. Now, why would Lenny leave a bloody rag in his dead father's house hmm? Oh yes, the State claims he left it as a warning to his father's wife but isn't that ridiculous? I mean really!"

That's all the asshole had to say. But he just kept pushing it.

"I'll tell you what I think ladies and gentlemen. I'll tell you what's more likely. You've already heard that Lenny was acquitted for the murder of his former partner Dennis Mazzani, the same man who Lenny's ex-wife Margaret seduced and eventually married. Well, Randy Head worked for Dennis Mazzani and was slated to testify in court that Mazzani had embezzled hundreds of thousands of dollars of client funds. Now, it seems to me that Randy Head's death was good news for Dennis and

The Seventh Illusion

Margaret Mazzani hmm? Is it possible that Mr. and Mrs. Mazzani had something to do with Randy's murder? And what about Dennis Mazzani's subsequent death? It's easy to see how that could benefit Margaret Mazzani, not only for the insurance proceeds, but also for the elimination of an accomplice. Yes, Margaret Mazzani, the same woman who lied in court against my client Leonard Boeski in an attempt to see him hang for a murder he did not commit! Oh, and how convenient for a bloody rag to suddenly appear at Leonard's father's house shortly after the Randy Head's murder. Let me share an important fact with you ladies and gentlemen. Listen very closely. Lenny's ex-wife, Margaret Boseki Mazzani possibly still had a key to Leonard's father's house. Listen very closely. Margaret Boseki Mazzani used to be Randy Head's lover in college. She could have easily lured Randy Head down to Blue Sink. In fact, we have a witness statement stating that she was sexually involved with Randy last year..."

"OBJECTION! OBJECTION! GOD DAMN IT!" I screamed.

It almost cost me the trial. I was removed from court and injected with something so powerful that I slept for over twenty-four hours. When I awoke, I was a free man. I refused to speak or appear with Reginald Corcoran. But I remembered Bruno's words. I packed my Volvo and began my mission immediately.

Who is this that appears like the dawn,
fair as the moon, bright as the sun,
majestic as the stars in procession?
                    Song of Solomon 6:10

Four

"I saw you on Lon Lacy Live Mr. Boseki, and I think you're right. Where can I purchase your book?"
                    – C. Thorndike, Tangerine Florida

"My husband is an adulterer Mr. Boseki, are you sure it's ok to kill him? If so, are you willing to make the arrangements?"
                    – Mrs. Francis Smith, Mobile Alabama

"You're a fucking degenerate and I hope you fry in hell!"
                    –Roger Oren, Charlotte N.C.

My ministry came to life after I appeared on Lon Lacy Live the evening of May 16, 1995. I was considered an oddity until then, someone with fifteen minutes of National fame after being acquitted for three murders. I took to the road with "Bible Truth" seminars immediately after my final acquittal, hoping to convince the Nation of our dire need to return to innocence. To my surprise, my message was violently rejected. I was spat upon, beaten and in one instance outside of Tupelo, narrowly escaped a gang rape from "escaped" prisoners of a road work crew. Still, I was not discouraged, knowing that apostles of Truth were often scorned in the early years. But within six months of preaching, I had become a pariah to the Pharisees and could not gain admittance to any church, chapel or

Kingdom Hall in America. I was on the verge of abandoning the cause altogether when I received that fateful call from Lon Lacy's handlers. A Lacy scout had picked up one of my pamphlets and thought I'd be an entertaining interview. Was I interested? I agreed only in the interest of spreading Truth. We made the arrangements over the phone and I had no further contact with them, other than a confirmation call two days before the broadcast.

I arrived to New York City and made my way to 30 Rock. I did not realize until after I was seated in the waiting room, watching the first thirty minutes of Lon Lacy Live, that I'd be sharing the interview with David Prince, the famous Televangelist.

"Coming up later in the next half hour, David Prince goes head-to-head with Lenny Boseki, the three-time acquitted murderer who now confesses he did it in the name of the Lord! Stay tuned."

I was shocked. "Head-to-head?" That smacked of a debate to me and I couldn't imagine how a conservative pastor like David Prince could possibly take issue with the Bible. I had followed his stellar career for years and agreed with almost everything he said. That would change.

I was slotted for the final fifteen minutes of the show. David had been on the full hour, first debating a Rabbi, followed by a Hindu and then a Muslim. I was bringing up the rear of what had been a contentious evening of religious argumentation. I was guided in during the break and took my seat. Mr. Prince would not shake my proffered hand nor establish eye contact with me.

"We're back." Lon Lacy started. "Now sitting in the hot seat is Leonard Boseki, a man acquitted for three separate murders that he now admits he committed. His motive? The Bible told him to do it."

The Seventh Illusion

"Lon," David Prince said. "I just want to say before we begin how despicable I find this man. He is despicable not simply because he is a ruthless murderer but because he professes to be acting under the orders of almighty God Himself to commit blood thirsty, unspeakable crimes!" And then he looked straight into my eyes for the benefit of the audience and said: "Young man, you say that the Bible told you to kill? Then let me ask you; have you ever read the Sixth Commandment? Thou shalt not kill! What part of those four simple words do you not understand?"

It's been suggested that the reason why David Prince came off so poorly during our first "debate" was because he had only a vague idea of who I was. He assumed I was simply another crazed killer who had heard voices coming from his Bible. He did not know that, unlike ninety-eight percent of the viewing audience, I'd actually read it.

"Yes sir," I said. "I'm familiar with the Sixth Commandment, but God commands that we kill those that break His Law. For your reference, God ordered Moses and the Israelites to stone a man to death for gathering sticks on the Sabbath in Numbers 15:32-36[22]. In Leviticus 24:13-16[23] God commanded the entire assembly to stone a blasphemer. Or review the book of

---

[22] *Num 15:32-36 - While the Israelites were in the desert, a man was found gathering wood on the Sabbath... Then the Lord said to Moses, "This man must die. The whole assembly must stone him outside the camp." So the assembly...stoned him to death...*

[23] *Lev 24:13-16 - The Lord said to Moses: "Take the blasphemer outside the camp... if anyone curses his God, he will be held responsible, anyone who blasphemes the name of the Lord must be put to death.*

Joshua where God orders Joshua's army to slaughter every man, woman, child and animal in thirty-one cities..."

"Son, you know just enough about the Bible to be dangerous! Very dangerous! Let me encourage you to read a book that may clarify things for you. It's about God sending his only begotten Son to earth as a sacrifice for our sins and therefore nullifying the law. Have you not heard of Jesus Christ?"

I stared open mouthed, so astounded by his words that I didn't respond.

"Well, this is going to be one short debate Lonny!" David Prince laughed. Do we have another guest in the wings to fill the void?"

"I'm sorry," I stammered. "I was just stunned by your viewpoint. I assumed a man of your stature would understand the Word."

"OH, I understand the Word, boy. It's you that need to learn the Bible and pray on your knees for Jesus Christ, the Prince of Peace to forgive you!" David said. "The Prince of Peace, not cold-blooded murder!"

"I'm familiar with the words of Jesus Christ." I offered respectfully. "Matthew 10:34 is very clear: 'Do not suppose that I have come to bring peace to the earth. I did not come to bring peace but a sword.'"

"Again here you are with just a smidgen of knowledge! Jesus is speaking of the sword of his Word. A new covenant of love and forgiveness that cuts through the earth like a sword!"

"I agree we must be full of love and forgiveness for those that sin. But we must still slaughter them according to God's Law."

"You just don't get it do you boy? Jesus Christ died for the sins of those you butchered. They were forgiven. You murdered those that were innocent in the eyes of

The Seventh Illusion

God. You hacked an ordained Christian minister to death!"

"Yes, I hacked him to death. I killed him because he was a sodomite. I executed him according to God's word in Leviticus 20:13[24]. But please understand that I was full of love for him as I devoted him to the Lord."

"I will say this again very slowly." David said. "Christ died for our sins. We are no longer under the Law. The Law is no longer relevant. Try reading the epistles of Paul, starting with Galatians."

"I'm familiar with Paul's Epistles. They contradict King David who said God's statutes were to last forever[25]. They contradict the apostle John that says to love God and keep his commands[26], they even contradict Jesus Christ who said in Luke 16:17: 'It is easier for heaven and earth to disappear than for the least stroke of a pen to drop out of the Law.'"

David Prince glared. "You shot your best friend from behind like a coward as I recall. What sin did he commit?"

"He committed adultery."

"Ah yes, with your wife?"

"Yes."

"Are you going to kill your wife too?"

A pause.

---

[24] *Leviticus 20:13 - If a man lies with a man as one lies with a woman, both of them have done what is detestable. They must be put to death; their blood will be on their own heads.*

[25] *Psalm 119:151-152: Yet you are near, O Lord, and all your commands are true. Long ago I learned from your statutes, that you established them to last forever.*

[26] *1 John 5:3 – This is love for God: to obey his commands.*

"She needs to be slain, yes." I said.

"And it's your position that every man or woman that has committed adultery needs to be killed?"

"It's not my position, it's God's position."

"We'll put an end to this right now," David Prince said, picking up his Bible and quickly turning pages. Then, he began to read John 8 in a low sonorous voice:

The teachers of the law and the Pharisees brought in a woman caught in adultery. They made her stand before the group and said to Jesus, "Teacher, this woman was caught in the act of adultery. In the Law Moses commanded us to stone such women. Now what do you say?" They were using this question as a trap in order to have a basis for accusing him.

But Jesus bent down and started to write on the ground with his finger. When they kept on questioning him, he straightened up and said to them, "If any one of you is without sin, let him be the first to throw a stone at her." Again he stooped down and wrote on the ground.

At this, those who heard began to go away one at a time, the older ones first, until only Jesus was left with the woman still standing there. Jesus straightened up and asked her, "Woman, where are they? Has no one condemned you?"

"No one, sir." She said.

"Then neither do I condemn you," Jesus declared. "Go now and leave your life of sin." – John 8: 3-11

David Prince, took off his reading glasses and smugly chided "John 8 3-11. You want the word of Jesus Himself, there is His word, there is proof by his very action!"

"I wish they were His words Mr. Prince, believe me. But they are not."

"Read it yourself, John 8!" And offered me the Bible.

"Mr. Lacy will you take it please and read the footnote associated with John 8?" I asked.

Lon Lacy took the Bible and read:

The Seventh Illusion

"The earliest manuscripts and many other ancient witnesses do not have John 7:53–8:11.

"It did not originally belong to the Gospel of John. Someone inserted this passage hundreds of years later." I said.

"Are you telling me you do not accept this passage as the word of Jesus Christ?" Prince asked.

"As you know Mr. Prince, John was written around 85 AD, about fifty years after Jesus was crucified. Biblical scholars have studied all the earliest extant Gospel of John manuscripts. This passage doesn't appear in the oldest and most reliable manuscripts. In fact, of all the Gospel of John manuscripts dated up to 500 AD, and there are many, only one has this passage. Most Biblical scholars don't believe Jesus said this or that John wrote it. The church inserted the passage hundreds of years later."

"Blasphemy! Lon, you can't argue with a mad man! This man is Satan's child!"

"Let's go to the phones." Lon said. "Hello Stacy from Charlotte…"

I'm told we stretched the phone bank to the limit that night and broke all records for number of calls received during a live broadcast. Most called to condemn me for being "evil", several went so far as to wonder if I was "The Antichrist" and one prophesied that I would suffer my "own medicine". A few of them though actually had questions.

From Florida:

"…Do you mean to tell me that God wants me to stone my neighbor if he mows his lawn on the Sabbath?"

"Yes sir. If you have a Bible handy, turn to Exodus 31:12-15[27]..."

From Kentucky:

"Are you telling me that it's ok to kill Muslims and Buddhists and Hindus?"

"I'm not telling you anything sir. God is telling you throughout the Bible. In fact, he's telling you to wipe out entire cities that don't worship him. Take a look at Deuteronomy 13:12-15[28]..."

From California:

"Let me make sure I'm hearing this nut case correctly: If my son calls me an (expletive) I'm supposed to kill him?"

"It's not me you have heard correctly sir, It's God. Leviticus 20:9[29] to be exact. And I must warn you that you are bordering on blasphemy to refer to His Word as 'nutcase'..."

From New York:

"What this (expletive) Boseki is advocating is genocide! He'll kill everyone in the Country if he can!

---

[27] *Exodus 31:12-16 - Then the Lord said to Moses...Observe the Sabbath because it is holy to you. Anyone who desecrates it must be put to death...whoever does any work on the Sabbath must be put to death.*

[28] *Deuteronomy 13:12-15 – If you hear it said about one of the towns the Lord your God is giving you to live in that wicked men have arisen among you and led the people astray saying, "Let us go and worship other gods" ... And if it is true and it has been proved... you must certainly put to the sword all who live in that town. Destroy it completely, both its people and its livestock.*

[29] *Leviticus 20:9 If anyone curses his father or mother, he must be put to death.*

The Seventh Illusion

"It's not my way sir. It's God's way. Re-read Joshua, re-read the Old Testament and you'll count over two million people slaughtered by God or under his orders as The Chosen Ones cleansed the earth of idolatry. Think about what a large percentage of the world's population that must have been. And by the way, this is why God is not active in the world today like he was in Moses' time. He's given up on us because the world is overrun with infidels. He's angry with America just as he was with Israel in the days of the prophets. We will never have God's presence again until the wicked are cleansed from the population of our great Country..."

"So, you're telling me" Lon interrupted "That God wants us to kill everyone that commits sin?"

"Yes. If you'll read Deuteronomy 28:15-68 you'll see how serious God is. If we don't carefully follow all the words of His Law, God will send plaques, our fiancée's will be raped and we'll be driven mad. We'll be invaded by a foreign nation and put under siege. In fact, God specifically warns that if we don't obey His Law then we'll be forced to eat the flesh of our children and our women will eat their own afterbirth. Verses 54-57[30] addresses the details..."

"This is outrageous!" Screamed David Prince. This is blasphemy pure and simple!"

---

[30] *Deuteronomy 28:54-57- Even the most gentle and sensitive man among you will have no compassion on his own brother or the wife he loves or his surviving children and he will not give to one of them any of the flesh of his children that he is eating. The most gentle and sensitive woman among you...will begrudge the husband she loves and her own son or daughters the afterbirth from her womb and the children she bears. For she intends to eat them secretly during the siege...*

"How can it be blasphemy when I'm simply reading from the Bible?"

"You are about Satan's work! You are twisting the truth and completely ignoring that Jesus Christ died for our sins and washed us clean in the blood of the lamb!"

"I accept Jesus Christ as my savior. That does not excuse us from obeying God's Statutes as you curiously seem to imply. Are you suggesting that I'm free to casually kill, steal, worship false gods and commit adultery?"

"No! I'm saying that Christ's crucifixion freed us from the Law!"

"I understand that you've ministered to condemned felons on death row is that correct, Mr. Prince?" I asked.

"Yes, and I've had many of them accept Jesus Christ as their Lord and Savior!"

"Shouldn't they have been freed from death row and prison after accepting Jesus Christ since they are now freed from the law?"

"Of course not. They owe a debt to society." David Prince said.

"Ah, then we agree after all! If someone has broken the Law they must pay..."

"You are on Satan's mission to deny the importance of Jesus dying for our sins. By his blood I am set free!"

"You insist that we're freed from God's Law. Jesus said otherwise on numerous occasions. I've already given you Luke 16:17 as a reference. Perhaps a few additional passages from Jesus for your next Bible study will help you understand His intentions. Matthew

The Seventh Illusion

5:17-18 [31] and Luke 12:49-51[32] clearly lays out His strategy…"

"VENGENANCE IS MINE SAYS THE LORD!" David shouted. "The Lord is giving me a clear prophecy at this very moment! *'You are an evil, conniving man doing the Satan's work!'* sayeth the Lord! God is giving me a clear prophecy that he is speaking through my lips. *'Ye shall be struck down by the Lord this very year!'* Death Mr. Boseki! Death!"

---

[31] *Matthew 5:17-18 – Do not think that I have come to abolish the Law or the Prophets; I have not come to abolish them but to fulfill them. I tell you the truth, until heaven and earth disappear, not the smallest letter, not the least stroke of a pen will by any means disappear from the Law until everything is accomplished.*

[32] *Luke 12:49-51 – I have come to bring fire on the earth and how I wish it were already kindled! I have a baptism to undergo, and how distressed I am until it is completed! You think that I came to bring peace on earth? No, I tell you, but division.*

Sun and moon stood still in the heavens
at the glint of your flying arrows,
At the lightning of your flashing spear.
In wrath you strode through the earth
and in anger you threshed the nations.
You came out to deliver your people,
to save your anointed one.
          -Habakkuk 3:11-13

I've never understood why God's Old Testament words aren't in red also.
          -The Aphorisms of Leonard Boseki (#53)

Five

Thus, began the busiest years of my life. I was inundated with correspondence after appearing on Lon Lacy Live, having made the mistake of providing my home address at the request of a caller. Most of the letters received were hate mail, death threats and other oddities from the lunatic fringe, but a few came from True believers wanting to organize. One particular letter planted the seed that would spread my message like kudzu throughout the South:

May 17, 1995
Dear Mr. Boseki,

I'm sure you don't remember me but I heard you speak at a Kiwanis Luncheon in Fayetteville, North Carolina last year. Although they cut you off only ten minutes into your speech, I want you to know I received your full message. I quit my job as a postal worker that afternoon, Mr. Boseki. I left my wife and four kids and devoted the next three months to reading the Bible. Now I'm preaching Truth to others just like you preached to my ex-Kiwanis Club.

I've established a church here in Hayton, North Carolina and the entire congregation watched you last night on Lon Lacy Live. Praise God, for He spoke through you with great eloquence! It would be our great honor if you would come preach at our church, which is growing rapidly. We are the <u>Swords for The Lord Assembly</u> located just off Highway 72..."

And so, I went and history was made. The SFTL Assembly welcomed me as though I was Ezekiel himself. They sat enraptured on folding metal chairs as I preached God's cleansing Truth that commanded his Chosen Ones to slaughter the unrighteous. It was invigorating to finally speak to Christians who understood God's True message of purity. Gazing out upon their adoring eyes, I realized my mission had truly begun. They rose to a standing ovation after I closed with Joshua 6:21[33] and I was mobbed like a rock star outside the chapel by awe struck Christian Soldiers wanting to touch the hem of my garment. A planned reception under a rented tent degenerated into a frenzied melee of the faithful as they poured into the pasture and trampled over folding chairs and tables laden with cold cuts, deviled eggs and sweet ice tea. It frightened me. Thomas created a diversion through his elders and managed to sweep me from the scene into his pickup truck, and we fled south, to a diner some ten miles from church.

"Do you feel it Mr. Boseki? Do you feel it?"

"Yes." I said, assuming he meant agitated fear.

---

[33] *Joshua 6:21- They devoted the city to the Lord and destroyed with the sword every living thing in it- men and women, young and old, cattle, sheep and donkeys.*

The Seventh Illusion

"The Sword of the Lord is in our very hands! We're going to lead the U.S. of A back to the Lord! It started this morning in Hayton and it's gonna spread across America just like in Joshua's time! We're gonna follow Joshua 6:21 into every unrighteous city in this Country starting with Atlanta. We're gonna destroy with the sword every living thing in it – men and women, young and old, cattle sheep and donkeys..."

I should have known then that I was dealing with a zealot and caught the next plane out of Ashville. Instead, I sat in the diner and reasoned with him, convincing him Atlanta was completely impractical given the respective size of its population and our congregation. He suggested Chattanooga. When I balked again, he bargained down to Murfreesboro.

"Mr. Conlin, we just can't start indiscriminately slaughtering everything that breathes. I know there are good Christians in every city you've mentioned."

He looked at me askance, as if I had blasphemed.

"Mr. Boseki, there are queers, adulterers and idol worshippers that make up the vast majority of each one of them towns I named. God didn't tell Moses and Joshua 'go to those thirty-one cities, politely knock on their door and ask them if they're Christians.' No sir, He said kill everyone! Kill the babies! Kill the children! Kill the cows!"

The people in the next booth seemed frightened. I asked Thomas to calm down. He tried, but his hands trembled badly as he raised his coffee cup to his lips. To distract him, I flipped over my place mat and we started writing the church Manifesto. It was subsequently photocopied, framed and prominently placed at the entrance of each of the Swords for the Lord assemblies that we eventually established:

Doyle Black

SWORDS FOR THE LORD ASSEMBLY
WHAT WE ~~BELIEVE~~ KNOW!

WE KNOW *that the Holy Bible is the infallible Word of God and therefore the supreme and <u>final authority in all things.</u> (II Tim. 3:16-17; II Peter 1:21)*

WE KNOW *that God and Jesus Christ are one and that He is the same yesterday, today and forever. (John 10:30; Heb 13:8)*

WE KNOW *God gave Moses HIS COMMANDS (LAW), which is clearly laid out in Exodus, Leviticus, Numbers, Deuteronomy etc. (Ex 20:1, Lev 1:1, Lev 27:34, Num 1:1, Num 36:13, Deut 5:4)*

WE KNOW, *per God, that <u>HIS LAW applies until the end of time!</u> (Deut 7:9-11, 1st Chron 16:14-16, Psalms 119:149-152, Matt 5:17-18, Luke 16:17, 1st John 5:1-3)*

WE KNOW *that where Paul and his Epistles contradict God, Jesus, or the Twelve Apostles, then Paul is mistaken, confused, and/or insane! (Gal 3:25 **vs** Matt 5:17-19), (Eph 2:8-9 **vs** James 2:14-25), (Gal 1:11-12 **vs** Matt 16:16-19) (Gal 2:11), (Acts 26:24)*

WE KNOW *God is ANGRY with those that do not believe and follow His Statutes. He commanded Moses (and other prophets) to march on a Holy Crusade to SLAUGHTER anyone that did not worship and obey Him (Joshua, Numbers, Jeremiah, Ezekiel, etc.).*

The Seventh Illusion

WE KNOW God no longer actively participates on earth because Moses and subsequent leaders failed to faithfully follow the Law and cleanse the earth of evil! It is our mission to finish what Moses and the others did not. Therefore:

WE KNOW that any form of ADULTERY, homosexuality, bisexuality, bestiality, and incest are perversions of God's gift of sex and that all sex perverts must be SLAUGHTERED.
(Lev. 20:10-21, Matt 5:27-28)

WE KNOW that every True believer should SLAUGHTER all non-believers and those who follow other gods. (Deut 7:16-25, Deut 12:2-3, Deut 13:1-10, Deut 17: 2-5). This includes entire cities if necessary! (Deut 13:12-16)

WE KNOW that anyone that does not obey God's Law or the ministers of our church must be SLAUGHTERED. (Deut 17:12-13)

WE KNOW that anyone not worshipping God on the Sabbath Day must be SLAUGHTERED.
(Ex 31:14 -16).

WE KNOW that any woman that is not (or was not) a virgin on her wedding night must be SLAUGHTERED. (Deuteronomy 22:20-21).

WE KNOW that any son that is stubborn and will not listen to his parents must be SLAUGHTERED. (Deuteronomy 21 18-21).

WE KNOW that witches, sorceresses, palm readers & fortune tellers must be SLAUGHTERED. (Lev 20:27).

WE KNOW that anyone that blasphemes the Lord must be SLAUGHTERED. (Lev 24:13-16)

WE KNOW that any people that do not obey God's Law will suffer plagues, disasters, and severe, lingering illnesses. Dreaded diseases, sickness and disaster will cling to them until they are destroyed. (Deut 28:58-68)

WE KNOW that the USA does not obey God's Law and therefore is suffering severe, lingering illness that will cling to the people until they are destroyed. We'll soon be forced to eat the flesh of our own children and our wives will be eating their afterbirth! (Deut 28:54-57) The only solution is to CLEANSE the sinners from this great land. Only after the guilty are SLAUGHTERED will God return! NOW, START THE FIRE OF REDEMPTION!!

"It is easier for heaven and earth to disappear than for the least stroke of a pen to drop out of the Law."- Jesus (Luke 16:17)

"I have come to bring fire on the earth, and how I wish it were already kindled!" – Jesus (Luke 12:49)

"Do not suppose that I have come to bring peace to the earth. I did not come to bring peace, but a sword. – Jesus (Matt 10:34)

"… and if you don't have a sword, sell your cloak and buy one." – Jesus (Luke 22:36)

The Seventh Illusion

"By God this is a historic moment!" Mr. Conlin said. "One day they'll change the name of this diner to 'Lenny's'!"

He was right of course; it was a historic moment. Word of my sermon spread throughout the South and SFTL's congregation tripled in size as we took our first step on the long march to reclaim America. As strange as it seems now, I felt a sense of hope then. We believed as a community that we were serving God and fighting for innocence.

* * * * * *

Although pleased by our rapid growth, I assumed that I'd soon die in accordance with David Prince's prophecy. I had long believed him to be a true messenger of God and persisted in this view despite his rude behavior on Lon Lacy Live. I continued watching Prince on his television program daily, as he spoke directly to the Lord and prophesied disasters against infidel nations and various gay cities. His message aligned so closely with Biblical Truth that I couldn't understand why he seem so misinformed during our televised discussion. Had he not warned sinners for years of their pending damnation? Why now the sudden softening of his fundamental faith? I was quite disappointed in his performance on Lon Lacy Live.

I learned shortly after the show that Mr. Prince was disappointed too. He'd been severely criticized by fellow televangelists for not convincingly renouncing my faith nor quoting enough scripture. They believed he'd not adequately exuded spiritual or scriptural authority during our nationwide debate, which in turn had a detrimental impact on Christian televangelism. To worsen matters, the press lambasted him for his "death" prophecy and viewed it as a thinly disguised temper tantrum. In short, David Prince was so unhappy with his performance that he wanted to debate me again at the earliest opportunity. Lon Lacy was happy to oblige, considering the high ratings and press coverage gleaned from the show. His handlers called me and pitched another session in July. I declined, explaining that I didn't like the world to see two men of God arguing with each other. They kept persisting and after weeks of my consistent "no", Lon Lacy called.

"Listen Lenny, you kicked David's ass on the show and he wants another shot. This will be a great way to promote that new biography of yours..."

I informed Mr. Lacy that I had not collaborated with the pretentious pedophiliac that penned my "biography".

"OK, OK, calm down. Shit, I thought you'd authorized it. Listen, this is a little unusual but we can offer you an appearance fee if you'll do the show. Say, a hundred thousand?"

To Lon's great disappointment, I hung up.

* * * * * *

Swords for the Lord Assembly grew rapidly during its first year and a half. I preached each Sunday morning and my sermons were recorded and transcribed for distribution to Soldiers in other locales. I usually picked one of the topics from our Manifesto such as false religions, homosexuality and keeping the Sabbath holy. It was wonderful to see the influence God's Word had on our congregation and they truly seemed to live their religion during that early period. They'd call me at all hours with questions and testimonies of their faith:

The Seventh Illusion

"I'm pretty sure I've got a Leviticus 20:18[34] going on next door to my trailer" a Georgia church member whispered one evening over the phone, "But I ain't altogether clear on the scripture..."

On another occasion half our church elders cleared out of our Tuesday night Bible Study when they heard an urgent message coming across the Church's ham radio:

"Breaker, breaker, I gotta Deuteronomy 22:20-21[35] at the Hideaway Bar and need some back up..."

... and at one Sunday afternoon church social I heard a small group of men planning a mission to Macon:

"Exodus 35:2[36] my friends. That's the only reason we need. Bring your shotguns..."

Oh, those early days of the Swords for the Lord, when we were hungry for the Word and gaining hundreds of new Soldiers weekly. We grew so large that we moved into an abandoned Kmart to handle the crowds. Elders of our ministry spread across the Southeast and opened additional churches, one as far south as Arcadia, Florida. We gave thanks to God for using the press to

---

[34] *Leviticus 20:18 - If a man lies with a woman during her monthly period and has sexual relations with her, he has exposed the source of her flow and she has also uncovered it. Both of them must be cut off from the people.*

[35] *Deuteronomy 22:20-21 – If however, the charge is true and no proof of the girl's virginity can be found, she shall be brought to the door of her father's house and there the men of her town shall stone her to death.*

[36] *Exodus 35:2 – For six days, work is to be done, but the seventh day shall be your holy day, a Sabbath of rest to the Lord. Whoever does any work on it must be put to death.*

spread our cause and strengthen Swords for The Lord. The newspapers were first to infiltrate my sermons and report the mass "brain washing" I was conducting on "mostly uneducated and gullible families of the rural South." Slow-witted reporters lifted excerpts of my text and placed them on their front pages, slothful editors ranted in long editorials against our "twisted faith" and liberal publishers called for the government to investigate the "great evil sweeping the Nation."

Television news crews quickly got on the bandwagon too. You may recall how Rock Phillips with National Broadcasting Network preened like an effeminate Roy Rogers the day we opened our first SWORDS FOR THE LORD AMMO Store in the Blue Ridge Mountains. He trapsed into the store wearing a white cowboy hat, hidden mics and video recorder, while posing with sissified friends as converts. They gushed with feigned enthusiasm as our store manager showed them our extensive display of Bibles, swords, shotguns, and mid sized stones.

"...you gotta stick with the mid-sized stones because if you go too big they die too fast; too small and all ya do is piss em off..." he told the "cowboys".

"What's this shrink-wrapped bundle of wood for?" Rock Phillips asked.

"Oh, that's our fire starter kit. Comes with a wood bundle, nautical rope, a stake, and gallon of gasoline. Everything ya need to get going."

"Get going?"

"For burning sinners, boys. Y'all need to get into the Word more ..."

All of this blared on national news at thirty-minute intervals for forty-eight hours while Rock Phillips breathlessly reported the "fruits of a fanatical faith exposed in Hayton, North Carolina". We never could understand why he thought he had to sneak into our store like a succubus to get his "ground breaking" story. We'd have gladly granted the interview had he just shown up at the front door with his camera crew. We weren't hiding our faith under a rock, you know. We wanted to shout Truth to the world and welcomed the opportunity to spread the Word. In any event, after the Rock Phillips "Investigative" Report, sales skyrocketed at the SWORDS FOR THE LORD AMMO Store and we eventually opened four more.

According to a CNN survey taken 18 months after the establishment of Swords for The Lord Assemblies, the general population was first curious, then outraged, and finally horrified, as it became increasingly clear that the national murder rate was rising. Our Church was blamed for the unusual spike in stonings, incinerations and general shootings throughout the Nation. TV news pundits howled their displeasure over America's increased anxiety, divisiveness, and general mistrust hovering over our Country. But, as is common with the liberal press, they failed to disclose the positive results found in polls. To wit:

- Those reading the Bible: up 58%,
- Those regularly attending Church: up 22%,
- Those practicing homosexuality: down 29%
- Those committing Adultery in the last 6 months: down 52%.

Obviously, the survey results reflected Swords for The Lord Assemblies positive impact on America. And as our influence increased, my videotaped sermons increasingly ended up in the hands of some TV reporter who in turn selected the most controversial passages for airing.

A segment of my October 6, 1996 Sermon aired on NBC Nightly News:

> *"Jesus told us that heaven and earth would pass away before the least stroke of the pen would disappear from the Law! And what does the Law tell us? To slaughter adulterers! Are we going to follow God's word, or are we going to be as unrighteous as Saul in the eyes of the Lord when he did not murder everyone as instructed?"*

CNN Headline News aired my November 24 sermon:

> *"Listen! We are marked by the Lord for a mission. Now watch this! Turn to Ezekiel 9 verse 4...The Lord says 'Go throughout the City and put a mark on the foreheads of those who grieve and lament over all the detestable things that are done in it.'*
>
> *That's us people! We grieve and lament over the idolaters and adulterers of this earth! And what does God tell us to do to those without the mark? He tells us in verse 5. He says to follow our leader 'through the city and kill, without showing pity or compassion. Slaughter old men, young men and maidens, women and children, but do not touch anyone who has the mark..."*

Even Lon Lacy got in on the act, airing segments of my sermons while David Prince sat beside him eviscerating me. Mr. Prince swore that I was "of the Devil" and that Swords for The Lord had pushed Christianity back five hundred years into the Middle Ages. He railed against the "spirit of fear and ignorance that pervades America" and that mine was a "ministry of hate." But throughout all his condemnation, he never noted the positive results accruing to America, thanks to Swords for the Lord.

Despite the efficacy of my sermons, our church elders approached me two weeks before Christmas, 1996 in a somber mood. I knew something was askew when they asked me to attend a "Prayer Breakfast" at Bighorn's restaurant. It turned out to be nothing more than a thinly disguised bitch session led by Mr. Thomas Conlin.

"Err, Pastor Boseki, the brothers and I want to address an issue that's been weighing heavy on our hearts."

"Yes?" I said, through a mouthful of scrambled eggs.

"Well, we've taken complaints from our congregations over the last few months. They say their members are starting to tire of your adultery sermons..."

"Oh, are they?" I asked, feeling immediately defensive. "So, they're tired of the Lord's Word, eh?"

"No, no, they're not tired of the Word, they're just hungering for more. It's Christmas. Maybe a sermon of the Nativity along with Jeremiah's call to take up the sword..."

"Adultery is against the seventh commandment!" I said. "I can't think of a better message than encouraging our members to obey the Ten Commandments!"

"We completely agree but, Pastor Boseki please! We did a little review of your sermons. Of the 67 sermons given over the last year and a half, 32 had adultery as the primary topic..."

And so, against my better judgement, I agreed to branch out further on Biblical topics. The elders seemed pleased and soon provided reports of our expanding membership and missions. I presume if there was a Golden Age of Swords for The Lord Assemblies it was during those early months of 1997. We were widely covered by the press, which thereby fueled our membership. Our members absorbed the Bible Truth and thereafter became Christian Soldiers seeking to cleanse our Nation. We received weekly reports of false god church burnings, executed adulterers, murdered homosexuals and slaughtered disrespectful teens. We were changing America, one corpse at a time.

But then, as with any rapidly growing movement, complications arose. Staff and church member problems grew so thick that I soon spent more time administering than ministering. I was overrun with issues of the Law; both Biblical and governmental. A sampling of my June 1997 Diary:

> - *Elmer Jackson, church elder of SFTL Tupelo, caught having sexual intercourse with his fifteen-year-old daughter, a direct violation of Leviticus 18:6. The pastor kicked him out of the church per Leviticus 18:29. Elmer was incensed and demanded a "face to face with Leonard". Upon meeting Mr. Jackson, he immediately requested readmission to the church, citing Genesis 19:30-36 as justification.*
>
>   *"Pastor Boseki, I'm a righteous man, like Lot. God knew Lot was righteous, so spared him and his daughters while killing everyone else in Sodom. Listen, I was a little drunk when they caught me fucking my daughter Becky. I admit that. But, Lot see, he fucked two daughters and got them <u>both</u> pregnant, while I only fucked one and she ain't pregnant! So, I ain't done nothing wrong! Read 2nd Peter 2:7-9 - Peter called Lot a righteous man despite him getting shit-faced, fucking his daughters, and knocking them up. Hell, same thing with me, that's all..."*
>
> - *Butch Welton from Macon arrived unannounced asking for a consultation. He wept openly and tore his t-shirt in anguish as*

he shared: "I was getting ready to burn down a Muslim temple in Atlanta and I was scared. I got caught up in the spirit of the Lord and vowed that if everything went ok, I'd sacrifice the first thing I saw when I got home. Hell, I figured it'd be that piece of shit cat that hangs out on the stoop or maybe my wife. Anyway, I burn down the temple and make it home round midnight and you know what? My daughter pulls in beside me, coming home from a movie. I gotta kill my daughter Pastor! God's calling for it just like in Judges 11: 29-40!"[37]

- Mr. Jay Moran, member of SFTL Blackmore SC, arrived via bus with seventeen church members. They demanded that their minister; Reverend Harold, be immediately fired under the charge of Discrimination and Eugenics. This from Jay Moran: *"It's discrimination Pastor Boeski! All of us here wanna be church elders and offer communion but Pastor Harold says we're not physically pure enough! He told Virgil here he's not fit because he's a midget! And he won't let Ray serve because he had testes cancer, and*

---

[37] *Judges 11: 29-40 - Then the spirit of the Lord came upon Jephthah...and Jephthah made a vow to the Lord: 'If you give the Ammonites into my hands, whatever comes out of the door to my house to meet me when I return ... will be the Lord's and I will sacrifice it as a burnt offering...When Jephthah returned home in Mizpah who should come out to meet him but his daughter...she was an only child...he did to her as he had vowed.*

Jesse's rejected cause she's got a club foot! He told little Macy here that she'll never be a church leader cause she's blind! What a thing to say to say to a four-year-old! In fact, he's told all of us that it's best we don't attend church at all, cause of our deformities! Pastor, I served in Germany during the war and this is the kind of shit the Nazis done! It wasn't just Jews they gassed you know; they were killing anyone with birth defects or deformities for their Master Race...

Appalled, I immediately called Reverend Harold and demanded an explanation for his abhorrent discrimination. He said he was simply following God's Word and offered Leviticus 21:16-20[38] as proof. Upon studying the passage carefully, I realized the Reverend might be correct as to what the Lord wants. I advised Mr. Moran and his fellow members that it might be best to attend our Columbia church instead; where it's less legalistic and more liberal.

---

[38] *Leviticus 21:16-20 - The Lord said to Moses: For the generations to come, none of your descendants who has a defect may come near to offer the food of his God. No man who has any defect may come near; no man who is blind, or lame, disfigured or deformed; no man with a crippled foot or hand, or hunchbacked; or dwarfed, or who has any eye defect, or who has festering or running sores, or damaged testicles.*

The Seventh Illusion

There were many other administrative problems that arose during June 1997. These three however, remain most prominent in my mind, due to what lay ahead, just five short months into the future.

The stars of heaven and their constellations
Will not show their light.
The rising sun will be darkened
And the moon will not give its light.
                    -Isaiah 13:10

Six

By Fall 1997 the church was in deep financial and spiritual crisis. We were low on funds; despite receiving several individual donations exceeding a million dollars the prior year. Maintaining churches, operating Ammo stores and growing legal fees were all major cash drains and expenditures now exceeded collections from tithes. I was using all my spiritual and accounting skills to keep Truth alive but things were now desperate. Aware of our problems, Thomas Conlin and the elders approached me for another "prayer breakfast". I declined. They insisted. I reluctantly agreed. That fateful meeting would eventually lead to the demise of our ministry.

"Pastor Boeski, the brothers and I have been seeking the Lord about how to heal our Church and Nation..." Colin started.

"Yes, we all have the same goals." I said.

"Well Pastor, I was deep in the Word Tuesday night and God spoke to me! He said we must rebuild Solomons Temple!"

"I beg your pardon?"

"Pastor! Who was the last man God appeared to?"

"King Solomon." I said.

"That's right! God appeared to Solomon in 1st Kings 3, and said 'I'm gonna give you a wise and discerning heart! No one will ever be as wise as you again!' And what does Solomon do as soon as he's blessed? He starts building God's Temple in Jerusalem!"

"Yes, that's true…" I agreed.

"And then while Solomon's in the middle of building it, God returns in 1st Kings 6 and says: 'As for this temple you're building, if you carry out my regulations and obey my commands, I'll come down and live with you again!' Do you see Pastor?! He'll come back and live with us again, just like in Mose's time! This is what we've been waiting for!"

"Yes, but Mr. Conlin…"

"And then, after Solomon finished and dedicated the Temple to God, The Lord shows up in 1st Kings 9 and says *'I'll establish your throne forever* as long as you obey all my Laws. But if you don't obey them, I'll bring disaster on you!' But the Jews didn't obey His Laws and God brought hell down on them! Well, we won't make the same mistake. This time, Pastor Boeski, we're gonna get it right! Now God tells us exactly how to build it in 1st Kings 6…"

It took me almost an hour to convince Mr. Conlin that our lack of funds and the time required for construction (Solomon spent thirteen years) made his plan an impractical solution for our current problem.

"But Pastor Boseki, we've gotta do something." Conlin insisted. "Membership is stagnant. Our pastors say their congregations are losing their zeal."

"Brothers I have a solution that will solve our financial and spiritual problems." I announced. "I'm currently writing a book on adultery entitled *The Harlot of the South* which should be a best seller and fill the church coffers. I'm about halfway through and believe I can finish the remaining 100,000 or so words by early next year."

Silence hung over the room. They exchanged sullen looks.

"I think that's certainly of the Lord but we need something now." Conlin finally said. "We need a religious revival! We need something to stir up our members! They're getting scared and starting to question the Word. We've gotta get them back on track before they back slide."

"What they need is a powerful new prophet." I said. "They need a Jeremiah or Ezekiel to warn them of the consequences of not following God's Statutes..."

"THAT'S IT!" Conlin jumped. "Pastor that's exactly what we need! And the first time I heard you speak I thought; 'this man is speaking the words of a great prophet!'"

"Thank you, Mr. Conlin," I blushed, "But to this day I struggle against being called by that title."

"Not you!" Mr. Conlin snapped then caught himself. "I...I...what I mean is certainly you are a prophet of the Lord Pastor Boseki, but I was thinking of the prophet that spoke to you when you were incarcerated."

I did not know what he was referring to. We stared at each other.

"Pastor Boseki, I'm talking bout the prophet that changed the course of your life! I'm talking of the Prophecies of Bruno!"

"Bruno?"

"Pastor Boseki! The German Shepherd that spoke to you while you were shackled by the Babylonians!"

"Oh yes..." I remembered.

"You wrote down his every word. He prophesied that you would be acquitted from your murders and you were. He prophesied that you would go on to form a great church that would sweep the Nation and you have. He spoke of many things to come, do you remember?

Pastor, we need to publish his words and put them in the hands of our church!

And so that very morning the elders followed me back to the church office and stood over me as I dug through old notebooks until I found the one containing Bruno's words. I felt uncomfortable as I photocopied the pages with Mr. Conlin at my shoulder. That night of revelation was now a dim memory and as sheet after sheet came through the copier I wondered; *Did Bruno really speak to me? Or was I having another nervous breakdown?* But didn't share my doubts with Mr. Conlin and the elders.

"Yes! Yes! I remember you reading these very words as you spoke to my Kiwanis club in Fayetteville. Look here..." Mr. Conlin presented a paragraph of barely legible scrawling midway down the page. He began to read the words of Bruno:

"And now you have heard what you must do. Do you have any questions of me Leonard? Ask anything; it shall not be denied you."
"Why was I born? Why? What's the use?"
"A SWORD!"
"I don't know what to do... what to do about Margaret."
"A SWORD!"
"Oh, shit I don't want to live."
"A SWORD!! Thou shalt be a great Sword for the Lord! Thou and thy Chosen Ones must sweep down upon the land and slaughter infidels so that God may return to a cleansed earth. Thou sha consume the wicked like a grilled cheese sandwich. Urrrrrr, ar you going to eat that beef barley soup? Slide it closer to the bars..."

After publication there was much debate over what Bruno meant by "beef barley soup". Some elders believed Bruno was alluding to Deuteronomy 8:8 in which he would lead us into the Promised Land. Others thought he was exhorting us to establish a church in the Dakotas where most of the Country's barley i produced. Either way, Conlin somehow knew in advance the interest Bruno would stir in our ministry and immediately had five thousand copies published in order to take them to our churches. Strengthened by Bruno, Thomas Conlin now became a passionate itinerant preacher, and single handedly revitalized our flagging flock.

I'm told he'd finish each sermon the same way:

"I want you to turn to page five with me. Now look at the answer to each question posed to Bruno. What is it? That's right, the answer is a SWORD! The answer is a SWORD, just like it was in the days of the Prophets. Do you know how many times the word 'SWORD' is used in Jeremiah? Sixty-eight times! And Ezekiel? Seventy-nine times! And Bruno, how many times does he mention SWORD? Ninety-two times!! The answer was and is the SWORD, and it's more important today than ever! We are the SWORDS FOR THE LORD!! AIIIIIEEEEE!"

He worked the congregations into such frenzy that post church sermon riots erupted on three separate occasions, each strangely occurring at Super Wal Marts 30 minutes after services ended. In each incident customers and employees were badly beaten and several vehicles burned before the local authorities were able to restore order.

None of this sat well with me. I was uncomfortable introducing "Prophecies of Bruno" as a new holy book and did not like the chaos that transpired whenever Bruno's words were preached by Brother Conlin. The church was becoming fanatical. Members were arrested weekly throughout the South for various murders and increasingly invoking Bruno's name in front of camera crews, police and judges.

I prayed without success for a solution to our volatility. I did however, receive a long overdue answer to another fervent prayer:

Doyle Black

Nov 5, 1997
Dear Lenny,

I have so much to say to you that I don't know where to begin. I've watched you on TV and can see that you believe everything you preach. Because of your faith I live in constant fear that you or one of your church members will kill me as I shop for groceries, or pick up Jenny after school, or wash dishes at my kitchen window. I plead for you to forgive me for my infidelity and beg you to tell your congregation not to murder me.

There is something else also. I want you to know that you have a daughter. She is five years old now and asks about her daddy often. I want you to meet her. Please come to Virginia so that Jennifer may see her father. I am too frightened to travel to North Carolina.

Margaret Boseki.

I must have read her letter twenty times, looking for a trace of the Margaret I had known a half decade before. I held the letter to my nose hoping for her fragrance, but there was nothing. I immediately responded that I would be in Norfolk in three days and would call upon arrival.

* * * * * *

I had my hair cut, purchased a camel hair sport coat, wool slacks and shoes at the Brentwood Mall and drove to Norfolk to meet Margaret and my daughter. I checked into Consulate Suites and immediately called her, but no one answered. I left a message that I'd be waiting in suite 354 all day and looked forward to seeing them. I poured a glass of water, sat down at my desk, and stared out the window.

Two hours later there was a knock on my door. I rose, put on my sports coat, checked my hair in the

The Seventh Illusion

mirror and opened the door. Jenny stood staring up at me with big, fearful eyes; a note penned to her pink Teddy Bear shirt. I knew instantly she was my child; the same green eyes and fair skin. I sank to my knees.

"Hello Jenny" I said softly, "Where's your mommy?"

She said nothing, only slipped a thumb in her mouth. I gently pulled the note off her shirt and read it.

Please bring her home when your visit is over.

On the back of the note was their home address. I stood up and held out my hand. She stared at it at length before finally accepting it. I walked her inside, closed the door and she started crying.

"Honey, don't cry. I'm not going to hurt you."

But she was inconsolable, and pressed her back against a wall; sucking her thumb. I picked Jenny up and took a seat on the couch with her, on my lap. I sang a lullaby for her and it seemed to help.

I see the moon and the moon sees me...
God bless the moon and God bless me...

"I thought you wanted to see me, honey. Your mommy said you wanted to see your daddy." I kissed the top of her head and smelled the soft fragrance of my daughter for the first time.

"No. Mommy said you're a bad man. But mommy made me come."

"Honey, I'm not a bad man. I'd never hurt you."

"Mommy said that you're gonna hurt her. Mommy said that we can't go outside because you'll hurt her."

I spoke soft and low, assuring her that I loved her mommy and that I loved her. She sat on my knee for a few minutes without speaking.

"Are you going to hurt my mommy?"

"I don't want to Jenny."

"But are you?"

I put her down and walked over to my desk for the Bible. I read the seventh commandment aloud and told Jenny that her mommy had committed adultery even though God said not to. He had given us Laws to follow and anyone that broke God's Law had to be punished according to God's instructions. I began reading Leviticus 20:10 to her but she started crying again.

"I don't know what it means!" She cried. "I love my mommy! I don't want you to hurt my mommy!"

I couldn't get her to stop crying. She wouldn't take anything to drink or eat, only ran to the door and kept saying "Please! Please don't hurt my mommy! I want my mommy!" I ended up having to drive her back home. As she jumped out of the car, I saw Margaret crack open her front door. She looked pale and haggard. Jenny ran into her arms and they quickly shut the door. I stood next to the car, staring after them for time unknown. Finally, I got back in and drove away.

That was the beginning of losing my religion.

Part V: I Am Dead

You Moon! Have you done something wrong in heaven,
That God has hidden your face?
I hope, if you have, you will soon be forgiven,
And shine again in your place.
              Jean Ingelow
              Seven Times One

One

I returned to Hayton, North Carolina in a somber mood. I abandoned my *Harlot of the South* manuscript, never to pick it up again. For the next several weeks I remained confined to my Pastor's quarters in quiet reflection. The elders grew alarmed after I didn't appear for Sunday church and were forced to improvise via a "Testimonial Service" in which members came forth to share their personal walks with God. When I didn't emerge the following Sunday, they called "Father" Conlin home.

"I'm leaving the ministry." I told him when he came to call. He asked why. I couldn't articulate a clear reason.

"You need to get right with God, Pastor." He said. "Get immersed in the Word. Look, I've brought you a gift."

Mr. Conlin placed a thin red leather-bound book in my hands. On the cover was a gold profile of a German Shepherd and the book's title in gold lettering:

The Revelation of Bruno
As related to Leonard Boseki
(Confirmed by Solomon Thomas Conlin)

"Confirmed?" I asked.

"I BEAR WITNESS THAT MY TESTIMONY IS THE WORD OF GOD!!" He exclaimed.

I had no idea what he was talking about.

He announced that God and Bruno had recently visited him in a motel room in Doraville, Georgia. As Mr. Conlin spoke, I heard fervency in his voice that had not existed before; saw zealotry in his clear blue eyes that troubled me greatly.

"I was at bedside, kneeling in prayer," Mr. Conlin said, "when I heard barking echoing behind me. I rose and turned to find Bruno trotting out of the bathroom. 'Behold!' he growled, and then I heard the shower curtain pull back and saw the Lord step forth! His head and hair were white like wool, his eyes were blazing fire. In his right hand he held seven stars..."

"Are you sure you didn't dream this?" I asked.

"SILENCE! I BEAR WITNESS THAT MY TESTIMONY IS THE WORD OF GOD!" He screamed. There was an awkward pause, and then he continued.

"When I saw Him, I fell at his feet as though dead. Then He placed His right hand on me and spake great prophecy. I saw the future and beheld America's great shame. God showed me we must save America by slaughtering President Clinton..."

"WHAT? Are you crazy?"

"HOW DARE YOU CALL GOD'S PROPHET CRAZED!" Mr. Conlin lunged. "Do you not understand that we are being led by an evil whore monger? Have you not read of the women confessing that they were harlots of our President? Have you not heard his bodyguards telling of his adulteries? Yea, God said that if Clinton lives, he'll continue shaming America with his insatiable penis! His perversions will consume our airwaves and America will witness his mocking of God's Law! They will become numb to his great sins and soon accept his infidelity as harmless! Even his wife shall stand by her man! Nay, we cannot allow our slut lusting President to degrade all that Swords for the Lord has accomplished!

"Thomas, listen to me! You can't kill President Clinton. It will devastate the Nation!"

"WE NEED DEVASTATION! We must kill Clinton so that righteousness will rein! America must return to holiness so that God can return to earth just as we've dreamed! Thus spake the Lord!: 'Just as Solomon attacked infidels in Jerusalem and used survivors as slaves to build My Temple, so you must attack Washington DC and build My Temple on the National Mall!' Only then will I return to live among you!

"Mr. Conlin, we can't attack Washington…"

"SILENCE! THUS SPAKE THE LORD!! CLINTON IS THE ANTICHRIST! He is destroying America by letting homos infiltrate America's military with his 'don't ask don't tell' hypocrisy! America's generals want the Antichrist overthrown! Go to the Pentagon! There, America's Armed Forces shall rise with you to destroy the Antichrist and his demons! Thereafter, Ye shall be My new Joshua, chosen to slaughter the unchosen on your march to reclaim the Promised Land! Start with Baltimore..."

Mr. Conlin was now unhinged, as he continued his "prophecy" at length, rambling of God's directive regarding logistical challenges and the difficulties of killing so many infidels. God told him to leave many of the unfaithful alive, and use them as slaves to rebuild cities. Afterward, the slaves would be sold as property, or willed to our heirs, just as God had suggested in

Leviticus.[39] God also quoted Scripture to Conlin as proof that He expected slaves to be part of the natural order[40]. When Conlin wandered into God's demands that SFTL start a slave trading company, I cut him off.

"Thomas..."

"GOD, BRUNO AND SOLOMON HAVE SPOKEN! Do not question God or you will be slain! Do not question the words of GOD or else a thousand arrows shall pierce your soul!"

That pretty much ended the conversation.

"Now brother, I must leave you." He said. "I will cover this Sunday's sermon for you. I want you to promise me you will get steeped in *The Revelation of Bruno* and pray for insight..."

He left so abruptly I didn't rise to see him to the door. I sat staring at my gift for some time and mulling over his diatribe before finally thumbing through pages to recall the words of Warden Bell's dog. As I read, I became first appalled and then frightened. Appalled

---

[39] *Leviticus 25:44-46 - Your male and female slaves are to come from the nations around you...you may also buy some living among you and they will become your property. You can will them to your children as inherited property and can make them slaves for life.*

[40] *Ephesians 6:5 - Slaves, obey your earthly masters with respect and fear, and with sincerity of heart, just as you would obey Christ.*

1 Peter 2:18 - Slaves, in reverent fear of God, submit yourselves to your masters, not only to those who are good and considerate, but also to those who are harsh.

Titus 2:9 - Teach slaves to be subject to their masters in everything; to try to please them, not to talk back to them.

because I saw that the words were simply the ramblings of religious fervor:

...thou shalt send four destroyers against them, the sword to kill and the dogs to drag the dead and the birds of the air and a wife that is a whore and Harlot of the South...

Page after page of nonsense,

...thou shalt place a bone up the arse of infidels and let the dogs drag them off unto the woods...

which no longer made any sense whatsoever:

...and yea, when the cole slaw is shunned, thou must slaughter the ignorant jailer.

I now realized that the words of a mad dog held sway over Swords for the Lord Assemblies. And as I read further, I came to a passage that greatly concerned me:

...but lo, there shalt come a time when Leonard Boseki, messenger of doG, will be replaced by Thomas Conlin, messenger of God! Then, Leonard Boseki saw through prison bars dimly, but soon, Solomon Thomas Conlin shall come bearing the message from his face-to-face meeting with God!

I dug out my notebook from the night of Bruno's prophecy. As suspected, Bruno had never mentioned Thomas Conlin. I turned back to *The Revelation of Bruno* and began reading chapter 2:

The Revelation which God gave in Doraville, Georgia to his servant Solomon Thomas Conlin (the Divine) to show what must soon take place...
<u>*To the angel of the church of Hayton, North Carolina write:*</u>

These are the words of Him who consumes the wicked like a hot grilled cheese sandwich. Bring Baltimore to its knees by bombing its highways and utilities...
<u>*To the angel of the church of Jackson, Mississippi write*</u>:
These are the words of Him who has the sharp, double-edged sword. New Orleans is full of immorality and must be burned to the ground...
<u>*To the angel of the church of Bithlo, Florida write*</u>:
These are the words of Him who holds the seven stars and seven A's in the Beef Barley Alphabet soup. Orlando if full of homos, harlots and haughtiness. Thou shalt slay the wicked as they visit their pagan theme parks...

Marching orders for our seven churches. He then veered into the "opening of sealed envelopes", each envelope containing orders to assassinate a specific individual. His writing became increasingly cryptic but I'm pretty sure his 1st and 4th seal called for the murder of the former Mrs. Conlin and the Fayetteville Postmaster respectively. There was no doubt as to who the sixth envelope applied to:

Then I saw a beast coming out of the earth. He exercised authority and made America and its inhabitants worship him rather than God. The beast hungered for whores, fed on them from Arkansas to Washington. He forced everyone to receive a mark on their forehead, which is the name of the beast or number of his name. The name of the beast is Willam Jefrsn Clnton. This calls for wisdom. If anyone has insight, let him calculate the number of the beast...

* * * * * *

I did not speak nor take visitors for the next month. remained ensconced in my Pastor's quarters, subsisting off bread and water, while praying to find a path out of great darkness. I left the TV tuned to the religious channel 24 hours a day, hoping for a word; a message that would lead me to the light.

I made it a point to devote complete attention to David Prince's "7777 Show" whenever it was on. And as I watched I saw that he had grown more fervent in the Lord since our meeting on Lon Lacy Live. He often started the broadcast by reporting that he'd received words directly from the Lord to share with his audience. I jotted them down daily for weeks:

"God told me last night that an earthquake will strike 'the Sodomizers of California' before year end..."

"...The Lord told me that I am to build a new church in New York City and that my listeners must send their tithes..."

And, his favorite recurring theme:

"God told me last night that Swords for the Lord Assemblies, that slithering Satan based enterprise, is filled with demons..."

"I was talking to the Lord last night and he said 'David, Leonard Boseki is causing Me great harm. He is casting thousands of My children into the pit of hell...'"

But even more interesting than his messages from God were his casting out of demons. Several times a week there was footage of him visiting small churches to rid evil spirits from possessed men and women brought before him. On many occasions while traveling the South, David Prince brought the cleansed forward afterward to testify that they were former members of the Swords for the Lord.

It was clear he had become obsessed with SFTL Assemblies and me, for he never missed a program without mentioning one of us. "Oh, and that coward and sniveling demon Leonard Boseki, leading thousands into hell from the comfort of his wicked church in North Carolina, will one day face God for his many sins! He is too cowardly to speak face to face with me for he knows that greater is HE that is within me than he who is in the world!"

And somewhere in the middle of his rambling, I made the greatest mistake of my life. I called Lon Lacy to arrange what would become David's and my last "debate".

We are like the moon. An empty landscape reflecting whatever light we receive. – Leonard Boseki

Two

To this day I'm not sure why I decided to appear on Lon Lacy Live with David Prince again. Perhaps I wanted to defend my faith or discredit his; but more likely I was searching for answers. I think I was hoping someone in America would call in during the show and convince us once and for all to let go of our delusions.

Lon Lacy and David Prince were elated to hear I'd finally accepted a return engagement. I'm told that despite the hastily arranged debate (only two weeks notice) a major ad campaign was launched that helped drive our appearance to the highest rating for any live show in network history.

Lon Lacy wanted to invite representatives from all major faiths to join us and offer their perspectives. I agreed but David Prince insisted that it be just him and me for the entire hour or else he'd refuse to appear. Lon caved and, in the end, it was just David and me again. But unlike our first meeting, David came well prepared for our second debate. We spent the first twenty minutes of the show firing scripture across the table in order to establish how wrong the other one was. Frankly, I found the exercise jejune and I'm told I looked bored and detached throughout the entire match.

"John 13:34, Boseki! 'A new command I give you: Love one another!"

"Yes, Reverend Prince, but the command does not nullify the Law. Jesus is saying it is in addition to, not in replacement of..."

"Clearly, you can't grasp Paul's epistles, Boeski!"

"Apparently you can't grasp Jesus, Mr. Prince. He told you in Matthew 5:17-32, that the Law stays until earth is gone and anyone teaching otherwise is wrong. Jesus then proceeds to actually *strengthen* the Law. He says, 'you've been taught not to murder? Well, now I'm saying that if you're even angry with a brother you might go to hell. You've been taught not to commit adultery? I'm telling you now that lusting is adultery. You've read in Deuteronomy 24 that you're allowed to divorce? Well, I'm telling you can't divorce'. Clearly, Reverend Prince, Jesus isn't abolishing the Law; He's bolstering it.

"As usual you've taken scripture out of context Boseki! The Lord is putting this word in my mouth for your benefit!"

He practically read the entire book of Galatians to me:

"Galatians 3:25 cannot be any clearer! 'Now that faith has come, we are no longer under supervision of the Law!"

"I'll state my position again, Reverend Prince: When Paul's words conflict with Old Testament scripture and/or the words of Jesus, we know that Paul is wrong."

"So, you don't think Paul has spiritual authority, Lenny?" Lon asked.

"No, I don't. In fact, I think Paul has set the faith back two thousand years..."

"Oh, that's rich, considering the source!" David Prince said.

"Let him speak David." Lon said.

The Seventh Illusion

"Paul has no authority to say that faith exempts us from being under God's Law." I said.

"Paul does have authority! Prince yelled, "He received the revelation directly from Jesus Christ!"

"Yes, Paul made that claim but it contradicts Jesus Christ, who said in Matthew 5:17[41] and Luke 16:17[42] that the Law continues until heaven and earth disappear. This contradiction should be no surprise though, since Paul wasn't interested in what Jesus said. Paul rarely mentions Jesus's teachings in his epistles. Paul never went out to hear Jesus preach throughout Judea, Paul never met Jesus in the flesh..."

"Paul met Jesus on the road to Damascus!" Prince said.

"Yes, Paul claims to finally meet Jesus;" I said, years after Jesus had been crucified and resurrected. Their meeting is well documented in the book of Acts but, nowhere in those passages does Jesus tell Paul we're no longer under the Law."

"Paul tells us he received his gospel of faith directly from Jesus Christ and that's good enough for me!" Prince said.

"Not good enough for me." I said.

---

[41] *Do not think that I have come to abolish the Law or the Prophets; I have not come to abolish them but to fulfill them. I tell you the truth, until heaven and earth disappear, not the smallest letter, not the least stroke of a pen, will by any means disappear from the Law until everything is accomplished. Anyone who breaks one of the least of these commandments and teaches other do the same will be called the least in the kingdom of heaven... (Matt 5:17-19)*

[42] *It is easier for heaven and earth to disappear than for the least stroke of a pen to drop out of the Law. (Luke 16:17)*

"So, Paul is lying?" Lon asked.

"No, we don't think he's lying, but we agree with Festus regarding Paul here."

"Who?" Lon asked.

"Look," I said, "Paul claims in Galatians 1 and 2 that the gospel he's preaching wasn't received from any man but rather by 'revelation from Jesus Christ.' Paul says that his exclusive news from Jesus trumps anything Apostles Peter, John, and James are teaching! Three of the very Apostles that Jesus handpicked for His earthly ministry. These three Apostles *lived with Jesus for three years and gained intimate knowledge of His teaching. They witnessed His crucifixion. They spoke to the resurrected Christ.* And, during all this time; starting with Jesus choosing them and ending after Christ's Ascension, Jesus never said that the Law no longer applied. If fact, he told them the exact opposite.

Then, two decades after Jesus has been crucified, here comes Paul; a man who never met Jesus when He lived, announcing that Jesus said to ignore the Law. Paul then confronts Peter, the very rock that Jesus was building His church on[43], and tells Peter he's wrong. No, we find Paul's claim quite ridiculous, when we see how contrary it is to Jesus' teachings. We therefore agree with Festus's opinion, as stated in Acts 26:24 'You are out of your mind Paul! Your great learning is driving you insane.'"

"It's you who are insane Boseki! Prince said.

---

[43] *Blessed are you, Simon, son of Jonah, for this was not revealed to you by man, but by my Father in heaven. And I tell you that you are Peter, and on this rock I will build my church and the gates of heaven will not overcome it. (Matt 16:17-18)*

The Seventh Illusion

"Mr. Prince, you know I'm not alone in my opinion. Here's a quote from Thomas Jefferson: 'Paul was the first corruptor of the doctrines of Jesus'..."

"We've got to take a station break." Lon interrupted. "Lenny, Give us a one sentence summary of your view of Paul."

"In sum, we believe Paul corrupted God's words and Jesus's crucifixion to fit his own delusional beliefs."

"David, your response?"

"Isn't that precisely what you've done, Mr. Boseki?"

* * * * * *

After the first commercial break, David Prince came out swinging:

"This crazed demon before us admits he ignores the inspired words of St. Paul, which were directly received from Jesus Christ. Yet, while he considers Paul's words worthless, this madman has published a "holy" book containing his conversations with a dog! A dog! He and his unholy church claim it to be the word of God!"

"I don't claim it to be the word of God." I said. "I acknowledge that part of the book is a conversation I held with a dog during a very stressful time of my life. I never said I believed it to be the word of God."

"This so-called holy book of SFTL Assemblies is advocating the assassination of President Clinton and the destruction of seven major cities in the United States!" Prince said, a copy of _The Revelation of Bruno_ suddenly appearing in his hand. "The assassination of our President! Where is our Secret Service? The destruction of seven major cities, and their inhabitants! Baltimore, New Orleans, Orlando, Atlanta, Pittsburgh, Philadelphia, and Fayetteville! If there are any viewers living in any of those cities be forewarned that Mr. Boseki's church wants to kill you! But fear not, I have already notified the White House of their evil plans!"

"I don't believe the book to be holy and don't agree with what is written in it." I said.

"Oh, you don't? Are you renouncing the very book that your church asserts to be a new revelation from God?"

"Some in the church may hold that view, but I don't."

By the 2nd commercial break David Prince was feeling victorious. As we waited off air, he joked with Lon Lacy about inconsequential things; acting as if I weren't in the room. Lon interrupted him and turned to me.

"I think he's got you on the ropes, Leonard. Let's see how the rest of the show goes for you."

Oh, and David orchestrated the second half quite well. He dominated the first few minutes, quoting scripture about false teachers and end times; waving his finger at me while intermittently; calling me "wicked" and "demonic". Then Lon opened the phone lines. I'm convinced David prearranged the first two callers:

"This is Sarah Boseki; the widow of Leonard's father."

"You're Leonard's mother?" Lon Lacy asked.

"She's not my mother." I said. "She married Father after Mother died."

"That's correct. And I just want to say that Leonard's father told me quite often how unstable Leonard is. He said that Leonard was possessed by Satan and had always been a great disappointment to him."

"Well, I'd be greatly disappointed too, if Beelzebub were living in my son." Prince smirked.

Sensing support, Father's whore kept going:

"Do you know that Leonard never even came to visit his father when he was dying?"

I was too taken aback to speak. And then the second call came through, without introduction. The tiny voice of a tired woman whom I did not immediately recognize.

"This is Margaret Mazzani, I'm Leonard's ex-wife...."

Vertigo. That is the only word I can use to describe the sensation, upon hearing her through studio speakers.

"I live in constant fear that Lenny or one of his Sword For the Lord soldiers will kill me. I can't sleep. My only daughter, Lenny's child, is terrified. She can't play with her friends. She sits in her closet with her toys because she says that's the safest place for her. I'm begging you, Lenny. I'm begging you to forgive me for whatever sins I may have committed against you." She began crying so uncontrollably that Lon Lacy dropped her off the line.

"That was you wife?" Lon asked.

"Yes."

"She committed adultery against you?"

"Yes."

"Well Lenny, what do you have to say? She's asking for your forgiveness..."

Oh, to have you before me now, my love. It would be me, begging forgiveness for the pain and madness I cast upon us. I feel you, my love, smiling beside me, as Chesapeake winds carry us toward Sandy Point.

"Lenny?"

"I do forgive her." I said after a long pause. "But God's law is clear on the penalty for adultery. She is to be put to death."

"Do you see?" David Prince announced. "Do you see that we are seated beside a man consumed by unadulterated evil? He has not a drop of love or sympathy for his wife! He has not a shred of love or sympathy for his daughter!" And then, Mr. Prince stepped in for the kill. In the interest of objectivity, I offer the transcribed manuscript below:

Prince: The Lord is speaking through my mouth tonight. Thus says the Lord! 'Cease your demonic ministry! Cease your wicked ways and return to My righteousness...'

Boseki: Oh, get behind me Satan.

Prince: Blasphemy! How dare you say God's Word is from Satan! You have a legion of demons!

Boseki: You think I'm demon possessed because I carry out what the Bible commands?

Prince: Not 'demon', demons! You have many demons!

Boseki: Cast them out for me then.

Prince:

Boseki: Cast out my demons! I beg you! Prove for me that the Old Testament is of Satan, and not of the Lord. That is my greatest hope!

Prince: You are the most evil man I have ever met.

Boseki: Reverend Prince, in your twenty-five years of Televangelism you have re-routed hurricanes, prophesied the word of God, cured the sick, cured the lame, and cast out demons. Tonight, I beg you, if you truly are the chosen man of God; cast out my evil spirits.

Prince: I believe you are beyond hope. I believe Satan himself possesses you! The Lord is telling me that you are beyond hope. I have a message from the Lord for you, Surely, ye shall die by the sword!

Boseki: Deuteronomy 18:21-22. Thus, sayeth the Lord: "You may say to yourselves, 'how can

The Seventh Illusion

we know when a message has not been spoken by the Lord?' If what a prophet proclaims in the name of the Lord does not come true, that is a message the Lord has not spoken."

Prince: Oh, it shall come true!

Boseki: Deuteronomy 18:20 – Thus sayeth the Lord: "But a prophet who presumes to speak in My name anything I have not commanded him to say...must be put to death."

Prince: It shall come true!

Boseki: When we met almost three years ago on this show, you prophesied in the name of God, that I would be dead within the year. Three years ago, Mr. Prince. It's you who should die according to Deuteronomy 18:20..."

That was the last scripture I was to quote on that last night of my ministry. Little did I know that it was David Prince's last night as well. Two hours later, as he stepped out of his limousine at the Waldorf Astoria, David Prince was shot to death by a Leonardite Dog.

Said the Wind, "What a marvel of power am I!"
With my breath, Good Faith,
I blew her to death -
First blew her away right out of the sky -
Then blew her right in; what strength have I!

But the Moon she knew nothing about the affair;
For high in the sky,
With her one white eye,
Motionless, miles above the air,
She had never heard the great Wind blare.
                    George MacDonald

Three

I did not sleep on the night of David Prince's murder. The major networks and newspapers called my hotel room, relentlessly asking the same questions: Had I ordered his murder? Did the Swords for the Lord Assemblies take credit for his death? Did I approve of his killing? I politely answered no to their questions and terminated the call. By 9am the next morning I'd had enough and checked out of the hotel. I was not half way through the lobby before I was accosted by a horde of reporters.

"Do you have a comment for the press?! A comment for the press!" They screamed.

"I've already made my comment. I do not condone Mr. Prince's death. I offer my sincere regrets to Mr. Prince's family..."

"We're not talking about David Prince," said a reporter in the front, "We want a comment regarding your wife's death..."

* * * * *

Margaret's neighbor, Mrs. Cathy Russell, had been surprised to find Jenny at her front door at 7:30 the morning after David Prince's murder.

"I can't wake mommy."

Mrs. Russell walked Jenny home and found Margaret on her back in bed, the TV on, still tuned to CNN. In her bathroom, an empty bottle of opioids and a wine glass were found beside the sink. She left no suicide note. That's all I want to say.

* * * * *

I flew directly to Norfolk from New York and over the ensuing week, tried to gain custody of Jenny. All my attempts were stymied. I decided to return to Hayton, resign from the ministry, gather my belongings, and return to Virginia to continue my custody battle. On the afternoon of my return to my SFTL Pastor's quarters, I was visited by church elders who handed me a note from "Alpha Omega", whom I quickly surmised to be Thomas Conlin. The letter, subsequently found in my trash can and held for evidence read:

To the Whore of Babylon!

Behold, I am coming soon! My reward is with me and I will give to everyone according to what he has done. The <u>cowardly</u>, the <u>unbelieving</u>, the <u>vile</u>, the <u>idolaters</u> and <u>liars</u> - their place will be in the fiery lake of burning sulfur! This is their second death. But even this will not be as painful as the thousand arrows that will pierce your soul for your <u>Apostasy</u> on national television!
　　　　　　　　　　　　-Alpha Omega

The Seventh Illusion

"Alpha Omega says you must leave immediately." One of the elders asserted. I agreed. It took me under fifteen minutes to pack my things into a trash bag and leave the compound. I stopped by Porky's Quick Mart just outside of Hayton for gas, bottled water, and a loaf of bread for the long drive home. It was right after I'd stepped back out of the store, with my bag of groceries, that I saw them.

"And the dogs shall lick up your blood as the word of the Lord declares!" Screamed a lardaceous redneck from the driver's seat of a rusted pickup. "SFTL" was embroidered on his soiled red baseball cap. *When did we order those huts?* I wondered as he raised a shotgun and fired from his seat. The blast blew wide and low of its mark, exploding my bag and left shoulder rather than my head as intended. As I spun backward and fell toward the curb he fired again. The second round blew over my head and shattered Porky's plate glass window. I struggled slowly to a seated position on the curb and waited for the final blast. The dumb shit only brought two shells with him. A rail thin man jumped out of the passenger seat, ran up to me and fired six shots from his pistol at close range. Only three of them hit me. My assassins managed to destroy a shoulder, spleen and lung but to our mutual disappointment, the poor impotent bastards couldn't accomplish what they'd come for.

* * * * * *

I am dead. Dead, while the world, and all its illusions live on. For three years now reporters, biographers and the lunatic fringe have made sporadic pilgrimages to visit me here in Lynchburg. They travel from all over the

Country to stare at an oddity, bobbing amongst the flotsam of Tennessee. Why they ask, why do I choose to live here in an assisted living facility amongst the elderly and insane? My answer is simple. It is because I am dead. And the dead can be buried anywhere.

I have shared this memoir in order for you to cease your endless pilgrimages and insipid inquiries. Your accolades and aspersions tire me. Your esoteric questions and editorial assaults bore me. To those of you seeking answers to your Biblical questions my response is: "I don't know." Please cease seeking guidance from me. To those asking whether I believe Thomas Conlin "Christo" rose from the dead three days after he was gunned down by the Secret Service, I can only say that I don't care. And that you're idiots. As to my own eternal question, still demanding response, I will answer again: I have no idea where my daughter is.

As for future historians, should there be any, who may ask whether I was ever truly possessed by the presence of God, I must confess that I don't know. I can only confirm that whatever once possessed me has passed. It has passed and left me stranded here, windless in Lynchburg. In the evenings I sit on the porch, thumbing through a tattered book of poetry; raising my eyes occasionally to watch distant headlights passing our mausoleum. Sometimes, I find myself staring blankly at the moon, feeling little; only the slipstream of the Seventh illusion.

Neti - Neti